First Born

JANELLE GABAY

www.janellegabaybooks.com

First Born by Janelle Gabay

First Born
Copyright © 2015 by Janelle Gabay
All rights reserved. Printed in the United States of America. No part
of this book may be used or reproduced in any manner whatsoever
without written permission except in the case of brief quotations
embodied in critical articles and reviews.
www.janellegabaybooks.com
janellegabaybooks@gmail.com

Library of Congress Cataloging-in-Publication Data is available
ISBN 978-0-9961588-0-0

First Born / Janelle Gabay.– 1st ed.
Summary: In future North America, nineteen-year-old Tarian Prescott
discovers his true identity as an immortal. A secret society of immortals
now relies on Tarian's DNA for survival.
 [1. Identity–Fiction. 2. Family–Fiction 3. Courage–Fiction 4. Science
fiction.]

First paperback edition, 2015

First Born by Janelle Gabay

To my mom and dad,
Who taught me how to love and filled my life with laughter.

To my husband,
Who always believed in my ability and encouraged my strength.

To my children,
Who never cease to amaze and inspire me every day, without
them there would be no stories!

Special Thanks:

Allison Newell
Sandy McCain
Tampa Writers Alliance Critique Group

First Born by Janelle Gabay

"Do not tell secrets to those whose faith and silence you have not already tested." Elizabeth I

First Born by Janelle Gabay

LONE SURVIVOR
TEN YEARS EARLIER

Joe Prescott opened the door leading into his son's hospital room. His wife, Carolyn, reluctantly lifted her head from their son's bed. Her face drenched with tears; her arms stretched across Tarian's sleeping body. She smiled when their eyes met.

"He's alive, Joe. Our baby is alive." Her voice sounded hoarse and dry, but she continued, "It's a miracle. His friends... all the other kids on the bus... died and --" The grief strangled her silent.

Joe saw her fight to keep the tears from forming, but they did not obey and fell from her eyes anyway. She didn't wipe them away because she wouldn't remove her arms from Tarian's body. Joe wondered if she would ever let him go.

"That horrible black ice on that stupid bridge! They should have canceled the field trip. I told Mrs. Middleton. Oh God, she's gone too!" She sobbed.

"I know honey. I know."

He wanted to silence her, to stop her pain, but the words spilled uncontrollably from her mouth.

"The bus skidded...the poor children...drowned in the icy pond. It's awful, Joe, just...just...not right." Her voice had gained strength but gave out once more.

Joe walked over to stand behind his wife. He kissed the top of her head, caressed her hair and gazed down at his second

First Born by Janelle Gabay

born son. He watched his small chest rise and fall. The minor movement filled Joe's heart with relief.

Joe had suffered death's sting for centuries, but tonight he had been spared. He thought about the many parents who had not been spared. Those parents suffered the most painful of all losses, the death of a child.

Joe reached down to hold the plump hand of his nine-year-old boy and felt the undeniable warmth of life on his skin. He knew what his son truly was; he also knew he could not tell anyone, not even his loving wife.

First Born by Janelle Gabay

ONE
CURRENT DAY – ENTENTE MILITARY ACADEMY (EMA)

Tarian casually studied his class notes on the *History of the Entente Reconstruction*. The mid-year exam was tomorrow. He was not worried about the test; he was merely passing time since he could not sleep. He had an A in the class. He enjoyed learning about the aftermath of the Great War, now known as the Entente War. The details of reshaping North America into one, united, closed-bordered nation intrigued him. It fascinated him to learn about the outdated practices of international trading. It boggled his mind to think of his homeland, the Entente, relying on any outside nation for resources.

At one o'clock in the morning, Tarian knew he had to rest. With one and a half years of intense physical training, Tarian had gone from a gangly, boney-shouldered, first-year to a strong, muscular, second-year, and his body ached all over. He rose from his desk, rubbed a kink out of his neck and collapsed onto his bed. His six-foot-two of newly acquired height consumed the entire length of his modest twin mattress. His long legs stretched outright, and his toes reached past the end railing. With his head resting on the palms of his hands, fingers laced, and his well-defined biceps spread triangular shaped on his pillow, he stared at the ceiling in anticipation. Tomorrow, his Cadet Sergeant had promised she would tell him the truth about his father's death.

First Born by Janelle Gabay

Tarian lay awake. For the past two months, the secret had chiseled away at his psyche in painful sharp cuts. Insomnia began in October when he had accidentally overheard the word 'murder' during a private conversation between his Cadet Sergeant, Audrey Gualtiero, and his dad's best friend, Senator Zachary Eastwood. The Senator was like a second father to him. He had lived with the Senator the year before he began the Entente Military Academy, but more relevantly, the year after his father's heart attack. So it surprised him that the Senator had never mentioned knowing Gualtiero, his classmate. Gualtiero was the head of his company in rank and one year ahead of him in school. She ruined his life every day with her constant orders of perfection. She was a walking megaphone. She expected nothing less than first, from bed making to underwater training drills. If her company came in second for anything, they suffered for it. Needless to say, Tarian made sure they never came in second.

"Why did the Senator kiss her on the forehead?" he asked himself as he had several times before. The Senator was an unsentimental man who rarely kissed his daughter. More questions filled his thoughts, *How does she know my dad? Why would she call his death a murder? I know that's what I overheard!*

He shut his eyes tight, exhaled and replayed the conversation inside his head but still had no answers. His brain remained stuck on the word murder. Tarian had been told his father died of natural causes due to a heart attack, so the mention of him being murdered struck him hard. *Who would want to murder an estate lawyer from Boston?*

First Born by Janelle Gabay

Finally, Tarian slipped into sleep. His imagination conjured up the many grotesque ways a man could be killed. As the bloody knife in his dream jammed its blade into his dad's chest cavity, cracking bone and gouging organs, he jumped awake with beads of sweat rolling down his neck. Anger consumed him. How dare someone kill his father!

Shaking his head and rolling over onto his right side, he forced the vivid images out of his mind. He wrapped his body in the cotton sheet and willed his brain to be still. He needed sleep. He had not been able to let his father's memory rest in peace since the horrid day he overheard their conversation, but tonight was the final night of his ignorance. Gualtiero had promised she would tell him the truth once off campus and on their way back to Salem for Holiday Break. No matter what transpired between now and then, he would hold her accountable for that promise.

First Born by Janelle Gabay

TWO
THE ATTACK

"Get up!"

Tarian vaguely heard the barking orders of Gualtiero in his haze of sleep. Distressing annoyance filled his brain. He resisted the urge to wrap the pillow around his head, cover his ears, and go back to sleep; but he could not disobey a superior officer.

"Now! Get up!"

Having finally slipped into a deep sleep, her shrill voice echoing inside his brain sent hot, irritating energy coursing through his veins, but he had to follow orders. He attempted to sit up but sleep lingered inside him. Slowly his eyes focused, and he saw her rushing towards his bed with fatigues and combat boots in her arms. She threw it at him. The sharp heel of the boot hit his bare chest like a solid punch. Now, he was pissed; she had gone too far with her superiority complex. Opening his mouth to yell back at her, he caught himself. She held rank. Then he heard the ear piercing fire alarm.

"Don't ask questions, just do as I say. Get dressed. Hurry!" Gualtiero ordered.

She did not leave the room or turn around to give him privacy; instead, she released weapons and a gas mask from her belt. As he rushed to get dressed, he noticed her usual steeliness had vanished. She looked frantic. He could tell by the color of the ceiling that it was still too early to be getting out of bed.

First Born by Janelle Gabay

When he looked out the window, he saw flames of fire devouring the grass of The Plain. The alarm was not a drill. Then he heard something. Gunshots?

"What's going on?" Tarian yanked on his boots.

"The Prevallers are attacking EMA. They've found you. Hide this just in case," she said, as she shoved the hand-cannon into his belt. She handed him another weapon, a bigger arm that could easily blast 3-rounds in a split second.

"Did you say found *me*?" He stood in front of her dressed, armed and ready.

"Come on!"

She pulled him out of his room and into the hall. Smoke rushed into his nostrils and clouded his eyes. He hurriedly put on the gas mask. His thoughts shot straight to his two best friends. He fought against Gualtiero's pull as he turned back to check two rooms. They were empty. His two best friends, Gabe and Maria, must have heard the alarm and already fled the building. He felt relieved and betrayed. They had left without alerting him.

Gualtiero clamped down on his elbow and dragged him toward the exit. Her strength amazed him. A flammable substance covered the doorway causing thick flames. They leaped through the vicious wall of red and fell to the ground: stop-drop-roll.

Back on her feet, Gualtiero tugged him up to his. They ran. He followed her not knowing at first what direction she was taking him. The dim early morning sunlight veiled everything in a color-blending, fuzzy haze, but he could see more cadets running with guns. Vermilion trails streaked the skies. Black smoke crept around corners. Patton's statue twisted into an

First Born by Janelle Gabay

unrecognizable heaping mess of bronze alloy. Thick, rich dust and scorching fire were everywhere. The Entente Military Academy was under full attack.

"Someone is following us," he told her.

Another cadet with a rifle ran after them. Gualtiero turned and shot the cadet dead without hesitation. Astonished, Tarian stopped running. *What the hell is going on?*

"Move!" she ordered.

He stared at Ian Khan's motionless body. "You killed Ian!"

"Yes, he was going to kill us. I'll explain later. We have to get to the boat!"

The sincerity in her silvery-blue eyes begged him to keep moving. He took one last scan of the magnificent yet formidable calamity surrounding him then ran. Buildings exploded behind him. Solid stone of impressive monuments tumbled into nothing but shimmery dust. He smelled the distinct odor of wood burning. The aroma was pleasant like a campfire, but the dangerous flames were only yards away from his flesh.

They ran alone now. They had escaped the crowd of cadets, but not the echo of pain infused voices. The sounds of screams reminded him of Ian's face. Haunted by Ian's eyes as they expressed his fear of death once the bullet pierced his skin. He remembered when Ian had provoked a fistfight and Tarian had been foolish enough to throw the first punch, an act that Ian could have easily used to get him expelled, but he hadn't. Tarian thought the two of them had come to an understanding. He was clearly wrong about that.

First Born by Janelle Gabay

Gualtiero and Tarian charged across Thayer Road and then Williams Road. She took him up a dirt road that ran along the shoreline to the south dock where a bearded man in an interceptor craft waited for them. Tarian jumped into the boat first, followed by Gualtiero. Tarian thought he recognized the man, but on second glance he did not know him. However, the man nodded at Tarian as if he did know who he was.

"Sit down," the man said before hitting the throttle. The boat sped away instantly at 35 knots, thrusting Tarian backward into his seat.

"Wait!" Tarian yelled to Gualtiero over the roaring motor. "We have to go back."

"We can't!" she demanded.

"I mean, Maria and Gabe. We have to find them.

"They're okay," she said then added, "I saw them. They escaped in a vehicle with Colonel Rigby."

He fixed his eyes on hers, and although she did not look away, he didn't believe her. He almost jumped off the speeding boat and into the freezing river, but she held his secret. She had promised him the truth, and that promise compelled him to stay with her. He was uninformed, and she was obviously very clear on the situation at hand.

He glanced down at the lethal weapon he held in his hands. He could aim it at her. He could force the promised information out of her right now. He began to lift the weapon but hesitated. He watched the man driving the boat as he dodged scattered debris in the river and falling from the sky. This man was no ordinary man; he was a trained soldier.

First Born by Janelle Gabay

He assessed Gualtiero. Her eyes alert like a watchdog, her stance athletic and her weapon ready. These two people were keeping him safe and alive. Slowly he accepted the fact that he had to trust them. The decision was made and hopefully it was the right one.

Tarian remembered the day he woke up and saw Gualtiero's face in the hospital. He had dropped into an unconscious state after taking the developmental drug, Sanoxine. EMA had given it to all the new cadets to build up their immune systems to fight advanced bioweapons. It was the only time she had spoken to him as a colleague. Her voice had been soft and caring that evening, and he knew she was more than his superior officer. He sensed she had a special interest in him that went beyond the academy, a connection.

Twenty minutes later they were exiting the craft at Tomkins Cove and boarding a sleek, black tiltrotor. The man abandoned his boat and jumped urgently into the tiltrotor with them. Sitting in the pilot's seat impatient and angry was yet another man, another stranger Tarian was supposed to trust with his life. This man was young, twenty-five looking, with large arms. The man took control of the tiltrotor the instant Tarian's feet left the dirt. Tarian stumbled to his seat as the aircraft lifted. He sat in the back balling his hands into fists desperately wanting to punch something; but instead, he took a deep breath and kept a keen eye on every person inside the aircraft.

After a seemingly endless flight, the pull of the descent stirred his empty stomach. As the tiltrotor lowered the last few feet to the ground, unpredictable vomit crawled up his throat but

First Born by Janelle Gabay

he managed to control it. He'd mastered self-control since his father's death.

The tiltrotor lowered onto a plain of snow in Battlefields Park in the Quebec District. The peaceful, pure white snow contrasted the chaotic grounds at EMA. A narrow road set in position by the sharp blade of time cut through the dense snow. It wound out of the park and into the city.

An unmarked, dark green sedan sat covered in white flakes at the beginning of the road. The crisp, subarctic air inside the vacant car engulfed the foursome. The engine froze by the relentless winter weather.

"Piece of shit car! Dammit, Eleanor! Invest in today's technology," the pilot, now driver, yelled as he attempted to start the ignition.

"Who's Eleanor?" Tarian asked Gualtiero.

"Our Chancellor," she responded.

The small, old sedan was not the vehicle Tarian would have chosen for the deep snow and expansive plain. Soon, however, the sedan was maneuvering perfectly within the tight streets of the city.

First Born by Janelle Gabay

THREE
HEADQUARTERS

Peering out of the backseat window, Tarian tracked the landscape noting landmarks, as the car approached the Quebec District. He watched as the car drove into the city.

"Where are you taking me?"

"To our village where you'll be safe."

"Are the Prevallers attacking other places?"

"Not at this moment, but we don't take chances."

"You promised to tell me the truth about my father. And now, I want to know who's after *me*!"

"I know. I will. You'll get your answers soon. I promise."

He sighed, wondering if he had the patience to wait any longer; however, a drastic change in the scenery caught his attention. Within the millisecond of his eye blink, they had left the city and entered a village, and Tarian had no idea how it had happened.

The long, cobbled street curved around old masonry homes and stores ranging in size from fat to skinny and short to tall creating a jagged skyline. The car pulled up to a wooden garage door with steel bands located in the heart of the village. The building surrounding the garage appeared centuries old and covered in stone and aged wood. Tarian admired the historic architecture.

16

First Born by Janelle Gabay

Once inside the garage, things changed. It was modern with flat walls and glass staircases. As he looked around more intently, he saw twenty dark green motor crafts ranging in size and model. A shiny sports car with a nine hundred, horsepower hover engine sat ten feet away from him, distracting his attention for a second. Returning his thoughts to the situation at hand, he wondered how had he ended up inside a gigantic car showroom after pulling into a single car garage?

"Cadet Sergeant Gualtiero --"

"It's Audrey, here," she interrupted.

"What?"

"Just call me Audrey."

"Oh, okay." He paused, finding it difficult to disengage from the strict EMA protocol he had followed for a year and a half.

"What?" she asked, resuming the conversation.

"I'm not loosing it, right? We did just go from the city, to here, instantly; and we did just enter a small garage, but now we are in a very large garage? Right?" These questions sounded crazy to his ears, but Audrey remained composed.

"You're not crazy. Have patience."

Patience, he thought. Tension covered his skin in prickly waves, and patience seemed impossible, but he had no other choice.

Moving out of the garage and into the belly of the building, Tarian noticed the four-story home filled with men and women of various ages. Each person nodded at him in recognition. Some of them patted him on the back, and one man even gave him a fist pump. They were all dressed in neatly

First Born by Janelle Gabay

pressed uniforms, the same dark green as the vehicles. He had
been taken to some sort of headquarters, as everyone swiftly
walked with purpose holding tablets, mobiles, and/or briefcases.
And like the garage, it was much more spacious than it appeared.

The foursome walked into a meeting room where two
men and two women stood to welcome everyone. They were
expected. Tarian sat rigidly in a comfortable leather chair that
was offered to him. He hoped for the answers he so anxiously
waited for.

"Hello Tarian," a middle-aged woman said. She wore a
broad smile of perfect teeth that spread her sagging jowls,
creating an unpleasant bulldog-like appearance that clashed with
her high-pitched tone of voice. "I am Margaret Davenport, and
this is Edward Corbet, Blaise Garneau, and Nicolas Giles," she
said as she walked from person to person. They were all intently
staring and smiling at him. She did not introduce a man in the
corner who seemed to appear out of thin air.

The man wore deep purple instead of dark green. He
looked rumpled even though his uniform was obediently pressed
like everyone else's. He appeared to be meditating. His eyes
remained closed, and he never acknowledged anybody else in the
room and no one acknowledged him. His presence, as well as the
strangeness of the entire building, made Tarian uneasy.

Was I the only one who could see him? Tarian thought.

"The attacks have begun for the mortals, and we have
been commissioned to help, but our priority is to find the person
assassinating immortals." She paused considering Tarian's
awkward expression and looked at Audrey. "He knows
nothing?"

First Born by Janelle Gabay

"No Margaret," she responded. "I was under the impression that I was supposed to bring him here first."

"Oh, well," she said, clearly under a different impression. "No, no my dear. This is not the place for him. We are handling Guardian profiles to find the traitor. Horrible, truly horrible work to pry into your colleagues personal lives. But unfortunately, it must be done." She turned her attention towards Tarian and continued her conversation. "I know you are ignorant about what I'm saying right now. That is why you will follow Audrey to the library where she will explain everything to you."

Audrey stood up quickly, but Tarian remained weighted to the chair. *What's going on? Assassin? Immortals? Traitors?*

"Go to the kitchen first. He needs a good meal," Margaret ordered.

"Come on, Tarian," Audrey said.

He remained seated, still in a daze, more questions piling on top of the previous ones inside his head. He thought of his family, especially his older brother Charlie. *Were they safe?*

"Let's go," Audrey said, tugging on his arm.

They left the others behind in the meeting room. Audrey zigzagged through the second level hallway then up a glass staircase. Tarian jogged to keep up with her. Finally, they walked through carved wooden doors into a rustic tavern-style eatery. It was the only room Tarian had seen, so far, that matched the historic style of the exterior.

"Sit here and don't move," Audrey ordered.

He definitely would not move from his seat without his guide. He was going through the motions but would not be able to locate this place if he had to.

19

First Born by Janelle Gabay

"Where are you going?" he asked.

"To get you food."

"But we can order here." He pointed to the ordering screen.

"No, too slow," she said, shaking her head and rolling her eyes.

She walked away before he could reply. The tablet for ordering lay on the table. Curious, he swiped the touch screen to view the numerous meal options. Before now, he had not even thought of food, but flipping through the images of delicious choices made his stomach growl and ache.

The mouthwatering aroma of herb-roasted turkey and stuffing wafted through the air. Scents of pecan and apple pie also tantalized his nose and teased his palate. He glanced around to view guests eating good old-fashioned, human prepared food. It had been a long time since he had eaten a meal that wasn't instantly generated. All the meals at EMA were scientifically created drinks and bars, specifically tailored to each soldiers' individual nutritional needs, adequate in calories, vitamins, fats, carbohydrates and proteins.

The chef paraded around the tables, stopping to accept the many compliments doled upon him. He appeared to be a man of importance. He looked jolly with his plump belly. In fact, he was the first overweight person Tarian had seen in this building. Like the rumpled man in the corner, the chef wore purple. His suit tailored for his profession but just as impeccable as everyone else's attire.

"I got you a bowl of chicken soup and a turkey sandwich," Audrey said.

First Born by Janelle Gabay

"Thank you," Tarian said, but it looked disappointing after reviewing the other plates of heaping piles of rare roast beef, honey ham, fluffy mashed potatoes, savory stuffing, corn on the cob and sweet sugary pies.

"And a cup of coffee," she said, sliding the steaming mug across the table.

She looked very pleased with herself, and he did not have the heart to complain.

"Where are we?" he asked, taking a sip of the bold, black coffee that was actually amazingly creamy and sweet. One bite into the sandwich and an explosion of Thanksgiving flavors infused his mouth. Tarian had never tasted anything like it. He peeled away the layer of bread to reveal a simple thick slice of turkey. He wondered how one slice could generate the many flavors of his mother's entire Thanksgiving dinner. He devoured every magical morsel.

"We're in the Quebec District," she said, staring at a remnant of sandwich left on his lips.

He awkwardly wiped his face with his napkin. "No, we're not."

"Technically we are. However, you will not find this particular village on any map. It is not a part of the Entente of Nations. We are independent."

With furrowed brow and pursed lips, he asked, "I need to call my mom and brother. They'll be worried."

"Your family was informed that you are okay. Of course they want to hear from you in person, so we'll arrange a contact soon."

"Are they safe?"

21

First Born by Janelle Gabay

"Yes, we have them under surveillance. EMA was a warning. The Prevallers chose the academy because you were there."

"Why do you keep saying that? Why would the Prevallers care so much about me? I'm only a cadet," he asked, swallowing a mouthful of soup.

"Tarian, you are very important to us. We are the Guardians of Dare. We are a dangerous threat to the Prevallers. Luckily, our Intelligence uncovered their plan before they had time to execute it fully. During the commotion of the attack, Ian planned to capture you after he killed me," she said, glancing around the tavern.

"Why?" he asked turning his head to view what caught her attention. He saw more curious stares directed at him. The chef strolled towards him.

"Are you done eating? I'd rather speak in private," she asked, assessing his empty plate and bowl.

He ate enough to feel comfortable, but the aroma left him wanting more.

"Yes," he said, embarrassed to look piggish.

"Welcome," a booming voice announced, as a friendly hand patted his back.

"Hello," Tarian said.

"Hello, Chef Richard," Audrey said. "Richard this is Tarian Prescott."

"Tis a pleasure to finally meet you. Ah, your plate is empty. Audrey, get him more food." It was an order but given in a gentle way. Nonetheless, it was still an order, and Tarian could tell Audrey did not appreciate being told to fetch food.

22

First Born by Janelle Gabay

"Actually Richard, we were just leaving."

"But he hasn't had pie!"

"I'll bring him back. Real soon."

The chef twitched his head and scowled at her, but then regained his amiable composure and smiled at Tarian.

"You must come to afternoon tea," he invited.

"Thank you. I will. It was delicious," Tarian said.

"Okay, let's go," Audrey said. "Bye Richard."

First Born by Janelle Gabay

FOUR
PIPER

Audrey once again pulled Tarian along, but he was happy to leave. The stares of the guests inside the tavern were making him uncomfortable. He felt like the seeker in a game of hide-and-seek that he was not aware he was playing. They ascended more stairs then entered a chilly, quiet room. Their loud, quick steps announced their approach, but the library's visitors were sparse and kept to themselves, immersed in their reading.

Audrey and Tarian retreated to a comfortable seating area in the back, hidden behind several rows of tall bookshelves. A welcoming fire burned warm and constant in a giant stone fireplace. She wasn't kidding when she said she wanted privacy. This worried him. *What horrible information is she about to tell me?*

Several uneasy seconds passed between the two, finally Tarian asked, "Why does everyone know who I am?"

She gave him a look of contemplation, as if she didn't know where to begin. Today had been an unraveling of new information and now he had more questions on top of the already daunting secret about his father's death. Only now, sitting across from her, the truth seemed frighteningly unwanted.

"You are inside Guardian Headquarters –"

"Did you tell him yet?" A girl popped into their intimate sitting area and startled Tarian.

24

First Born by Janelle Gabay

"Not yet," Audrey said through gritted teeth obviously annoyed at the girl's interruption.

"You are the first immortal to be born in five hundred and thirty-three years." The girl spat the words out with uncontrolled excitement.

"What are you talking about?" Tarian looked from the girl to Audrey and back.

The jumpy girl heightened Tarian's anxiety and Audrey's irritation.

"Shhhh! Settle down, Piper," Audrey said as she guided Piper into a chair. Audrey kept one hand on Piper in an attempt to keep her still. It failed.

"Oh what a story it is!" Piper said rocking back and forth.

Tarian feared she would pounce on him at any moment.

Audrey turned toward Tarian and tried to regain her composure. She took a deep breath and continued, "Tarian, I'm six-hundred and twelve years old. I'm an immortal. I was born Audrey Ballard in 1499. My parents were Loriners, ordinary people who made bridles for horses. Your dad's father owned a spice shop and his mother was a powerful witch. We were neighbors. We grew up together during the time of Tudor London."

"What?" He replied loudly as he jerked forward in his seat to inspect her.

She appeared to be twenty years old, at the most. She smirked and tilted her head. She must have expected this reaction.

"I'm five-hundred and ninety-eight," Piper added with a wide toothy smile.

First Born by Janelle Gabay

"As strange as it seems, it's very much true," Audrey said.

"But you are twenty and my dad was in his forties and she is...I don't know...she looks sixteen." He glanced at Piper.

"I know. That is our physical age, not the actual number of years we have lived. We've studied our phenomenon for centuries, and we still don't know why some of us age farther than others."

"That's what differentiates us from vampires," Piper said.

"What?" Tarian asked.

"Oh, yeah, and they drink blood," Piper added.

"I don't believe you. You're kidding right?" Tarian tried to laugh at the absurdity of Audrey and Piper's words. His faint laughter turned to panic. His head began to ache. He sat back placing his weight on the cushiony chair and closed his eyes in an attempt to stop his head from throbbing.

"Piper stop talking! I know it's a lot of strange information. We are unique. We are immortal. We are unsure exactly how we became immortal since our births happened long ago during a time of little scientific data. During the fifteenth and sixteenth centuries most people explained away strange phenomena as divine intervention or witchcraft." Audrey said the words as kindly as she could. She let the meaning hang in the air.

"Yes, yes. And now, we can see our DNA. We have an abundance of methylation bookmarkers and as a result the mechanism is showing curative for any human disease in us, although we can't pinpoint how. We have regenerative stem

First Born by Janelle Gabay

cells. All sorts of unique traits that mortals don't have," Piper said.

As Piper's words flew out of her mouth again, Audrey closed her eyes and looked as if she was defusing a bomb set to detonate inside her head.

The information spun inside Tarian's mind. He closed his eyes, regained his composure and asked, "If I'm to believe this story, then how could my father die?"

"Death Serum!" Piper yelped, then covered her mouth with her hand. She looked as if she had just said the most insulting curse word.

"Piper, let me explain," Audrey snapped and Piper cowered into the chair. "Out of all of the other creatures inside our borders, we could not be killed. We had no weaknesses until recently. A Death Serum has been developed, we assume, by the Prevallers. It's an extremely advanced bioweapon. Our most skilled scientists here at Headquarters have failed to make an antidote for it."

Tarian shot to his feet and began to pace. "Then we're all in danger. The Prevallers are eliminating the immortals before they begin a war."

"Exactly. We have hundreds of years worth of strength, wealth and knowledge. We have made this nation great since the Revolutionary War. Plus, we are the most reliable and organized of all the creatures. Destroying us is brilliant strategy."

"And my dad was killed by this Death Serum?"

"Yes and thirteen others."

"So how can you say I'm safe or my family is safe? None of us are safe!"

First Born by Janelle Gabay

"The village has a magic shield." Piper jumped into the conversation. She nodded her head and widened her eyes.

"No one has been murdered within the protection of the village," Audrey said.

"And why is my birth any different than yours just because it happened hundreds of years later. I don't get it!" He continued to pace, wearing a path in the rug.

"It's a long story," Audrey said.

"I don't care. I'm sure Piper can tell me," Tarian said. He glanced at Piper.

"Yes, yes." She sat upright, leveled her gaze but did not get the chance to speak.

"No, I'll tell it. Sit down," Audrey ordered. "Have you ever heard of the lost Colony of Roanoke?"

"No," Tarian said. He sat in the chair running his fingers through his stubbly buzz cut hair.

Piper resumed rocking, eyes wide with excitement, but she bit her lips closed.

"Well, those of us within the walls of London began to gather together. We traveled to the New World as the Colony of Roanoke in 1587. Our assumed mission was to become a settlement for Queen Elizabeth and Sir Walter Raleigh. At the time, they were competing with Spain to conquer the New World. That part is in the history books, but our real mission, our immortal secret mission was strictly to protect Eleanor White Dare and her unborn child, hence the name, Guardians of Dare. In the history books, we vanished and many theories have been made explaining our demise, but in truth, we disappeared on purpose." Audrey took a breath.

28

First Born by Janelle Gabay

Piper stared at Audrey, lips quivering. Audrey rewarded her with a nod of permission.

"Eleanor's baby was foretold to be the last born immortal, but she died of illness as a teenager. Eleanor is our Chancellor. She was the last immortal to be born back in 1568. She never had any more children." Piper finished the story.

"All of our children have died, all except you," Audrey added.

"But I'm only nineteen. How do you know I'll survive?"

"You've already survived," Audrey said.

"The bus accident," he said soberly.

He always knew he should have died when the Salem Academy school bus skidded on black ice and sank into the icy pond. Everyone perished except for him - all of his friends. He had no recollection of the events. He had blacked out. All he remembered was waking up inside a hospital. Several doctors called his recovery a miracle.

"Yes. You should have died when you were nine. Since that day, your father knew. He gathered a few of us together, and we have been studying your miraculous existence ever since."

"If I'm the only birth, I mean…new…immortal…How many of us are there?" he asked. Keeping his thoughts in order became a difficult task.

"Right now? Three hundred and twenty-nine. We are continually searching the world for immortals, but it has been over two hundred years since our last discovery. However, even those immortals were all born in fifteenth, sixteenth century Europe. So you see why you are so important. You were born recently and with the Death Serum--"

First Born by Janelle Gabay

"The Prophecy is coming true," Piper interrupted, her excitement gone.

"Piper!" Audrey growled.

"What? Tell him about the Prophecy," Piper said.

"What's she talking about?" Tarian quieted his movements and listened, fearing this news would be overwhelming.

"I told you your father's mother was a witch."

"Yes," he nodded.

"Well, her coven foretold of a new and final birth followed by the horrific destruction of our kind. During Queen Elizabeth's reign anyone suspected of witchcraft, and of course, cheating death would fall under that category, suffered torturous studies and deaths. We assumed the prophecy meant we were soon to be discovered and hunted and killed. So that's why we fled England with Eleanor Dare. She was the only immortal pregnant at the time. We thought Virginia Dare was the foreseen final birth, but she was not. And no one has fit that description until you."

"You're it Tarian. You are the only hope for the survival of the Guardians of Dare," Piper said in a surprisingly mature voice.

"What?"

"Well, the prophecy has changed. I mean it has evolved. I guess that's the best way to explain it. The coven has said that our extinction can be stopped."

"How?"

"Well that's just it. Prophecies are vague. Something about a tomb and other creatures."

30

First Born by Janelle Gabay

"No, it goes like this. The savior lies in a tomb where grown men die. A young child of many is the key soon born of mortal witch and man of unending years. Do not fear other creatures from the south for their help will bring life," Piper chanted.

"Do you see what I mean? Jibber jabber. Why can't they just tell us in English?" Audrey threw up her arms.

"It makes perfect sense. Tarian is one of four children: 'one of many,'" Piper said.

"Yes, but he's not lying in a tomb with grown men."

"Not yet," Piper added.

"Great! Something I can look forward to. What about the kid thing? None of you were able to have children? My dad was the only one?" He questioned.

"Not immortal children. We've had children and families throughout the centuries but they're mortal," Audrey explained.

"Have you ever had kids?" he asked Audrey.

"Yes," she said. "A girl, Isabella. She was beautiful. She died many, many years ago."

She did not elaborate and Piper remained silent too. Audrey's eyes moistened at the mention of her daughter's name, and he saw her swallow a lump of grief in her throat. He knew that rock-hard lump of pain. He, too, had experienced the inability to form words through the thick grief that clogged the throat.

Time had not healed her pain. Everyone at his father's funeral had promised him that time would heal his heart and his

31

First Born by Janelle Gabay

memories would bring joy, but her pain was alive after all these years.

"I see," he said.

Then an even worse nightmare consumed him. He would outlive his family and his girlfriend, Delia. He would watch them grow old and die, and everyone else that he loved would die too. He would have to endure heartbreaking losses over and over forever. He once had his immortal dad, but someone had taken that gift away from him.

"Tarian, are you okay?" Audrey asked.

"I want to find the person who took my dad's life, and I want to kill him. I could have had decades of memories. You did. Centuries! I barely got seventeen!" He said with enormous breaths and flared nostrils. "What good is this gift of life if everyone you love dies?"

He glared at her, and for the first time, she looked away. He turned to Piper but she was gone. Vanished. For a second Tarian felt bad for scaring her away, but he could not calm his rage.

"This is a damn curse!" he yelled but still Audrey had no words. "It could have been a very special gift but someone took that from me. Who?" He pounded his fists into the chair. His lunch stirred in his stomach.

"I don't know!" She yelled back at him then inhaled deeply to recompose herself.

The fire in the hearth began to feel hot instead of warm. Glances from a couple of green-suited library patrons turned into haunting stares. Now he knew why they all looked at him as if he was an infamous celebrity. He had been twice cursed, first

32

First Born by Janelle Gabay

with immortality and second with the link to their survival or death.

"How can you not know who is killing your...our kind? This looks like quite an elaborate organization. Someone knows the truth," he said and saw Audrey flinch. "It's one of us, isn't it? You mentioned a traitor earlier."

"That's the fear."

Eyes wet with tears, hands clenched into fists. The blood in his veins raced, filling his muscles with the need to move.

"I know how you feel," she said trying to calm him down, but those were the wrong words.

Strike one!

"No, you don't." He directed his irritation towards her.

"Yes, I do," she said adamantly. "Lower your voice."

Strike two!

"Well what do we do now?" he asked in the same voice. "I want justice. I'm an Entente soldier. I'm trained to fight. Take me to the person in charge of us, the Guardians."

"You do nothing but stay here where you are safe."

Strike three!

"Hell no! I will not." His voice boomed another decimal louder.

"Shhhh! You have to. You are a protégé. We don't know your state. We need to study you and protect you."

"I'm not a lab rat."

"No, you're not. You're the first Guardian of Dare born in centuries. Do you realize how important you are? Your father died protecting you, protecting our kind. If you die, then he died for nothing."

First Born by Janelle Gabay

"How dare you use my father against me!"

Holding her hands up in retreat, "I'm sorry; that's not what I meant. Your father was my best friend. He loved you," her eyes softened. "Forget the Prevallers. Forget the prophecy. Your dad thought you brought hope to us all. He thought if you could be born than maybe others could too. Maybe we all could birth immortal children and stop suffering the unbearable pain of their deaths."

"If you knew my dad, you'd know he wouldn't want me hide behind your magic curtain. He sent me to EMA! The orders were in his Will."

"Zachary's back!" Piper popped back into view, rocking in her chair as if she had never left.

"Senator Eastwood?" Tarian asked.

"Yes," Piper said.

"That fits…Right…He's immortal too isn't he?"

"Yes," Audrey stated.

"That's why you were talking to him… about my dad…I get it now…you and Senator Eastwood sent me to EMA…not Dad. You said the Guardians are soldiers. Not an attorney, never a lawyer like I thought, like my dad. I was supposed to work in Dad's law firm. Everything changed after Dad died, and now I know why." He talked without thinking, words spilled from his mouth, words of comprehension.

"I think it's time for you to go to your room and get some rest," she said.

"What about Delia?" he asked.

"She's mortal, Tarian," Audrey said.

34

First Born by Janelle Gabay

"Of course, because I'm the only one." Tarian nodded his head. His eyes remained focused on a distant intangible image.

"Come on, let me take you to your room." Audrey placed her hand on his forearm.

"It's one o'clock in the afternoon!" He snatched his arm away from her.

He looked at Audrey then Piper. He paused then he whipped around and stormed out of the library.

Audrey's strides were on his heels immediately. He erratically paced the maze of hallways and the other floors, looking for an office that felt important. There were a lot more than four floors as he had originally thought.

Frustrated, he turned to Audrey. "This place is gigantic. Where are they?"

"Follow me."

They went to the fourth floor and walked straight back to the last door on the left. They entered a lobby area with a set of monstrous, solid, oak doors. A mahogany desk sat empty of its receptionist. Steel framed windows with old stone on the outside, and bulletproof panes of glass broke up the walls. It smelt like his dad's law office: wood, leather and a smokiness that had rooted its odor inside these materials a long time ago.

Audrey knocked on the door.

First Born by Janelle Gabay

FIVE
ELEANOR

"Come in," a female voice said.

Audrey and Tarian walked into a palatial room with richly embroidered tapestries and spectacular tables made of petrified wood, as well as, all the technological advancements of any Government Intelligence Agency. This room could not possibly fit in the space provided by the quaint village street venue. It had to be an illusion. Ten feet tall screens lined the back wall that extended at least one hundred and twenty yards the length. Even the Entente Military Academy with all its modern technologies had nothing to compare to this room. Misty images of charts and maps levitated in the air.

"Tarian, this is Eleanor Dare," Audrey said. Her words pulled him out of his awed state and back into his rage. She turned to face the gentleman in the room and introduced him. "And you know Zachary. I mean, Senator Eastwood."

Tarian surveyed the two of them before he spoke. Eleanor was what he now thought of as the Purple People. She wore a blackberry business suit, and the Senator wore his usual well-tailored, steel gray business attire. A few other people in dark green, the Green People, studied charts and gathered information on tablets in the far back of the room.

"I'm not staying here to be a lab rat," he finally said to Eleanor. "No matter how elaborate your chemistry set is." He turned his attention towards the Senator. He felt the urge to

36

First Born by Janelle Gabay

punch him in the face; angered by all of the secrets he had kept. The Senator was his father's best friend. This man was Delia's father. Resentment stung his esophagus like bile, but Tarian swallowed it and maturely, but sternly, directed his conversation to the Senator. "You should have told me."

"As you can see," Audrey said, "Tarian is very upset with all the secrets. His new world is confusing and --"

Tarian cut her off. "I can speak for myself. I'm a fighter remember. I'm EMA, the pride of the Entente. If I die, then I die. Take my DNA; take my blood, my whatever you need. Keep it, study it. I don't care. But you can't keep me here. I'm going to find my dad's murderer."

"You will serve Joe best by staying inside this village," Senator Eastwood said.

"Bullshit!" Tarian became even more infuriated as his father's name slipped from the Senator's lips.

"Listen, Young Man, I did not bring you into my home for you to throw everything away," the Senator said with finality.

Tarian remained stubbornly silent.

"Zachary, I agree with Tarian. He's not Virginia. I promise you. He is going to survive," Eleanor said.

Tarian could feel Eleanor's confidence and strength. She had a steady stance that emitted unabashed truth. She looked at Tarian with pride and concern. She sat down behind her desk and gestured for everyone to sit. Senator Eastwood stood, visibly upset that she had rebuffed his position, but it was obvious, no one questioned this woman's choices. She held the superior position in the room, and Tarian wondered where the Senator and Audrey fell in the line of command.

First Born by Janelle Gabay

"What is our position?" Eleanor directed this question to Senator Eastwood.

"I'm not going to marginalize the situation. The attack on the Entente Military Academy was a huge breach in security. The President is reeling. The press is having a field day ripping apart the safety of the Entente's closed borders."

As the Senator spoke of EMA, the image of the Academy lifted off of the large screen in the distance and appeared next to Eleanor like a levitating hologram. Tarian assumed Eleanor had a unique device to create holograms, but she held nothing. She simply waved her hands, and things happened. With another flick of her wrist, the two people dressed in green disappeared from their posts in the back of the room and materialized standing next to Tarian.

"Incredible." Tarian gasped. He touched the man's arm to find he was flesh and bone, not a holographic light field.

The moving picture that floated in the air clearly showed some of Tarian's professors examining the rubble looking for students. Next Tarian viewed a similar image of the Government District.

"As you can see the Government District in Boston is secure, and our resources have not been targeted," the Senator explained.

One by one the holographic light fields of these places materialized for review. Silently, they examined each important resource facility of the Entente. The uranium pits were not damaged. The diamond mines still swirled into the earth's crust and the phosphate mines still cut across the land. The electricity-producing fusion power plant remained operational, as did the

38

First Born by Janelle Gabay

space based solar power farm. And so on, and so forth. As far as Tarian could tell, the Entente nation was still very much intact.

Eleanor threw the three-dimensional images back onto their flat surfaces one hundred feet away with one flick of her wrist. The two Green People also vanished but reappeared at their stations in the distance.

"EMA was a deliberate attack. The reasons are known to the President and us, but obviously, we cannot tell the public," the Senator said.

"Why?" Tarian asked.

"Many Guardians hold positions at EMA, and you were there. That was the target. The Prevallers' mission was to capture and kill as many immortals as possible. Luckily, we had Recon Intelligence and were able to get all of the Guardians out in time, but there were far too many mortal casualties."

"Maria, Gabe," Tarian said almost to himself.

Everyone looked at him with sympathetic eyes, but no one assured him of their safety. He hoped his closest friends were alive, and someday, they would be together again.

"We were lucky. We cannot risk Tarian's safety again." The Senator turned his back towards Tarian to speak to Eleanor.

"He's perfect for reconnaissance," Eleanor said.

The Senator scoffed. "You are using him as a decoy."

Tarian cleared his throat getting Eleanor's attention. "I want to know more about the assassin."

She politely redirected her explanations towards him. "Yes, yes. You, as well as the rest of the public, are aware of the threat to our way of life by the outside alliance known as the Prevallers. It is no secret that when we closed our borders and

First Born by Janelle Gabay

ended trade amongst other nations, we created many enemies. While we've thrived, the outside world has not."

"It was only a matter of time before the other nations destroyed each other. We had the insight to prevent such ruination from crossing the seas and affecting our nation. We fought hard to erect our borders, build lethal drones and secure our lands," the Senator stated.

"Correct, Zachary." Eleanor acknowledged his interruption then continued, "Without the strength of the Guardians, the Entente would not exist. We helped build the peaceful society we live in today. We have battled in secret for the security of this land and our freedoms since the Revolutionary War. Our existence and contributions have always been a secret until now. Someone has not only leaked the existence of an immortal race to the Prevallers but has created a Death Serum to kill us. And that informant is feared to be one of us."

"Why?" Tarian asked.

"We don't know," Eleanor said.

"And that is who killed my father? One of our own," Tarian asked.

"We believe so," Eleanor said. Her eyes fell. Tarian saw that she mourned the loss of her beloved immortals. With one subtle sigh, she looked a lot less powerful.

Tarian wanted to fight for this woman. "I'm ready," he stated. These were his people, his dad's family and now his. He felt a surging need to protect them and punish such an evil betrayer.

"I don't like it; we have other alternatives," Senator Eastwood said.

First Born by Janelle Gabay

"Zachary this is my final decision," Eleanor stated.

Tarian caught a look of resentment the Senator aimed at Eleanor. Tarian had never seen the Senator receive orders from anyone.

Eleanor turned all of her attention towards Tarian. "You need more training. We need to test your special abilities, see how far you've developed. However, I need you in the lab first."

"How long do you need him?" Audrey asked.

Tarian felt like a pawn in a very real chess match.

"In 24 hours you can take him to the Realm."

"Agreed," Audrey said.

"Tarian, I will escort you to the lab," Eleanor said.

They all stood to leave. Once out the door, Audrey and Senator Eastwood headed in the opposite direction.

"Senator." Tarian caught him before he walked away. "How's Delia?"

"She's fine," the Senator said.

"When can I see her?"

"I'm not sure. It's too dangerous."

"I understand. Please tell her I'm sorry."

"I will. She knows nothing of this. If and when you see her, it must all remain a secret," the Senator said.

The Senator gave Tarian one of his sanctimonious downward glances that Tarian had received several times during his yearlong stay at his estate after his father's death. Only now, Tarian surpassed him in height, and his tone did not have quite the same effect. However, Tarian still felt like a boy that owed him a great deal. He took Charlie and Tarian into his home, helped their mother financially, prepared Tarian for EMA and

41

First Born by Janelle Gabay

Charlie for Harvard. *Would he feel obligated to him forever*? He wondered.

First Born by Janelle Gabay

Six
The Lab

Eleanor led Tarian up two flights of stairs to the lab. Tarian watched her closely. Everyone who noticed her made sure to say hello, and a couple of people stopped to ask for her signature.

"We are not all Guardians. We do have mortals here too. I trust the mortals in this building. They know our kind. Most of their families have been working for us for generations. It's a shame with Joe's and the others' deaths that we have all become very suspicious of one another. I honestly cannot imagine anyone in our organization as a traitor," she said.

"You must have your suspicions," Tarian said.

"Clever boy." Her emerald eyes twinkled, but she did not expound. "Your father was curious too. You know Joe, Audrey and Zachary were inseparable for many, many years. Then Audrey met Marco. Oh, how she went through the wringer with those two! Your dad and Zachary were ruthless on poor Marco. No one less than perfect would suffice for their best friend. Your dad was a shape shifter, did you know?"

"No," Tarian said, surprised.

"You've probably noticed the dress code around here."

"Of course."

"Purple identifies those among us who have uncommon abilities. We have discovered these special talents are due to

43

First Born by Janelle Gabay

witches' blood. Some of the people you see dressed in purple are not immortal. They are in fact witches."

"Really?"

"Well, I generalize, but in some way or another these witches defy natural law. Call it magic, clairvoyance, paranormal, and so on. Personally I do not like labels. We all have some unique gift."

"If my dad had unnatural abilities, do I?"

"Not sure yet, all of us were conceived by two mortals. You were not. These tests will give me more answers."

She opened the door to the laboratory and concluded the conversation with a smile. Everything about Eleanor from the gait of her walk to the expression in her smile radiated confidence. She seemed too important to be escorting him around, but he guessed he was an interesting new development in her several, long-lived lifetimes.

The laboratory wafted ten degrees colder air and hummed a guitar solo. The style reminded Tarian of music his dad used to listen to. Fresh, clean smells of lemon and lavender filled his nostrils. Four long chairs that resembled dentist chairs, but looked much more inviting, stood in each corner. The chairs were designed to be comfortable, and Tarian assumed he would be sitting in one for a long time. When he saw the needles a chill slid down his spine, but he convinced himself he could handle a few pricks and pokes.

"Tarian, this is Henry. He is the best. Hasn't lost a patient yet," she said as an attempt at comic relief, but she was not a funny person, and the joke went stale fast.

First Born by Janelle Gabay

Henry just rolled his eyes and gave Tarian a look of sympathy.

"I'll check back in later." She left as regally as she had entered.

"Your job is to sit back and relax. The tests take thirteen, maybe fifteen hours but you can go to sleep," Henry said.

"That's okay. I'll stay awake," Tarian said, but the idea of sleep was tempting.

"The tests don't require anything on your part except to be in proximity to the equipment because of the wires and tubes. I've been doing this a long time and found the newer versions, the wireless versions, are not always better. In fact, their results have been erroneous. I like to stick to the old-fashioned, wired impulses and injections," Henry explained.

While Henry spoke, Tarian dozed off. Attempting to lift his eyelids, he noticed Henry wore a mask covering his nose and mouth. A sleeping inhalant now controlled Tarian's consciousness. His bravery, anger and confusion slipped away into the numbness of drug-induced sleep.

He awoke several hours later with stiff muscles and a cramped neck. The fog of sleep inside his brain slowly thinned, and he became aware of his surroundings. Henry still sat at his computer nodding his head and tapping his pencil to the beat of the guitar solo. Tarian attempted to speak, but an embarrassing dribble of drool leaked onto his chin. He quickly wiped it away.

Henry gave Tarian a thumbs-up and said, "Well, my friend, you were a delightful patient. Snoozed like a baby. I got what I needed, and you can be on your way."

45

First Born by Janelle Gabay

"Great," Tarian said. He opened his mouth to complain about being tricked into unconsciousness but decided sleep had been beneficial. He had not realized the toll the stress had taken on his body. Whatever concoction of sleeping gas he had been given, it was the perfect combination for satisfying, restful slumber.

"And here is your lovely guide," Henry said.

"Hi Henry," Audrey said, obviously used to Henry's bantering style. "How did he do?"

"Very well, very well," Henry said. "I captured plenty of cell division for Eleanor to look at. Did some carrier, predictive and presymptomatic testing. Amazing cell development." The complex words seemed misplaced inside Henry's lazy drawl.

"Really, that's fascinating," Audrey said but with her back turned to Henry, she looked at Tarian with wide silvery blue eyes and raised eyebrows. "Okay Tarian, let's go. It's time to leave the poppy field." She held a hand out to assist him from the comfort of the cushiony, leather chair.

In the hall, she looked over at his drowsy face and said, "Enjoy yourself?"

"Yes," he said, a bit ashamed at his need for sleep. Fatigue did not seem very soldier-like to him.

"Hey, don't feel bad. He does that to everyone. Henry has a way about him that makes people calm. We call him Dr. Doze," she said. "For many reasons."

"Well, I feel better than ever. I'm ready for training."

"There has been a change while you were sleeping."

"What happened?" He wondered: *good change or bad change.*

First Born by Janelle Gabay

"It's okay. We will train in the Realm in four days. We captured one of their men. He's not here in the village, but Eleanor is in constant contact with Central Intelligence."

"Has he confessed anything about the Death Serum?"

"No, he's not talking but we have gathered an abundance of information from his devices."

"That's good but what about the killer," Tarian asked.

"We believe he's in Boston. We also believe he went after your family."

"What!" Tarian halted his walk, squared his shoulders in Audrey's direction and began yelling, "You said they would –"

"They're safe. Everyone is okay."

"How?"

"Your house was broken into while your mother was home."

"Did he hurt her?"

"No. She didn't even hear or see anything. She was in her bathroom taking a shower while the person rummaged through the house. When she came out of the bathroom, the house was ransacked, and the person was gone."

"And Chloe, Teresa and Joe Jr.?"

"They're fine. Thankfully, they weren't home at the time."

"So where's my family now?" he asked.

"They're on their way here," she said.

"Good! I want to see them."

"I know you do. It's an important time for you to be with your family, and we need them to remain here where it's safe. We postponed training so you could spend Christmas together

47

First Born by Janelle Gabay

and convince them to stay here. But I need to explain a few things first," she said.

"Okay, explain." His patience waned.

"We have an Inn for people like your family. They can't know about the Guardians."

"What do I tell them?"

"As far as they know, this is a safe house for the Entente Military and Congressmen. Your mother and older siblings think the burglary has to do with Zachary since he's a senator. It's not a stretch for them to think Government officials and their families would be targeted by the Prevallers," she said.

"Okay. That's fine. I will make sure I don't tell them anything they're not supposed to know."

"Good."

An almost visible uneasiness floated around her.

"What are you not telling me?" he asked.

"Nothing, I don't like waiting."

"You don't trust this new information?" he said.

"Having a traitor among us is a new phenomenon. I'm not sure who I can trust."

"Do you trust Eleanor and Senator Eastwood?"

"Yes." She answered without hesitation, but she still looked troubled.

"Tarian!" Senator Eastwood rounded the corner, determined to gain their attention. "Thank you, Audrey, I will take it from here."

She gave Tarian a diluted smile and handed him over to the Senator. If Tarian had not known better, he would have thought she was disappointed to leave him.

First Born by Janelle Gabay

SEVEN
AN UNLIKELY PICNIC

Delia's lips met Tarian's before he had a chance to say hello. The kiss turned into a passionate production that extended past the point of etiquette. Tarian knew she had missed him, but he also recognized her mischievous intentions. Making her father uncomfortable was her favorite sport.

Trapped by his desire for her, Tarian would have kissed her for hours if she chose, but she released him. Awkwardly forced to look at Senator Eastwood, he tried in vain to blink away the haze of lust lingering in his eyes. He knew better than to speak any words and forced the smile to leave his face. The three of them stood in triangular formation in the center of the Inn's lobby for what felt like an eternity.

"Tarian, your family is not expected to arrive for another couple hours. You may take Delia into town if you like, but do not leave the village and remember what we discussed. You too, Delia. We have limited time and even though it is safe here, we must use all precautions," the Senator explained.

"Yes, Father, I know."

Delia locked her hand in Tarian's and rushed out of the Inn. She guided him through Rue de la Magie and drew him inside a door beneath a sign that read *The Perfect Picnic*. The store was empty of customers but filled with woven picnic baskets and checkered blankets. Most normal people did not picnic with snow on the ground, but he knew Delia well and

49

First Born by Janelle Gabay

guessed that she planned on keeping him quite warm despite the chill in the air.

Several minutes and a few zigzagged maneuvers through alleyways later, Tarian unfurled two heavy blankets in front of a secluded bonfire.

"How did you know this was here?" Tarian asked.

"I've been here before." Delia laid out a variety of cheeses and a baguette to snack on.

"Should I be concerned?"

"Yes." She sat cross-legged on the blanket and ripped off a piece of bread.

A twinge of guilt tried to destroy this moment. Tarian closed his eyes refusing to acknowledge the invasive thoughts about his father's killer. Tonight he wanted to banish his duties and focus on Delia's happiness.

She leaned in and caressed his face. Her eyes were filled with concern. She kissed him then backed away. She ripped off a piece of bread and handed it to him.

He took the bread and watched a smile spread across her face. The sight of her smile lessened the distractions inside of his head.

"Why aren't you eating?" she asked.

He grinned in response. He hungered not for food. He pulled her on top of him in one bold move. Tarian did not usually initiate aggressive, romantic advancements, as she's the Senator's daughter.

She giggled with delight and stretched the length of her body on top of his without refusal for several minutes. His hands found the small of her back, then wound around her narrow waist

50

First Born by Janelle Gabay

to grasp the sharp edges of her hips. She did not pull away; instead she pressed her body harder into his. He hungrily kissed her neck, and she moaned into his ear. Entwined in ecstasy, they explored one another with mouths and hands. Somewhat to his relief, since he knew he could not refuse her if she wanted more, she peeled her body off of his.

She rolled onto her back still holding his hand, looking at the dark cloudless sky. "You know this fire never burns out. Isn't that weird?"

His labored breathing prevented words. Eventually, his animalistic desire turned into a manageable ache, and he answered her question, "Yes that's weird. Are you sure?"

"Yes, every time I've come here, day or night, it still burns. And I've never seen any person around tending to it."

"Strange." He knew it was the work of a Purple Person, but he kept the secret.

She propped herself up on one elbow and ran the soft tip of her slender finger along his cheek. "What have they asked you to do?"

"It's classified. If I tell you, I have to kill you." He pulled her towards him again.

"No seriously." She pulled away.

"How many times have you been here?" he asked.

"We've hidden here a few times, thanks to Dad's work. And now he's gotten your family in danger too."

"No, he hasn't."

"Yes, he has!"

He wanted to tell her about the many circumstances that brought him to this village, but how could he explain it and not

First Born by Janelle Gabay

reveal the truth? He'd have to lie or evade her questions. He'd have to act just as her father did, and he knew she resented her father for his secrecy.

"I'm going to be fine," he said. "And what about you?"

"I'm fine."

"You're still very thin."

"I know." She turned away from him.

"But you're healthy?" He tread lightly, knowing she was sensitive about her illness.

"Yes, I've already told you I'm fine." Turning back around to face him she asked, "When do you leave?"

"What do you mean?"

"Tarian don't do this to me. You know me." She looked into his eyes with strength and wisdom.

"Christmas day, our training begins in four days." He braced for the onslaught of powerful words that she would cast upon him.

"We will spend every minute together." She tucked her head into the crook of his shoulder and snuggled up to his robust body.

He was surprised she did not complain about government brutality or unnecessary military actions. Normally these conversations would end in a long debate over many of the Entente's policies. Today, however, it ended much more pleasantly.

First Born by Janelle Gabay

EIGHT
UNWELCOME TOURIST
DELIA & TARIAN

The aged cobblestone road of Rue de la Magie stretched long with crooked wooden signs swinging from creaky metal chains. Bells rang crisply when vendor's doors swung open and shut. The magic and music of Christmas filled every nook and crevice of the unique village as the shoppers gathered last minute presents. The smell of baked cinnamon bread, pumpkin pie and brewed apple cider with hints of mulling spice made shoppers stop to purchase one last item for dinner tonight. It was Christmas Eve, and even the venom from the Prevallers' attack could not poison the spirit of the village.

From the stationary shop across the street, Delia watched Tarian laugh and dine on baked Brie and chestnuts with a woman. The clerk shot annoyed glances at Delia, but she had no intentions of leaving her watch post. To appease the wicked clerk, she snatched a Christmas card off of the shelf and paid for it. The clerk looked at her quizzically as she placed the card inside a paper bag. The card read: *To my wonderful wife: Meet me under the mistletoe.*

Delia plucked her purchase out of the clerk's hand and resumed her post. She was not about to leave the store, not while her boyfriend ate lunch with a beautiful woman. She continued her spying. The clerk cleared her throat, but Delia ignored her and rolled her eyes. *I bought a fricking card!*

53

First Born by Janelle Gabay

****

Tarian and Audrey sat in front of Café de la Nouvelle Natuche, a popular gathering place for the villagers and Guardians. They were lucky to get a seat, even an uncomfortable scrolled iron chair outside. The heat from the outdoor fire pit kept them surprisingly warm as tiny snowflakes cascaded to the ground.

"The weather is far more enjoyable than I thought it'd be," Tarian told Audrey as he glanced at the snow piled high on the peaks of the rooftops.

"It is," she said with a wry smile.

Tarian caught the nudge of a lie. "What?" he questioned.

"I can't have any secrets," she huffed. "That's my gift."

"Oh my God, you're a Purple Person!"

"Shhhh! Yes, I have a small gift but it's not very helpful really. Nothing like your dad's shape shifting. You would've been amazed."

Audrey's many memories of his dad slipped out during their conversations. At first it had bothered him. He had been jealous and hurt over his lost memories, but soon the pain turned to fascination. Seeing his dad through someone else's eyes began to feel like a present being opened.

"What do you do?"

"I can change the weather but only a small circumference of air. I can't cause a tornado or anything like that. But it helps on a cold day like today."

First Born by Janelle Gabay

He smiled to himself reminiscing about how Delia had been able to keep him warm in a very different way.

"What?" she asked.

"Nothing," he said. His cheeks filled with heat.

"Oh, you can have secrets. I get it." She crossed her arms and smirked.

The Audrey Tarian had known at the Entente Military Academy had softened. As her subordinate, he had suffered her constant barrage of orders throughout his first year and a half, but the woman that sat across from him now demanded only camaraderie. She had guided him into his new life, with patience, in less than four days.

"Why won't you come to Christmas Eve dinner tonight?" he asked.

"I told you, I always spend it with Eleanor and the Guardians."

"Come over afterward."

"No Tarian, you enjoy this time alone with your family. We begin training the day after Christmas, and by the New Year, if we're lucky, we'll have our assignment. It won't be peaceful for long."

"I know. At least come over a little while before we have to leave? I want to introduce you to everyone."

"I'll try," she said.

He had seen her every day for a brief few minutes. She informed him of the Prevallers advancements and setbacks, updated him on the antidote serum and so on, but inevitably the briefing turned to talk of his father or EMA.

First Born by Janelle Gabay

She slid an envelope across the table. "This is why I asked you to meet here."

"What is it?"

"Open it. It's your witch's blood test results. Let's see if you're a Purple Person too." She whispered the last part.

He ripped it open with one swipe of his pointer finger then paused. His heart pounded, but did it matter to him? Maybe since he had just discovered she could control the weather, he now felt competition.

"I don't really understand most of these markings, but I'm a Purple Person," he said with a grin. Relief rushed through him, and again he wondered why he cared so much.

"Congratulations. Cheers!" She lifted her mug full of cider, and he lifted his. "Cheers!"

"So what can I do?" he asked.

"Let me see the report." She reviewed the papers. "Your ability is to be determined, but look here." She pointed to a percentage notation. "This means you have more than 50% witch's blood. I bet your mother is a descendant from a witch. She probably doesn't even know it."

"Cool," he said still feeling dismayed by this new information. Every day he learned a new, unbelievable fact about himself or his father. He began to wish for a normal, boring day.

"Don't worry. When your ability comes, it will feel natural. You'll see. Mine came after I had lived forty years, but your father had the gift at sixteen."

****

First Born by Janelle Gabay

The sharp ringing of bells startled Delia, and she nearly knocked over a glass angel for sale on the display table in the stationary shop. Once again the clerk furrowed her bushy brow and squinted her dark eyes at Delia. Delia realized she had better get out of the store before she was thrown out.

She needed to know what was in that envelope. It must have been good news since they toasted their cups with a smile. Jealousy filled her lungs as she breathed. That woman was one of the horrid village people, and she was luring her boyfriend into this strange world.

Her eyes burned from the constant squinting, and her shoulders ached from the tension of holding still for too many minutes. A fist-sized knot bunched in the crook of her neck. It built in size with every pretty smile from the desirable woman sitting next to her boyfriend. She knew Tarian had other things to attend to while here in the village; she was hoping the agenda needs were not so attractive.

"Delia!"

Her father's sharp voice startled her.

"What are you doing? I told you not to leave the Inn alone. It's too dangerous, and you are too weak."

"But it's Christmas. And I'm not weak."

"Honey." He softened his voice. "Your illness and the Prevallers do not care about such things. Let's go."

Delia hoped to catch Tarian's eye as she left the store, but he remained focused on the other woman. To her dismay, the only eye she caught was the disapproving gaze of her father.

"What?" she asked her father. *Did he know I was spying?*

"You should have stayed at the Inn."

First Born by Janelle Gabay

"Why can't I interact in the village?"

"I've told you."

"No, you haven't. You just say 'because I said so.' I thought this was a safe place for us?"

"It is."

"Then I should be able to walk around freely. I'm eighteen."

"We are not discussing this. Do not leave the Inn unattended!"

"Whatever," she sighed.

As always he gave orders, not explanations. She knew her father loved her, but it was a strange love, distant and controlling. He was a secretive and powerful man.

She had been to this village several times before but still felt like an unwelcome tourist. As they walked in bitter silence, she recalled her first visit; they had come during a summer month. At eight years old, and much healthier then, she and her mother had enjoyed visiting the fanciful shops. When she was young, the peculiar patrons dressed in purple and green had made her joyful. Today they made her inquisitive and suspicious.

An uneasy memory came to her. She remembered strolling this same path, looking up at her father as he gazed straight ahead as if he belonged to this place. As a young girl, she could not explain the impression the town made upon her. Now it seemed clearer but still indefinable. Everything about the unique village filled her stomach with tingling anticipation.

First Born by Janelle Gabay

NINE
CHRISTMAS EVE

The door swung open wildly, and Tarian knew it was his little sister excited to see both of her brothers at the door with presents. Tarian had met up with Charlie after lunch to purchase gifts for the family. Neither of them ever bought Christmas presents before Christmas Eve. At least this year they had an excuse. Their sudden rush into hiding did not make for good shopping conditions.

Chloe hit Charlie like a miniature bull causing all of the presents to fall onto the floor. Chloe looked healthy as her youthful pink skin and beautiful blonde curls bounced as she ran. Teresa and Joe Jr. also came to greet them, curious about their outing into town. Teresa, Chloe, and Joe Jr. had been promised a visit to the shops and ice rink, but their mother had been too busy turning the room into a homey Christmas experience.

Tarian's mom had decorated for hours. Somehow she had managed to make the Inn's suite look like home. The balsam fir Christmas tree stood in the corner of the living area. Evergreen filled Tarian's nose and twinkling colorful lights consumed his sight. Shiny, inviting presents were placed neatly under the branches wrapped in silver and gold ribbons. Seeing this stunning display and knowing how hard his mom had worked to make an inconvenient Christmas seem spectacular made Tarian realize just how much the traitor had stolen from his dad.

59

First Born by Janelle Gabay

All through the night as they ate dinner and played board games, Tarian's mind dipped in and out of the past. They laughed and cried over silly minor details that had been forgotten. When Charlie rolled snake eyes, everyone went silent remembering that was Dad's famous roll. He could turn out two dice with a one on them whenever he needed to.

Tarian enjoyed this precious time with his family. He made every minute of this night count, right up to bedtime. Mere seconds had infinite value, now that he knew what he was.

"And they lived happily ever after," Tarian said, as he closed the bedtime story book.

"I love happily ever after," Chloe said in a sleepy voice, eyes closed.

"I thought you were asleep."

"Nope." She smiled her sweet smile.

Tarian's heart melted. "Goodnight Chloe." He slipped one leg off the bed and began to sneak away from his tired little sister.

Chloe pulled him back towards her. "Cuddle! Just a little longer."

"Of course." He kissed her forehead and sank back onto the pillow.

"Love you," she whispered. Her body squirmed its way under his arm and her head nestled on his shoulder.

Thirty minutes later he untangled her blond curls from his neck, removed her sleeping body from his, and tiptoed out of the bedroom. He went downstairs to help his mother clean up and prepare for gift opening in the morning.

First Born by Janelle Gabay

"Thank you, Sweetie," his mom said, her hands soapy from cleaning dishes. "Chloe misses you. She has put all of her dolls away and only plays with army toy soldiers now. She makes her own mini EMA in her room, and all the boys in the neighborhood play at our house now."

"She's a character." Tarian smiled, but inside he worried that his little sister may never return home to play with her neighborhood friends.

"I know. The attack scared her to death. I'm so grateful for this place. Thank goodness Zachary took us all here."

"It's a nice village, so old and different from the districts."

"It's a …" she paused, mouth pursed, eyes searching, "wondrous place, but it's not home. At least it's very Christmassy, for now." She smiled.

"Yes, almost elf-like isn't it?"

"Yes, that's it. I wouldn't be surprised to find Santa Claus living here," she said.

He understood how she felt. He wished she knew the real magic of this place. "Has Senator Eastwood told you how long you have to stay here?" he asked.

"No. I wasn't going to worry about that just yet. At least the kids are off of school. But I do realize I have to stay here to keep my children safe. Charlie is the only one who wants to leave. He insists he's going back to Harvard after the New Year."

"I figured. He told me the same when we were shopping."

"Where are you going tomorrow?" she asked.

First Born by Janelle Gabay

Tarian knew it was a loaded question. He saw the obvious disbelief in her caramel eyes. "I'm going to be trained for a special mission. One that could put a stop to all of this."

She looked at him with knowing eyes.

He had more information, but he could not tell her. Her awareness heightened his guilt. His eyes fell to the floor.

"Your father had secrets too," she confessed. "I've been here before, you know. Joe took me here twenty-seven years ago. It hasn't changed at all."

"I didn't know that."

They silently continued to clean up the dinner mess. Tarian felt his mother's stare upon him, and he could not face her.

"Be safe," she said softly.

"Mom, it's going to be all right. I promise." He hugged her. "Go to sleep, you look tired." He pushed her out of the kitchen.

"I have to set the coffee," she protested.

"Go! I'll do the rest. You've done enough already. Love you mom."

"Love you more." Her mouth smiled, but her eyes remained doleful.

First Born by Janelle Gabay

TEN
CHRISTMAS MORNING
DELIA

Christmas paper and fir needles scattered under Chloe and Joe Jr.'s feet as they scampered around the tree delivering presents to their intended recipients. Delia finally plopped down next to Tarian and sunk into the plushy couch. All morning she had been recruited by Chloe to be one of Santa's helpers and had not had a minute of peace since she stepped through the door.

Delia clung to Tarian and refused to let Chloe steal her away again. His arms wrapped around her, her head on his shoulder, relaxed. All presents had been opened. Breakfast sat comfortably in their bellies. The two of them only wanted to embrace one another for the remaining couple of hours they had left.

Chloe sat on her knees on the floor arranging her new army figures and the new combat tank. She organized and reorganized the figures. Joe Jr. whizzed by riding her new hoverboard and knocked down all she had built.

"Joe! That's mine! Get off!" Chloe yelled.

"No! Catch me."

He sped away but did not get far before he fell off and began to cry. Soon Teresa had set him up with some of his Christmas toys to play with, and both youngsters were happy. These gifts would help the children forget Tarian's absence.

First Born by Janelle Gabay

Delia's age and knowledge prevented the luxury of such distractions. Her space would be empty; her heart would be broken. Her time robbed from her because of what? Who exactly was taking Tarian away from her? Tarian would not tell. Her father would not tell. This confirmed her decision to take that job offer in the Government District. Once Tarian left on his secret mission, she would leave on hers.

At this moment, there would be no discussion of training or job offers. She ran her teasing fingers over Tarian's arm catching his attention. She kissed him lovingly until the objections from Joe Jr. and Chloe forced her to stop.

"Ewe, gross, kissy face," sneered Joe Jr. and Chloe.

Seconds later, Audrey walked through the door escorted by Senator Eastwood. Delia stiffened at the sight of them and held tight to Tarian's arm. She saw a smile spread across Tarian's face as he took in the vision of Audrey. She had to turn him over to this beautiful woman like feeding him to the wolves.

Together they rose from the couch. Tarian introduced Audrey to Delia and then to his entire family. They all gathered around the kitchen counter for coffee and more pastries. Delia and Tarian stood as one, arm in arm. She wanted her connection to him prominent in both her father's and Audrey's minds.

Her father gave her a look of sovereignty. Tarian was his jurisdiction now, but she would not surrender him without a fight. Her father was removing her boyfriend from her arms and delivering him into the arms of another. She cast glances of contempt upon him, and he countered with domineering, dark eyes. She would never receive empathy from him. In her

First Born by Janelle Gabay

eighteen years, she had never seen compassion in his eyes and questioned his love constantly.

As a child he had hugged her, he had read her bedtime stories, he had taught her valuable lessons but all with distant emotions. That distance spread with every year she aged, but it had made her strong. A hardened sense of duty had come from her father. Work always trumped family, especially secretive, never discussed jobs. He left in the middle of the night, locked his office door and refused to answer any of her questions concerning the state of affairs of the Entente or this mysterious village he called a safe house. She loved him, but could not honor him because what constituted honor for her was honesty and trust, something she had never received from him.

Now her beloved Tarian kept secrets from her too. The strange intuition that always crept into her bones when she visited here told her she was losing him. He was joining her father's mysterious village.

"So when will we all be safe again, Daddy?" Delia asked.

Her snide tone caused Tarian to snap his head around and look at her with drawn brows and tight eyes.

"Oh Sweetie, you give me too much credit. I wish I had the control to determine the movements of the Prevallers. I do not," her father said.

"What about you, Audrey? What's your level of control around here?" Delia turned her plastic smile towards Audrey. Delia's grasp of Tarian's arm became a vice grip.

"I'm just a soldier like Tarian. Going to do whatever is asked of me," Audrey volleyed.

First Born by Janelle Gabay

Delia took it all in. She glared at all of them including Tarian and his mom. She loved Tarian but at this point her delicate rage threatened explosion. She was too smart to start a sparring match with her father in front of everyone's company, so she removed herself from the room.

"Where are you going?" Tarian chased after her. "I have another hour or so."

"I don't," she said bluntly.

"Please don't leave like this."

"Like what?"

"Angry."

"I can't be happy to see you off to God only knows where!"

"Don't worry." He placed his hands on her hips.

"Don't patronize me!" Her deep blue eyes glared at him.

"I will tell you everything when I get back," he whispered.

This sparked her attention. Would he be completely honest with her?

"I love you," she whispered, and her eyes softened.

"I love you too." He pulled her into his arms and pressed his lips upon hers.

She kissed him back with passion. She wanted her kiss to weaken his knees, to be a kiss that would live in his dreams forever. She slipped out the door as a tear cut a path down her mocha face.

The whisper of "Goodbye," achingly forced out of her breath.

First Born by Janelle Gabay

ELEVEN
DAY ONE

With one step over the threshold, Tarian, Audrey, and the Senator walked from the charming cobbled street of the village and onto the slick, rigid tiles of the training facility. The building had Entente identifiable markings everywhere, straight lines and precise people in gray. A few familiar Guardians dressed in green and purple suits dotted the otherwise colorless environment.

"Tarian this is a joint training facility for both the Guardians and the elite Entente military. You will be safe here. The protection from the village extends into this building as well," Senator Eastwood explained.

Confused, he studied the gray walls. They emitted a dull coldness, and yet, at the same time, he knew they cloaked and protected him.

The welcoming tour included all the usual venues but also numerous virtual simulation rooms. Suddenly, Tarian realized he would never leave the building. The fresh air he had smelled outside was gone and substituted with imitation air designed by human beings to enhance the senses. But it smelled too perfect. At once he missed the harsh odors of EMA from the stench of ground-in sweat to the bittersweet smell of the fresh cut lawn.

"Here we are, your room for the next few weeks." Senator Eastwood stopped in front of a door labeled 3344. "Audrey you are right here, across the hall."

First Born by Janelle Gabay

"Weeks?" Audrey asked.

"Yes, I've brought in a team. I want Tarian to train with them and a few days is not sufficient. He has a lot to learn, and we have a lot to test."

"Exactly what am I being tested on?" Tarian asked.

"Your immortal senses and strengths. I need to know how far you've developed before I'll send you on a mission."

"We don't have much time," Audrey said.

"I'll be the judge of that. Get some rest, both of you." The Senator turned on his heels and left.

The fury on Audrey's face made Tarian nervous. He reached for the doorknob to escape into his room. Feeling empathic towards her, he turned around to invite her inside but saw only her door slam shut.

The lushness of his room outclassed any place he had ever stayed at before. The room and the entire building did not seem real. Some sort of magic hovered around and inside these walls. Like the Guardian Headquarters, the size of this building deceived and fascinated his senses, but in addition to that, it felt as if he had stepped out of the village and into the Entente Military District five hundred miles away. However, he could not recall ever seeing any Entente military personnel walking the village streets, and yet they lined the halls here.

Early the next morning he changed into a training uniform hanging in the closet, a camouflaged snug bodysuit made out of an extremely pliable yet indestructible material. The label read 'bulletproof' but offered no other information. Tarian wondered what he would encounter today that would require a bulletproof bodysuit. The boots were high and came up almost to his knees.

First Born by Janelle Gabay

Even though he was covered from neck to toe, he felt barefoot and naked. Everything was designed to fit him snugly and made from a flexible material that stretched over his muscles and melted into the creases of his skin. All sizes were accurate, even the high arch of his shoes.

All items of clothing inside the closet were individually wrapped. The first container labeled The Game hung next to those marked Day 5 through Day 21. He knew uniforms 2-4 were not missing. The Guardians' obsessive-compulsive organization would not make such an error. Days 2-4 did not exist because he would not be changing out of this bodysuit for four days.

Audrey and Tarian collided as they exited their rooms. She wore an identical bodysuit, but she had a backpack.

"Where's your backpack?" she asked.

He quickly ran back to his closet to find an identical backpack hanging on a hook. It weighed a hefty forty pounds at least.

"Have you played this game before?" he asked her when he returned to the hallway.

"Yes," she answered.

He waited for her to elaborate, but she offered nothing. They walked several seconds in silence.

"Care to explain?" he finally asked.

"It's basically a complex and challenging Capture the Flag set inside the Realm."

"The Realm? I thought we were in the Realm."

"No, we're not. This is the training facility. It houses many rooms."

First Born by Janelle Gabay

"The Realm is a room?" he asked.

"You could say that," she replied.

"Err, uh," he murmured then asked, "How many of us are playing this game?"

"Two or possibly three teams of 25 soldiers," she answered. "The main subject of this game is you."

"Me?"

"Yes, your immortal abilities will be assessed. You'll be put through strange tests to see if your extra strength or extreme vision have developed."

"Cool. Maybe I can even fly," Tarian laughed.

"Maybe," Audrey responded with a serious tone.

"What? Seriously? Can I fly?"

"We don't know what you can do yet, hence the test."

She might as well have ended her sentence with 'Idiot' because that was how she made him feel.

"Did I hurt your feelings?" She mocked then pushed him so hard he fell into the wall with a loud thud. "You need to toughen up."

"I'm tough." With a bruised ego, he remained silent.

"Not all eyes are on you, so don't worry."

Still repairing his ego, he did not answer.

"The Realm also trains the Elite Forces. This facility houses one percent of those who graduate from all of the EMA's across the Entente. Those with the right credentials train here to become the Elite Forces. They are some of the few mortals that know about us."

First Born by Janelle Gabay

"Okay. Why is this place full of military personnel, and yet, I never saw anyone wearing a military uniform inside the village? Do they never leave the building?"

"Something like that," she said.

"We're no longer in the village are we?"

"Something like that."

"We're in both places at one time."

"Something like that." She smiled but offered no explanation.

Maybe there was no explanation, he thought. Maybe it was just plain magic. Before he could ask her more questions, they reached the door of their destination.

Approximately sixty trainees gathered into a circular all white room, no windows, no furniture. Tube-like compartments big enough for one maybe two people lined the curved wall. Each trainee stood in front of a cylinder. Tarian fell into an open spot in the circle, as did Audrey. Directly across the room stood an athletically built, brown-eyed girl with severe bruising covering the left half of her face. Next to her stood a tanned skinned, square-shaped man with a blood red suture split across his cheekbone.

Maria? Gabe?

Her hair was shorter and dyed blue, and he had a terrifying scar, but it was definitely Tarian's two dear friends. So much had happened since he last saw them. What had they gone through? By the looks of their faces, quite a bit of pain.

Guilt crushed the carefully constructed fence of bravado Tarian had built to endure the craziness of the last few days. He bowed his head. He could not look into the eyes of true soldiers.

First Born by Janelle Gabay

He had been rescued and whisked off to safety in a fancy tiltrotor. The Guardians had coddled him while his friends battled the Prevallers to stay alive. If he had not abandoned his friends, maybe their faces would be undamaged, but then again, maybe it would have been worse for them to be with the so-called 'First Born.'

Maria caught Tarian's attention with animated facial expressions. She looked excited to see him but how would she feel after he told her his story. He wanted to run across the room and embrace them both. Ripples of uncertainty swelled into giant waves of apprehension the more he waited. He needed to get the truth off of his chest, face his sentence. However, the massive Commander General that stood in the center of the room made it impossible for him to act on his eagerness.

The Commander was a huge man, as tall as he was thick. His sharply, defined muscles bulged under his shirt. These were not decorative muscles of body builders; these were functional muscles of a disciplined war hero.

Do they make superheroes here? He wondered.

"Move!" The Commander shouted in Tarian's face.

Tarian realized he had not heard one word of instructions. The giant man had been talking, but Tarian had been drowning in his culpability. Now he was holding a weapon that he could not remember accepting nor did he know how to operate it. With a reluctant step inside the tube, the door snapped shut, and he could no longer see his friends. He was encased inside a narrow metal tube that began to shake violently. The powerful elevator sucked him towards the sky with tremendous speed, although he had no visual reference point to judge this fact.

First Born by Janelle Gabay

The ascent stopped abruptly but without a jolt. Quite easily, Maria, Gabe and Tarian emerged from their tubes. The others were gone, and so were the tubes. A forested, mountainous jungle surrounded them. And it was warm, very warm. The three stood still and silent for a moment as the dizzying effect of the transport subsided.

"So this is the Realm." Tarian looked around the vast environment. He thought about what Audrey had said. She had called the Realm a room, but this was no room. *Was it?*

"Have we been tractor beamed to like… outside the borders?" Gabe asked.

"Impossible," Maria said. "It's just a sophisticated simulation center."

"I no longer know what is real and what is simulated anymore, but I do know they call this place the Realm," Tarian answered.

Stress in the form of laughter unexpectedly burst from the mouths of all three of them. They felt like children trapped in a fairytale existence where all their wildest dreams and nightmares were possible. All three of them had experienced a surreal week that seemed to climax here in a magical forest. Tarian's guilt vanished. It seemed no time had passed between them, and they exchanged explanations of their survival. His friends did not consider his rescue to be abandonment instead they encouraged him to embrace his amazing future. They had already been informed about the Guardians and most of Tarian's story, so they were prepared for his wild tales. He knew nothing of their past week and listened as they told him frightening accounts of the

First Born by Janelle Gabay

attack. Tarian could not believe they were lucky enough to make it out alive.

"You should see the lawn, it's awful. The beautiful grass burned to ash," Maria explained to Tarian.

"And our barracks: Eisenhower, Pershing, Bradley and Washington Hall. It's a pile of stones. It's like the Prevallers were aiming their weapons at that spot," Gabe said.

"They were," Tarian said. Accountability washed over him once more. Those buildings were destroyed because of him, and who he is.

"Oh yeah," Gabe said.

Dark emotions trounced their joyous reunion.

"Cadets Stacey and Tommy didn't make it Tarian," Maria said the familiar names through clenched teeth, and Tarian bowed his head. "Professor Novak and Major Steinhart are gone too." She opened her mouth to list more names when Gabe nudged her arm.

"It's alright. I need to know. They're who we're fighting for," Tarian replied.

"For the Black and Gray and Gold!" Gabe shouted.

"For the Black and Gray and Gold!" They all three shouted in unison paying tribute to the nation's colors.

Saddened by the details of death and destruction, and yet exuberant to be with each other, they began their new journey into the Realm. Filled with patriotic pride Tarian marched onward holding his weapon. Embarrassment hit him when he realized he had no idea how this particular weapon worked.

"I feel really dumb right now, but did the Commander explain how to use this," he asked holding up the arm.

First Born by Janelle Gabay

"You are too much. It's a stunner." Maria rolled her eyes and explained the mechanics to him.

"The effects are severe. One hit will send a two hundred pound man to the ground instantly. The convulsions last two minutes and from what I've heard, hurt like a mother," Gabe warned.

"That's when you get away from the enemy, or you take your victim as a prisoner," Maria said.

"Don't shoot the guys in green like us. Only shoot the guys in black camouflage," Gabe said.

"Got it," Tarian replied.

Tarian was thankful to be with Maria and Gabe but wished for Audrey's experience. He guessed they had been separated on purpose. Someone controlled the game; therefore, every move was strategic, a test of survival.

Within an hour, they met up with an enemy game player. Squatting and hiding like wolves ready to pounce, they watched. The opponent girl was alone, moving stealthily through the woods. She had not seen them. The threesome turned to one another and nodded. Jumping from the foliage, armed and ready, they had her surrounded. Without hesitation, she shot her stunner but missed. Gabe grabbed her weapon while Tarian wrestled her to the ground, trapping her under his weight. Without warning an enormous man appeared. She was not alone after all. Suddenly he fell to the ground with a loud thwack and Tarian thought he felt the ground shake. All two hundred, thirty pounds, six-feet-five-inches of him crashed to the dirt. Legs thrashing, arms flailing and eyes rolling.

"Mike!" The girl cried out.

First Born by Janelle Gabay

Gabe stood motionless; his stunner still pointed at the position where the giant man had been standing before he fell.

"Let's go," Tarian ordered to Gabe and Maria.

He had the girl's stunner, and Maria grabbed the giant man's stunner. Before lifting his weight from the girl, Tarian pinched a pressure point in her neck, paralyzing her long enough for them to get away clean.

As they ran through the thick bushes and tall trees, Tarian sensed someone watching. He cast his glance upwards to find the trees filled with red-eyed, scorpion-tailed animals. These animals hung upside down; tails curled around branches while they observed. Tarian pondered if they were possums or monkeys, but as long as they did not attack, he did not care. A few of them threw clumps of dirt and rocks, but other than that, the animals remained tame.

Night finally arrived after a grueling day of running, fighting and hiking. Maria, Gabe and Tarian made camp under the cover of the trees. Tarian guessed by the stars and moon in this sky the time was around nine o'clock.

"I can't believe it is so light out. According to the stars, it should be 9 o'clock," Tarian said.

"What are you talking about? It's pitch dark," Maria said.

"Really?" Tarian asked.

Maria and Gabe looked at him inquisitively. Tarian glanced around. Through his eyes, he saw an eerie haze of light. He clearly saw moonlight shimmering off of droplets of misting rain. It must just be a difference of opinion.

"I'm freezing," Maria said.

First Born by Janelle Gabay

The damp cold also besieged Tarian's bones. They unpacked the backpacks searching for something warm. Tarian watched as his friends stumbled in the darkness, they really could not see anything. Tarian found his sleeping bag first then a snaplight. He shook the stick until it glowed.

"Is that better?" Tarian asked.

"Much, thanks," Gabe said.

"I guess you can see in the dark," Maria said.

"Yeah, I guess." Tarian shivered but not from the cold. Having his immortal senses develop in the presence of mortals rattled his nerves. He didn't want his friends to look at him differently, or worse, be scared of him. He missed Audrey.

The threesome formed a triangle on the hard, uneven ground. The thin sleeping bags helped with the cold but did nothing to make the ground less forgiving and uncomfortable. They talked about what they had seen today inside this enigmatic jungle. It had been hard enough to plod through the thick underbelly of bushes, but having strange animals and shadows crossing their path was frightening.

"This place is like nothing I've ever seen before. But it feels real, doesn't it? The humidity, the smells," asked Maria.

"Yes." Gabe stared up at the stars, heavy breaths leaving his lungs. Exhausted.

"I hope I can make it," said Maria.

"You will. Just keep your mind straight. Remember it may seem real but it's not," Tarian said.

"That's just it. It's scary as hell, and it's not even real. I've been through real, and this is almost as bad. Soon it'll be up

First Born by Janelle Gabay

to us to find and defeat the Prevallers. These people can kill immortals. What chance do I have?" Maria asked.

"We have to remain optimistic," Tarian said.

He, too, was feeling the forest's spookiness but knew the visions he had seen did not exist in reality: phantom shadows, mechanical scorpion-tailed monkeys, burning water. It was a game; he kept telling himself, a psychological and physical test of will. But the strange and magical sensation of this place obscured reality.

"Yeah, well, I'm trying. Watching friends die, getting the shit kicked out of me. You weren't there. You don't know," she jabbed at him.

Tarian saw Gabe nudge her with his hand, but he didn't want them to change or filter their words. He didn't need his friends to tip toe around any topics just because his life was now a bizarre circus. He needed them to remain constant even if it meant getting his feelings hurt. His skin had thickened since his father's death. He had survived EMA's tough regimen. He had kept his calm today under a canopy of strange creatures. He could handle the truth.

"No, you 're right. I was enjoying a nice Christmas." He said back to break the tension.

"I still don't understand why Maria and I were picked for this. We haven't even graduated from EMA. This facility is for Elite Forces and Immortals. We're neither," Gabe said.

Tarian had not thought of that point. He hadn't had time to think. He had been too busy running and fighting, but Gabe was right. Why were his friends here? He remembered the

First Born by Janelle Gabay

Senator said he had picked a team. He must have chosen his friends for a reason.

"Did you see Delia during Christmas?" Maria asked.

"Yes."

"That's good," Maria said, followed by a long uncomfortable silence.

Maria liked Delia, but they were from two different worlds. Maria was a poor farm girl while Delia was a wealthy Senator's daughter. When Delia visited EMA, and they all went out together, their easy threesome conversation became forced and awkward. This was because Delia and Maria were both confrontational. Their different upbringings made for extreme opposites of opinion, so disputes were constant. Both women stubbornly voiced their views, which never concluded in any agreement. There were no hard feelings between the two women; in fact, Tarian suspected they both enjoyed verbally sparring with one another.

"What were those things that threw rocks at my head?" Maria asked of the strange monkeys they had encountered earlier that day.

"Machines," Tarian answered.

"Did you see their eyes?" Gabe asked.

"Yes, blood red." Tarian shivered. "They were lenses, not eyes. Cameras. They are tracking us. I'll bet whoever is running this game uses them to judge our progress."

"Did you see its tail?" Maria asked again clearly disturbed by the monkey creature.

"Well, they are vile creatures," Gabe said.

"How incredibly messed up is this jungle?" Maria asked.

79

First Born by Janelle Gabay

"I can't tell if it's a jungle, a forest or a mountain range," Maria added.

"You should see Guardian Headquarters. It's amazing but in a good way, not like this," he said then stopped, unsure of what to keep secret.

"Well, I still can't call Cadet Sergeant Major Gualtiero by her first name. A…Au… Audrey. See it doesn't want to get off my tongue. That's just too weird for me. Remember what a bitch she was at EMA?" Maria said.

"She's still hot though."

"Shut up, Gabe!" Maria jabbed him hard with her foot.

"Yeah," Tarian said and joined Gabe in a series of manly catcalls.

"Yeah?" Maria scoffed. "What about Delia?" Her words were meant to finish the manly grunts. She knew how to drop a bomb on the guys' chauvinistic playfulness.

"She's hot too," Gabe responded just to annoy her.

"I wasn't talking to you," she said.

"I think she is fine," Tarian said.

"Oh, she is fine." Gabe continued to tease.

"No, Stupid, he means she is doing fine," Maria tut-tutted.

"You think?" Gabe questioned jumping to conclusions. "Did she dump you?"

"No, I mean I saw her, and it was great. She's just very thin."

"She was thin before. She kept getting sick," Gabe said.

"I know, and she has never explained what made her sick. She just seemed different. I can't explain it."

Maria burst into laughter.

First Born by Janelle Gabay

"What's so funny?" Tarian asked.

"Everything is different. How is a girl supposed to act? Her boyfriend is immortal --"

"She doesn't know I'm immortal," he interrupted. "Her father won't let me tell her or anyone, for that matter."

"It's going to work out, don't worry. Let's just take one messed-up crazy task at a time, okay?" Gabe joked.

"Sure," Tarian and Maria agreed in unison.

"Do you hear it?" Tarian asked, and they fell silent.

"I don't hear anything?" Maria said.

She looked at him, and he knew what she thought, another freaky immortal sense. Minutes passed as the music's volume gradually increased, but still only Tarian could hear it.

"Taps," Maria and Gabe finally said in unison.

The historic horn melody played every night before bed at EMA. A tradition that still held strong even after the Entente War.

"It must be ten o'clock," Gabe said.

"Why are they playing it here?" Maria questioned.

Tarian wondered the same thing. Was it simply a reference of time or did the Realm know *Taps* kindled deep internal feelings for him? It conjured up images of Delia. The long C Major notes played on the bugle inspired inner reflection. *What was going to happen when this was a real game? I had survived one attack, could I survive another? Could I survive without Audrey's help? What if I never did see Delia again?*

Tarian's thoughts drifted to his dad. As a child, Tarian shadowed him. He admired and loved his dad more than anyone else. He was an unusual child in that he would sit contentedly for

First Born by Janelle Gabay

hours at his father's office as if he were thirty years old. The staff and partners nicknamed him Master Tarian A.I.T., Attorney in Training. He even had his own letterhead printed with that title scrolled across the header in fancy lettering. The hopes of a father and son law firm died after the funeral, once the Senator thrust him into the military. He let out a sigh, lost in the thoughts of what was supposed to be.

He closed his eyes. The image of a Prescott and Sons, Esq. sign drifted into his dreamlike state, waving in midair like a proud flag, and then blackness eclipsed him. He slipped into a fitful sleep.

First Born by Janelle Gabay

TWELVE
DAY TWO

Day two of the strenuous game began at first light. By noon, they had traveled miles in the stiflingly, humid heat and still had not found the allies they now sought.

"I have an idea," Tarian stated. "See that cliff." He pointed to a shelf-like ledge protruding from a large mountain.

"Yes," Gabe and Maria said.

"We need to get there," he said.

"I see. Get to high ground," Maria said.

"Yes. Then maybe we can find out where the enemy base is," Tarian explained.

"Or find Green's base. It would be helpful to have more than the three of us," Gabe said.

"Maybe we can even see the flags," Maria said.

The idea was simple; whatever group captured the enemy flag first, won the game. But the location of the flags remained a mystery. Lack of communication from the rest of their team made Tarian miserable. He felt lost and trapped on a giant chessboard, but he did not know which end was which. Getting to higher ground would help him collect his bearings.

"Eeeekk!" A high-pitched voice screamed from behind a rambler bush.

A young woman dressed in green camouflage jumped out of the tangled vines. Tarian had thrown a rock at her, barely

83

First Born by Janelle Gabay

missing her head. Gabe and Maria jumped, spread their legs into ready position and aimed their stunners.

"Don't shoot!" She yelled, arms up.

"Sorry," Tarian said. "I saw you hiding but could not tell which team you were on. You're lucky I didn't stun you."

"Thanks," she hissed. Her eyes bored into him.

"I'm Tarian."

"I know who you are, First Born." Her face puckered as if the nickname left a sour taste in her mouth.

"Who the hell are you?" Maria spat.

Tarian grinned at Maria for coming to his defense.

"Jen." No smile.

Tarian wished he'd hit her with the rock.

"Well, Jen, I'm Maria, and this is Gabe. And unfortunately, it looks like we're on the same team."

"Looks like it," Jen sighed.

"Are you alone?" Maria asked.

"As of about four hours ago. My partner got shot and captured."

"Do you know where our base is?" Tarian asked.

"No, I was hoping you did. Scott and I searched miles and found nothing," she confessed.

"Same here. We're going up there now to get a better look at this crazy place," Gabe explained. "Do you want to come with us?"

She did not answer.

"Fine, we'll go without you." Maria began to walk away.

"Look, I don't like leaving you behind, alone," Tarian stated.

First Born by Janelle Gabay

"I don't need your help," she spat.

"What do you have against Tarian?" Gabe asked.

"He's the reason we're in this mess. The Guardians are supposed to protect us, not the other way around."

"You signed on to this when you chose to enroll in the military. Protect and serve," Gabe said.

"I didn't know immortals existed when I enlisted."

"If it's any consolation to you, I didn't know about the Guardians and immortals either, and I sure never wanted to be the 'First Born.' But I do want to train hard and stop anyone else from losing their life."

She gave Tarian a long, hard look. No smile. Begrudgingly and without a word, she took the lead and began to climb the mountain.

It was not an easy journey. They encountered more manmade creatures they had to outsmart, and they could not find a clear path to follow. Thick branches of overgrown weeds and plants buried the trail and covered the mountainside. Vines wrapped around their ankles as they dug hard into the ground with their boots. They had to climb quickly, using the deep traction on their soles to propel themselves upward. An occasional slip in the wet, dark patches brought their focus back and put a heavy scare into them. They jammed stakes into the slope of the cliff, pulling the weight of their bodies upward through the slimy mud and jagged rocks.

A bright fuchsia colored insect landed on Jen's hand. The brilliant color mesmerized her, and she did not shoo it away. Prisms of color danced on her skin as the insect fluttered its tiny translucent wings.

First Born by Janelle Gabay

Catching up to her Tarian stopped and saw the insect. "What's that?" He looked closer. It had stripes and a needlepoint nose.

"I don't know," she replied then the insect stung her. "Ouch! The little a-hole bit me!"

They all watched as she instantly slipped into sleepiness. A smile fanned across her face, and her head swayed side to side. Then her fingers lifted one by one from the stake driven into the mountainside keeping her from falling to her death. She let go. Tarian leaped to grab her but missed then Gabe managed to catch a loop on her backpack, but she slipped out of it and fell. They all screamed.

"Help! Help!" They cried.

She looked up at them still smiling. She was going to hit the ground on her back, and Tarian winced at the thought of her spine shattering into tiny fragmented pieces. Suddenly, he realized maybe this was a test to see if he could fly. He could save her. He positioned his feet to push his legs off the side of the mountain for more speed. He jumped.

"Tarian!" Maria screamed.

Tarian fell fast. He could not fly. First, fear burned throughout his veins but he managed to douse the panic with reason. Next, his mind searched rapidly for a logical solution. *I can't fly but I won't die, so maybe I can land on the ground before her. I can catch her.*

"Look out," Gabe yelled.

Swoosh! A winged creature the size of a horse whirled by them. The creature dove gracefully placing its mouth around Jen's falling body and hooking Tarian with its clawed hoof. The

First Born by Janelle Gabay

bird-like creature flew over the ledge and dropped Tarian then it flew away with Jen locked inside its beak shaped mouth.

More fuchsia colored insects flew around Gabe and Maria's exposed hands and heads as they continued to climb upwards.

"Move!" Maria screamed at Gabe.

They began to jab their stakes into the mountainside without care. Driving the metal sticks in a ladder pattern. Their feet following up and up and up. As they climbed they shook their heads and swatted anything that came close to their exposed bare skin. Finally the two of them threw their torsos over the top edge of the ledge. Tarian grabbed their hands and pulled. Rolling onto their backs their chests heaving with oxygen gulps. They were all safe.

"Do you see anymore of those things?" asked Gabe still lying on the ground.

"No," Tarian said.

"Where do you think that flying...horse...hawk...thing...took Jen?" Maria asked.

"Probably she is out of the game now and back at the training facility. That's my guess," Tarian answered.

"I thought she was so dead. I thought we'd be picking up body pieces at the base of this mountain." Maria spoke slowly, her eyes to the sky, back on the ground, head swaying back and forth rhythmically. "And you! Did you think you could fly?"

"No," Tarian lied, then stuttered out an explanation. "I..I..just...thought...knew if I fell I wouldn't die...so maybe I could soften her landing."

"Whatever," Maria scoffed.

87

First Born by Janelle Gabay

The three of them fit nicely onto the spacious ledge without fear of falling. Looking down the side of a mountain, two hundred feet in the air, instantly brought a better perspective to the game. The idea worked. They could see the layout of the playing field as if it was drawn on a map in front of them. The size, now visible, was daunting. From their vantage point, the enemy camp was set up north of the mountain. They had built their headquarters in a circle, and it looked as if the prisoners were being held in the center. Very clever, they all mused, since this made it difficult to recapture their teammates.

"Look over there," Tarian pointed south of the mountain. "Is that our base?"

"Maybe, I can barely make out some tents." Gabe strained and squinted his eyes.

"Yes it is. The others must have banned together to create it. It looks well organized, but I like the circular idea of the enemy's better. Our prisoners are too exposed," Tarian said.

"What prisoners?" Maria asked. "I can maybe see tents but not people."

"I believe the tent to the left of that large pine tree is housing three prisoners. It's hard to see them form this far away."

"No, it's impossible. It must be another *immortal* sense. Some sort of super sight," Maria said.

"Maybe," he said, wondering. "Well, we need to get some food and rest."

Once again Tarian felt uneasy discovering his new strengths in the presence of his normal friends. He busied himself setting up camp for the night. His body ached from

First Born by Janelle Gabay

fatigue. Even immortal muscles were subject to weariness and discomfort.

The ledge was comfortable and provided a cool breezeway. The cold air made Maria shiver and it reminded him of Delia. The Eastwood Estate remained a constant sixty-five degrees year round, and Delia was always chilled. She wandered around dressed in sweatpants, sweatshirt and slippers during the evenings before bed to avoid freezing. He missed her.

A smile crossed his lips as a mental image of her paraded around his closed eyelids. He raised his arms and put his hands behind his head, keeping his eyes closed until her image had vanished. He listened intently to the moaning of the rushing wind. He heard the rustling of leaves in the trees as they settled back into place after the air had passed threw them, only to be moved again and again as the wind kept blowing softly but steadily. The sounds of animals made him listen more intently, concentrating on the grunts and groans, trying to decipher if the noises were indeed animals. He did not hear *Taps* tonight.

"I really think we have been transported," Gabe said.

"Still impossible," Maria said. Her voice was drunk with sleep and her tone annoyed. Gabe's words awoke her and she rolled over in her sleeping bag.

"After everything I've seen in the past week, nothing is impossible. These people can bend space. I'm not sure how they do it, but it can be done. I've seen it. We are inside it right now," Tarian said.

"Am I the only one who feels like I'm in over my head?" Gabe asked.

89

First Born by Janelle Gabay

"No," Maria answered and it was the shortest answer she had ever given. She was always one to respond sarcastically, to criticize any weakness. For her to think inwardly meant true concern.

Tarian hoped her brevity was just due to exhaustion.

"I guess that's why we're here training so hard. It seems unnecessary or repetitive but they have a reason. I'm sure of it," Tarian said trying to bring back their conversational pattern. They had their roles. Tarian was the optimist. Maria was the smartass critic. Gabe was the suspicious theorist. Any conversation that dipped out of this pattern was foreign for them.

First Born by Janelle Gabay

THIRTEEN
DAY THREE

Six hours later beams of bright sunshine shone on their faces. The mountain faced east and was no longer cooled by shadows, but instead, heated by the sun. By the time the haze of sleep lifted, and Tarian became fully aware, he had already overheated inside his sealed sleeping bag. He peeled it off of his sticky skin and tried to cool his extremities with wiggling movements, but it was no use. A sweaty, frustrated, miserable day lay ahead.

The climb down the mountain proved to be just as difficult as the upward ascent. They had to rely more on feel and less on sight, causing them to lose their footing several times, and thus, falling a few feet. Gabe twisted his ankle dodging one of those fuchsia insects, and worried that once he was on the flat ground, he would not be able to walk fast enough to keep up with the others. He had warned Maria and Tarian that he would slow them down, and they must leave him behind to fend for himself. Of course not, they had protested.

One, two, three, thud, thud, thud – six feet landed safely at the base of the mountain. The ground gave a little but not enough to protect Gabe's ankle, and he fell to the grass in pain. Tarian wrapped the ankle with the supplies in his backpack, but Gabe still moved too slowly and clumsily.

The slowness of Gabe's gait agitated Tarian. Gabe's left side sunk with every step as if he was the only one walking on

91

First Born by Janelle Gabay

lopsided quicksand. Tarian looked ahead to his destination, eager to get there. Knowing that without Gabe's weak ankle he could be there hours sooner. Then the inevitable happened. Gabe collapsed to the ground again. Instantly, Maria and Tarian turned back to him, and in a split second, realized he did not fall because of his ankle. Without a word, they both pivoted around and ran at full speed. They knew Gabe was a goner, and their only hope was to escape. They never looked back. For one, they had been trained not to since it would slow them down, and two, they refused to witness their friend convulse in pain.

Once they knew they were safe, they stopped to catch their breath. "Did you see them?" he asked.

"No! Not at all. I feel like scum. Thankfully this is a simulation. That is scary as shit!" she said, with huge gasps of breath between each sentence.

"Yeah, scary as *shit*," he repeated her descriptor with a grin.

"Let's get moving; I feel like I'm being watched," Maria said. Her face tense and eyes shifty.

Tarian felt it too. He looked behind him but saw no one. But he still could not shake the ghostly feeling of shadows lingering around him. Then he wondered if they were spared stunning on purpose. Maybe that was the game plan all along. *Follow the leader*.

"Maybe we are," he whispered to her. "Let's not head directly back to base until we know for sure we are not being followed." His voice was barely audible, and she gave a slight nod of understanding.

First Born by Janelle Gabay

He led Maria into an overgrown forest of thick trees, sharp holly bushes and low spreading junipers. He stopped once engulfed by foliage and they both sat in silence, hunched low, eyes keen but seeing only various shades of green. Tarian held his breath to listen. Nothing. No one. His legs began to tighten, but he refused to kneel. Then he heard it, the faint rustle of human footsteps stalking. Snap. Snap. Branches broke under the feet of their pursuer. Tarian could tell by the pattern of noise that the enemy did not know their exact location.

He stayed motionless and pondered whether to take action or lie in wait. Maria would not make a move unless he did. He measured the choice on the fact that he had only heard one person in the brush. He sprang and attacked.

Tarian was stronger than the man he wrestled to the ground. That was helpful, but the man was larger. Tarian lost his leverage. Knees hit ribs, fists cracked jaws, heads butted. The man managed to pin Tarian's shoulders to the ground until Maria's thick, muscular leg kicked him hard to the gut giving Tarian an opportunity to rise to his feet. The man's melon sized fist charged into Maria's right side. Her ribs crunched, and she stumbled. Rage whirled inside Tarian's blood giving him a strength and courage he had never used before. The man did not stand a chance against Tarian's immortal strength. Hogged tied and gagged the man finally stopped fighting.

"Why didn't you just stun him?" Maria asked, visibly and mentally exhausted by the events that had gone down. She held her side and bent slightly in pain.

Tarian's jaw throbbed as the blood rushed to it.

First Born by Janelle Gabay

"I need to know if there are more of them and where they are," Tarian answered.

He stared down his opponent and repeated the words in a question.

"Of course there are," the opponent spat.

"Where are they?" Tarian asked but received a defiant stare. He pulled the stunner out of its designated pocket and repeated the question.

"You think that's going to make me talk, First Born?"

"I don't know. Let's see!" Tarian stunned the man without delay.

The man had a look of surprise on his face, believing Tarian would stall before stunning. Tarian surprised himself too. He had not hesitated to use such a pain-inducing weapon. As the man lay convulsing noisily on the ground for two minutes, no other opponents came.

"Well then, I guess you were lying. There is no one else with you," Tarian said and turned to walk away.

With a serious, wide-eyed look of amazement Maria asked, "What about him? Are you just going to leave him here in the dirt?"

"Oh yeah," he said and put the gag in his mouth.

"No, that's not what I meant. We aren't going to take him with us?"

"No. He will only try to slow us down. That tracking monkey," he pointed to brown fur and crimson eyes peeking from behind a tree, "will report a man down. Come on. We have to hurry."

94

First Born by Janelle Gabay

Maria followed after him as the man squirmed and attempted to yell through the gag. Tarian marched confidently on. The fight felt good. The pain made him feel alive with power. He impressed himself with his quick decision-making under pressure.

"Stop," Tarian whispered after they had been walking in the direction of the camp for a while. Maria knew they were close but did not know why he advised the halt. He put his finger to his lips and with his other hand, pointed two feet in front of them. At first glance, all she saw was grass and sticks, but then she noticed the very fine black wire zigzagged from tree to tree for about ten feet.

"Do you see any wiring over there?" He pointed to the right of the pine tree.

"No," she said. "Let's go."

They cautiously approached the clearing. He felt every minor movement inside the fibers of his muscles and carefully controlled each advance. His vision seemed to be clearer and brighter, watching for the enemy. His mind keen, working as a computer to calculate escape routes if needed. He located every obstacle to overcome. His acute hearing heard the flutter of a bird's wing, the crunch of pine needles under his feet and the unwanted sound of 'click.' In an instant, he saw Maria fall to the ground. Next he heard a second click but felt nothing.

"What the hell!" barked a voice from an enemy opponent in the bush. "You're the First Born!"

He stood up and proceeded to tackle Tarian. In that split second, Tarian roundhouse kicked the man in the head. Tarian knocked him out cold. Tarian swung the convulsing Maria over

First Born by Janelle Gabay

his shoulders and started to run full speed the remaining fifteen hundred yards to the camp.

Her convulsing stopped halfway, but he refused to put her down. She pounded his back with her fists and cursed at him viciously. He ran faster. She gave up. Once past the secure border, he dropped her to the ground roughly and doubled over breathing heavily.

"Smooth landing. If you are going to sweep me off my feet, at least have the courtesy to put me down gently," she said, wiping the dirt from her hands. "I'm not a small girl. Are you all right? That was a long haul."

"Yes, fine," he said between breaths. "Yeah! That felt awesome." He grinned from ear to ear. He loved the thrill of the hunt. With every brutal exhale of air, he felt the warrior inside him.

"You know that stunner hit you?"

"Yeah, how did it feel?" he asked.

"No, I meant weird that you did not react. But it felt like shit," she said.

"Really? What does shit feel like? Honestly, Maria, you need to find better descriptors."

"Okay. It felt really, really, really horrible. Is that better? Did it look like it felt good? What kind of stupid question is that?"

"Are you two finished bickering?" A blonde haired man said in an annoyed voice. "How'd you find us?"

"Where's Audrey?" Tarian asked.

"In the captain's quarters," he said. He pointed to a very large tent.

First Born by Janelle Gabay

"Audrey?" he politely asked, standing outside of the tent. He was unsure of the correct procedure before entering someone's tent. The three-knock rule could not be used on a door made of fabric.

"Come in, Tarian," she said recognizing his voice.

Tarian held the flap open for Maria then followed her inside. Audrey leaned over a table studying charts. He could tell she was working her atmospheric magic as the interior felt dry and cool. She sized the two of them up with one quick glance.

"We have set up a makeshift bathing area by the stream. I would suggest you two go for a swim and tend to your wounds."

"Yes ma'am," said Maria, still in EMA mode but Audrey did not correct her.

"They captured Gabe, and we know where their camp is," Tarian said.

"Yes, I, too, know where the camp is," Audrey stated.

"What else do you know?" Tarian wondered if she had been observing him through those monkeys.

"That you need a shower."

He stared at her trying to read her unreadable face.

"What is it, Tarian?" Audrey asked.

"Nothing," he said.

Her Cadet Sergeant persona offended him.

"You've all done well, now tend to your wounds. You both can sleep in Tent Seven tonight," Audrey said courteously but abruptly.

At the stream, Maria stripped down to her underwear without inhibition. She was tall and built solid like an athlete. She jumped into the water. Tarian undressed then cannonballed

First Born by Janelle Gabay

into the stream. She splashed him back, pretending to be annoyed. She challenged him to a breaststroke race, but Tarian won.

They dove into the refreshing water and let the liquid clean their dirty, sweat-covered bodies. Tarian burst through the water's barrier into the air and let the clear droplets fall away from his face. Eyes closed. Relaxed. It felt good. He didn't want to exit the revitalizing water but knew it was time to return to camp.

"That's a nasty cut you've got there on your shin," Maria commented on his gash while he stood soaking wet with only his underwear on.

He felt uncomfortable, but Maria was like a sister to him. "Yeah, I know. Watch this," he said.

She focused on the sliced skin. Slowly and ever so slightly, she saw the droplets of blood return into his body. The tiny fibers of tissue wove their way back together. Even the purple tinge of the bruising steadily faded to match his natural color tone.

"Wow! That's amazing!" she blurted mouth agape.

"I know. I'm getting better at it. Of course, I did not know what I was doing at first. The more I concentrate on healing, the faster it happens."

"I wish I had that ability."

"How's your side where he punched you?" he asked her.

"I've had worse. I have brothers. Just a scratch."

"Here, let me help you."

He offered to wrap up the dressing around her elbow. The slice and lump came from a nasty fall she took after Gabe

First Born by Janelle Gabay

went down from the stunner. She fumbled to secure the tape with one hand.

"Thanks," she said with a look of defeat in her eyes.

"He's fine you know. It's just an exercise. You could not have done anything differently," he said, reading the look of concern on her face.

"I guess so, but I feel so stupid. I should have had his back."

"You did. It was an accident. He got injured, and that was the problem."

His words made them both think about Maria's delicate mortality. The responsibility lay within Tarian. He was the immortal. Like Jen had said, 'The Guardians are supposed to protect us, not the other way around." He was beginning to understand the power of his new position and what his eternal role as a Guardian meant. He was born to protect the weak.

Tarian finished her dressing, and they proceeded to find Tent Seven. It was smaller than Audrey's tent with no special climate control and two cots for beds, but it was a thousand times better than sleeping on the hard ground of the mountainside cliff.

At two o'clock in the morning, Tarian awoke abruptly. His dream had been vividly disturbing. Touching his lips with the ends of his fingertips, he sensed the phantom presence of a girl's mouth, but which girl. The sensation of pleasure lingered inside his body as the feeling of deceit pumped through his heart. In his dream, he had been enjoying an intimate encounter with Delia. As his lips kissed hers, she morphed into Audrey. To his surprise, his hunger increased, and he wanted more. Then

First Born by Janelle Gabay

someone slapped him in the face. Blackness engulfed him, and he woke up. The sudden leap out of dream world left him disoriented. It took him seconds to regain his bearings. Embarrassment crept into his conscience, and he turned to look at Maria. Relief washed over him as he saw the rapid eye movement of REM sleep upon her.

He cast off the sheets in the hopes of hurling away the pleasurable heat he felt sweeping through his body. With the humid air clinging to his skin and pulsating pain beating into his head, he knew the comfort of sleep was gone. The throbbing sensation that seeped into his brain increased. Soon violent pounding consumed his head. He needed water. He realized he had not eaten or drank much in the last forty-eight hours, and it was catching up to him. Carefully he snuck from his cot, as to not wake up Maria. Her eyelids twitched, and her mouth dripped saliva. She looked as if she was running from something wicked. It was comical, but he was in too much pain to laugh; plus, he was afraid if he woke her, she would punch him hard.

He took his backpack outside to try to find a painkiller and water for his headache. He located the medicine and wondered if it would be strong enough for immortal pain. Maybe he just needed water. His mouth was parched. He rummaged some more, but no water; then he remembered the stream. He could use that as drinking water.

Halfway down the path he heard Audrey's voice. He froze. *Where was she? North, she was north.*

Audrey walked through the moonlit woods with someone. He bent low and found a thick Mountain Laurel bush to hide behind. Once hidden, the guilt of his romantic dream rushed

First Born by Janelle Gabay

back to him, and he prayed for invisibility. The other voice he heard was high-pitched and familiar. He lifted his eyes above the Laurel bush, watching the two figures walking in the distance. Shadows from the full moon laced their faces, but he could see the other person was a Guardian. The woman was wearing a green Guardian suit. The face was recognizable, but the name would not come to him.

They argued, but he only caught general words at the end of their discussion. Audrey pressed her mouth into a thin line while she furrowed her brow. The lady dressed in green showed Audrey photos and paperwork that made Audrey scowl. Then the lady kissed Audrey on the forehead and walked away. Tarian felt an urge to approach Audrey, but she quickly turned on her heels and marched back to camp.

"Margaret," he whispered. "That's her name."

It was the lady he had met right after the attack, the lady who was profiling Guardians. The vexing fog of forgetfulness lifted. Soon his suspicions got the best of him, and many possible scenarios flaunted themselves in his brain. Trust was a tricky thing. It was easily doubted.

Within seconds and distracting him once more, his headache screamed in protest to this delay in hydration. The vicious thirst returned to his throat and cast away all his suspicious thoughts. He continued to the stream and knelt down to retrieve a cupful of clean spring water. He not only drank it, he violently threw it against his skin, wishing it would sting or hurt him in some way. He needed to rinse away his mixed emotions of shameful lust and infuriating distrust. He poured one

101

First Born by Janelle Gabay

last douse of chilly water over the top of his short, dark hair, pinning it to the surface of his skin like a tight ski cap.

It had been a dream, *hadn't it?* He desperately wanted to trust Audrey. He tried to grasp the meaning of the dream. For some reason, the dream had driven him into the woods where he found her.

Why? What did it mean? The water turned frigid once the breeze hit his skin. The cold liquid dripped from his scalp eliciting energy from his flesh. He was hoping for clarity not zest. He ran back to his tent.

First Born by Janelle Gabay

FOURTEEN
THE FLAG

Before he had reached his tent, Maria appeared and snapped, "Where've you been? I've been searching for you!" She looked at him sideways as if to ask him why he was soaking wet.

"I had a headache and needed water. What happened?"

"They've ordered us to line up."

"Whose orders?"

"I don't know who they are. We just met them two days ago. Someone woke me up and got me out of bed," she spat.

Maria and Tarian ran to their tent to retrieve their gear then fell into line. Audrey, Sophie and John handed everyone a small device. Tarian turned the flat, oval shaped, lightweight object over in the palm of his hand.

"This is the egg, as we call it," John said then he touched it.

At once, all of the eggs lit up. It was similar to a mobile phone only much lighter in weight with no visible controls. John slid open the thin top layer of his egg splitting it into two parts revealing a secret compartment where a miniature egg-shaped piece hid. He stuck the tiny egg behind his ear.

"This smaller piece," he said, "controls the egg. Once placed behind your ear, the conductor responds to your thoughts. These tiny devices have many functions, but we will use it mainly to communicate to one another as we attack the enemy

103

First Born by Janelle Gabay

camp and get our prisoners back. These devices also work as trap finders and a GPS to help us find the base as well as each other. Audrey's team will be in charge of capturing the flag. The sooner you find it, the sooner we can get out of this muddy hellhole."

The tiny egg showed no visible signs of adhesive, but when Tarian placed it behind his ear, it stuck to the side of his head like a magnet. He held the larger egg in the palm of his hand. A map appeared on the egg's face, and Audrey informed them that this was the guide to the enemy flag. According to the device, the flag was 9.6 miles away, which would take them three hours of hiking. The enemy camp, however, was three miles away. Seeing these vast distances on a map was startling. How could this all be an illusion? Tarian desperately wanted to know how they made this Realm possible. Was it magic or advanced science far beyond his comprehension? He was beginning to agree with Gabe's theory of teleportation.

"Let's go," Audrey ordered, and they began trekking through the woods.

Tarian placed the egg inside his pocket, but it zipped out into the air where it hovered in proximity. It remained a constant companion to Tarian as he marched on with his troop. He could hold on to it if he chose, or he could let it float by his side.

After an hour of treacherous plodding, a thick curtain of heavy rain swiftly blew in, and they were forced to take cover under a canopy of trees. Rain-soaked leaves dripped water onto their heads, prolonging the agonizing journey. Maria and Tarian huddled close together to try to stay as warm and dry as possible and examined the egg.

First Born by Janelle Gabay

"This thing is helpful," Tarian said partly to himself and partly to Maria, but Audrey was close by and smiled at him. "Can it get wet?"

"Yes," Audrey said.

"Did you help develop it?" he asked.

"Yes. It's a Guardian advancement, but we've run into some problems with it."

"It barely has any weight to it," Tarian said.

"It's made from digitally fabricated carbon fiber filaments," Audrey said.

"It's also cold," he said.

"Very observant, Tarian," Audrey said with that smile again.

This was the Audrey he trusted; however, she seemed preoccupied with something, and he wanted to know what. She must have felt his gaze upon her, for she looked back at him, then stood up abruptly.

"The rain has stopped. Move out," she ordered.

Audrey waited for everyone to exit. Tarian was the last one, and she walked behind him. She whispered, "Boron arsenide; it's a fantastic electrical insulator."

He grinned as her breath brushed the back of his neck.

After another hour of hiking, their V-formation scattered. Audrey held the position in the front with Tarian left of her. Maria had been left of Tarian for a while until she encountered a large spider's web, and in removing its sticky fibers had shifted her position right. Without warning, everyone to the right of Audrey fell into a deep cavity. Audrey and Tarian were the only two people left standing above ground.

First Born by Janelle Gabay

"Dammit!" Audrey hissed and shook the egg as if it had not worked properly.

"Maria," Tarian called out.

"I'm okay. It's a long drop, but the ground is level. Ugh," she moaned in aggravation. "Those jerks put out a trap."

"Is anyone hurt?" Audrey called down into the pit.

Several 'no ma'am's' were voiced from below.

"Keith, survey the damages for our men. Lori, walk the perimeter. Let me know if there's an escape."

Immediately both went to complete the tasks and within minutes reported back to Audrey. They were all in good health, no sprained ankles or broken bones. The pit was roughly ten feet in perimeter with an opening of five feet. There were no visual signs of an exit.

"I will alert John and Sophie of our setback. Sit tight, help will come for you soon. Tarian and I will continue. We have to capture their flag before they capture ours. Winning means eating steak instead of canned rations," she said to the disappointed grumblings of those stuck in the hole.

Tarian felt miserable for Maria.

"Move!" Audrey ordered when he hesitated.

In the forty-five minutes it took to hike, walk and swim to their destination, neither of them spoke a word. Visions of his dream and what it meant, moreover how it made him feel, continued to penetrate his conscious thoughts no matter how tightly he closed his mind. Furthermore, he sensed that she wanted to talk to him as well. Numerous questions swirled in his brain. He had not stopped thinking of what he witnessed between her and Margaret during his trek to the stream. He knew he was

106

First Born by Janelle Gabay

new to the world of the Guardians, but he disliked being omitted from any conversation. This jealous feeling engulfed him. His thoughts began to jet off into opposing directions. Audrey and her Guardian friends had centuries of memories and secrets.

"What's going on, Audrey?" he finally blurted out.

Their rough marching through the root and rock-filled, uneven ground came to a halt. She looked at him with confused eyes, then turned away and began trudging on.

"We have to capture the flag," she said, still focused on her forward motion.

"I saw you with Margaret in the woods," he said. He still could not remember the lady's last name, but he was certain the first name was Margaret.

"I don't know what you think you saw."

"You were arguing with her," he said. He had gotten the ball rolling, and the momentum of the conversation pulled him forward.

"This is complicated. I cannot share all my information with you." She kept her head forward facing as they walked side by side.

"Why not? Back at Headquarters I seemed pretty important to everyone," he said still walking.

"After the game," she said, finally bringing her eyes to his.

"I want to know everything. I'm an integral piece in this puzzle. People hate me because of it."

"What?"

"Never mind."

107

First Born by Janelle Gabay

The conversation halted at the site of the enormous river they had to swim across. They had exited the forested mountaintop and landed next to an embankment. Opposite of the shore was a vast meadow where the flag stood waiting.

Tarian's tense body relaxed under the buoyancy of the fresh spring water, and the frigid temperature soothed his inflamed muscles. The water prompted an unsolicited race between them. She won, again.

Once out of the water, they moved on. She still did not speak, but he assumed she was looking for more booby traps. The beautiful meadow of yellow wildflowers and green grass seemed too good to be true. It simply could not be as easy as walking through a flower-filled meadow to capture the flag.

As soon as Tarian had stepped one foot into the calf deep grass, his throat swelled shut. Panic filled his senses. His eyes bulged from his head. He fell onto Audrey like a zombie clawing at her for life. She pushed him to the ground, placed both hands on his chest and pumped twice.

"It's okay. Don't panic," she said as she looked down at his face while straddling his torso. He looked up at her choking. "Shhhh. You're not dying. It's a trick." She gently stroked his chest and arms.

He wanted to believe her, but the feeling of no air terrified him. He gathered every ounce of will he had and managed to calm his chaotic nerves. Little by little, second by second he felt oxygen creep into his lungs.

"Don't gasp!" she ordered. "Breath steady."

He tried, fighting all of his instincts to gulp in the air around him. His eyes never left hers, and he appreciated her

First Born by Janelle Gabay

patience. He mocked her slow breathing pattern and regained normal oxygen levels. He fought the tears.

"What was that?" he asked still a little breathless.

She crawled off of him and said, "It's an oxygen dump. It's an immortal weakness. We already have a much higher blood oxygen level than mortals."

"But I felt like I had no oxygen."

"I know. It's a strange phenomenon, and actually, the reaction should not have been that bad since your body was cold from the water."

"Why didn't it affect you?"

"I'm trained to recognize this trap. You're not."

He staggered to his feet still feeling weak. Together, they moved a few steps in the direction of the flag.

"Stop!" Audrey said. "There's an electric barrier."

Tarian stopped as ordered, but did not see the barrier.

"Right there," she said pointing low to his right. "Can you see that disturbance in the grass?"

"Yes," he said amazed. It was barely visible, but the grass vibrated. Once he noticed it, he could see the faint line encircling the flag.

"You think the stunners are bad, this would have thrown us twenty feet," she said with experience in her voice.

"The stunner did not affect me."

"It didn't?" she asked.

"No. Is that unusual?"

"Well, it's rare," she replied, and he saw her eyes narrow.

Was she impressed or envious? He wondered then asked aloud, "Why didn't the egg detect this?" The egg had been

109

First Born by Janelle Gabay

extremely valuable for navigation and communication, but it missed both booby traps.

"Like I said, it's still in the developmental stage. It should have warned us," she said. "I've seen a lot in my life, and human intelligence and instinct are still the best weapons."

"How do we disarm the barrier?"

"We don't. We have to find the hole. There is always a hole. I'm sure the disarming device is in the hands of the enemy. Whether the enemy is close by or not is something we will find out soon enough."

She began to walk the perimeter of the barrier shaking the egg device violently. She expressed a slew of expletives at the ineffectiveness of the egg. Twice they walked it, and Tarian felt as useless as the egg. Finally, she saw the gap.

"The opening is less than two feet," she warned. "Enter sideways, turn your shoulders and suck in your gut."

Her pixie-sized body walked straight through.

"We're in, and I didn't have to suck in my gut." He sneered at her.

"That's not what I meant. Geez. Touchy. Now watch out. If it were me, I would've installed ejection pedals all the way to the target. We'll see," she said.

With her gift she froze the grass into tiny icicles, he assumed to stop any pedal ejection devices, then she ran full speed for the flag. He followed her lead. Without interference, she snatched the flag and sat down.

"Now what?" he said in huffing breaths after the last sprint.

First Born by Janelle Gabay

As she relaxed, he stood in an athletic stance ready for action. She smiled and motioned for him to sit down.

"We wait. We've got the flag, and that's the end of the game."

"Oh, okay."

It all seemed very anti-climatic to Tarian. Now he did not know what to do with himself. After four days of intense field simulation, suddenly, he was supposed to sit still and relax? His arms became cumbersome and awkward until finally he just let them hang at his side, trying to look natural. Audrey looked at ease and did nothing to calm his nerves.

"Well, I can't fly." Tarian sat down and tried to relax.

She laughed for several seconds then said, "If you had, you'd be the first."

"So no immortal can fly?"

"Nope. What else did you discover about yourself?"

"I can see in the dark and very far into the distance compared to Gabe and Maria. My hearing is also much acuter than theirs."

"You're displaying soldier traits."

"Compared to what?"

"The immortals that work in the labs inside Headquarters don't usually display soldier skills."

"What are their strengths?"

"Things like being able to look inside a cell without a microscope and photographic memory. These different and unique skills separate us into soldiers or scientists. This organization of abilities leads me to believe that God did

111

First Born by Janelle Gabay

intentionally make us the way we are. We're not some mutant race. We serve a purpose."

"We sound like some overgrown ant colony."

Audrey laughed, and Tarian joined in.

"I did feel a surge of super strength during a fight. Maybe it was simple adrenalin," Tarian said.

"Did this come after one of your friends was threatened or hurt?"

"Yes, how'd you know?"

"It's common in us. We have an aggressive protection extinct. Sort of like the vamps but different."

"Vamps? Like vampires?"

"Yes. There are all sorts of creatures in this world Tarian."

"Are there red-eyed, scorpion-tailed monkeys?"

She laughed, "Yes, outside the borders. Let's just say they're the result of an animal weapons experiment from fifty of years ago that went awry. Maybe they've all died out now. I haven't had a mission outside the borders in a long time."

Tarian had spent his entire life inside the Entente. No one went outside the borders anymore. There was no need. Plenty of wonderful cities spread across this nation to fill up a lifetime of vacations. Now it seemed ridiculous and narrow-minded. He began to realize just how incredibly sheltered his perfect little life had been.

One tubular pod appeared out of thin air. They squeezed inside. The compact space was not suitable for two people. Cramped and entwined together, Tarian once again desperately

First Born by Janelle Gabay

tried to banish all thoughts of his prior dream from his conscience mind.

They were uncomfortably but successfully delivered back to the familiar room where the game had begun. When the door opened, their twisted bodies stumbled awkwardly out into a room filled with cheering soldiers. Maria and Gabe hurried over to congratulate them. Their team had won the challenge. That evening they were treated to a buffet of scrumptious food prepared by Chef Richard, but taking a hot shower and sleeping in his downy bed was Tarian's best reward.

First Born by Janelle Gabay

FIFTEEN
FENG AND JUSTICE
DELIA & ROMAN

Delia's heart dropped when she stepped into the law offices of Feng and Justice. The last time she had been in this building, Mr. Prescott was alive and in the prime of his life. She remembered traipsing through the halls and hiding in secret rooms at age ten with eleven-year-old Tarian while their fathers discussed important business matters. These visits were a typical occurrence during her adolescence, but then they had ended. As she grew older, she lost interest in playing with Tarian. Their silly childhood games turned into thorny pre-teen anxiety. Looking back, she wondered why things changed so vastly. When and why do children become self-conscience?

Today, two days after Christmas, she walked into this office as a striking woman ready to begin the New Year and her new life. She vowed to be independent and never be smashed under her father's thumb again. Mr. Feng had promised her an internship where she could gain on-the-job training while continuing her Harvard education virtually. She deserved this job. But no matter what she told herself, the guilt still crawled under her skin. She had deliberately kept this opportunity a secret from Tarian. She told herself she was sparing his feelings. To tell him she was going to work for his father's old partner would just bring back the pain of his death. In truth, if she was honest with herself, she wanted a secret of her own. He had left

114

First Born by Janelle Gabay

her. He had gone away with a beautiful Entente agent doing who knows what for the government. None of it made sense. It helped her sanity to have her own undisclosed affair.

In preparation for her interview, Delia did a background check on Mr. Feng. She found very little information about him as a young adult due to his secretive Xia heritage. Rarely did a Xia marry, educate or work outside the community. She did learn they are required at least two years of college-level medical school before deciding on another major. Most Xia adults worked in the medical field and lived close to home on the west side of the Entente. Mr. Feng did neither. In fact, Mr. Feng had become an attorney; he had sued the world-renown Xia Technologies Inc., received millions for his victory and lived on the complete opposite side of the continent from his family.

Joe Prescott had promoted him to partner at the young age of twenty-eight and by thirty, when Mr. Prescott died, he was the senior partner. But what intrigued her the most was his refusal to work with her father. His law office was in the center of the Entente Government District, and he worked closely with many other Senators. Mr. Prescott had handled all of her father's business affairs when he was alive, but now, Mr. Feng would not take her father's calls. She had her reasons for alienating herself from her father, but what were Feng's reasons?

"Follow me, Miss Eastwood."

The young, well-dressed male receptionist led her down a lengthy plush hallway she did not recognize, and into Mr. Feng's office. Everything was new. Ms. Lucy, Mr. Prescott's old receptionist, no longer greeted clients and the dark wainscoting she used to run her fingers across replaced with modern, textured

115

First Born by Janelle Gabay

designs. She reached out allowing her fingers to skim the new walls. Sadness washed over her, but she only allowed herself a moment of nostalgia. She erected her posture and squared her shoulders. The past was the past.

But the past would not rest. As she passed Mr. Prescott's old office, her mind drifted back to Ms. Lucy. She had been the one to find him lying dead on his office floor. Tarian's mom had called her at three a.m. after her husband had not come home that evening. It was normal for him to work late, but one a.m. was always the latest. When Carolyn could not contact him, she called Ms. Lucy. Ms. Lucy insisted Carolyn stay home with the little children while she went and checked the office.

"Miss Eastwood," the young man said again.

"Pardon," she said, snapping out of her reminiscence.

He held the door open for her and said, "Come in, please. Mr. Feng has left you instructions on the desk."

He shut the door leaving her in solitude. She swiped the tablet and read the note. It instructed her to write an essay about herself and then turn on the wall display. She did as she was told, finding it all extremely strange.

Roman Feng watched the lanky young woman in his office from behind hidden walls. He had already researched her and knew she was overly qualified for his low-level internship position, but like everyone else, she would have to start at the bottom and work her way up. They had met at Joe's funeral where she never left Tarian's side - a day that changed Roman's life for the worse.

116

First Born by Janelle Gabay

"Delia Eastwood," Roman whispered to himself as he watched her. He studied her as he kept her in his office far past the conclusion of his required instructions. He wanted to see how she reacted to his absence. She fidgeted in her chair and then rose to walk around the room. He admired her long legs and choice of classic style dress. She leaned over to view the photos on his table. In no way did she seem inhibited or nervous. He continued to ponder her true motives.

"Do I hire you? This will change everything," he spoke to himself in his secret room. He had read her anonymous blogs. He had followed her short but impressive Harvard career, but had she left her home? He wondered if it was an act, a trick. She may be a spy for her father.

Roman did not want her because of her intelligence nor because she was Zachary Eastwood's daughter. He wanted her because of the disease. Her overly thin frame secured his suspicion. He needed to work on her. He needed to delve into her fascinating medical history, but would she let him?

"Hello, Miss Eastwood," Roman introduced himself.

"Hello." She spun around to find him standing behind her.

He seemed to appear out of thin air. She feared he had been in the room, possibly sitting in a chair in the dark corner all along, and she had not noticed him.

"It's a pleasure to see you again, Mr. Feng." Delia did not spook easily and regained her composure without a hint of a derailment.

First Born by Janelle Gabay

"Welcome to the law firm of Feng and Justice," he said, still holding a firm, warm grip on her cold, rigid hand long after the handshake had ended.

His yellow eyes frightened her, but she managed to remain poised. She remembered how his eyes had entranced her at the funeral. It was an eye color she had never seen before on a human being. Now she knew, after her research, it was a popular Xia trait.

"It's an honor to be a part of this firm."

"Do you have a place to live?" he asked.

"Yes, I'm staying with a friend," she replied.

"Very well," he stated. "Let's get started. We have much to accomplish."

First Born by Janelle Gabay

SIXTEEN
EBONY6

The last seven days consisted of one thing: extreme physical exertion. Get up at 500 hours, eat, run, weight train, eat, simulation room, cardio train, eat, sleep, and repeat. Inside the simulations, Tarian fine-tuned his immortal abilities and overcame his immortal weaknesses. To say the least, he was exhausted. So, today, when he received the note under his door that read, "Meet in the library at 800 hours," he almost jumped with joy.

Ten minutes early and proud of himself, Tarian strutted into the library grinning. He wanted to get a head start on the assignment before anyone else showed up.

"Always the bridesmaid," Audrey joked when she saw his arrogant gait.

"Hello, Audrey." He narrowed his eyes at her and gave her a smug smile.

Of course, he was second. He hadn't beaten her at anything yet. Her perfection was getting old. Plus, the constant help she gave him teetered on fanatical. Worst of all, he knew she thought of him as a boy, and that irritated his manly ego. He secretly hoped he would age to thirty, ideally, maybe even thirty-five. He would still be young but old enough to be respected by mortals without question and, best of all, older than Audrey.

"You look happy," she said.

119

First Born by Janelle Gabay

"Oh do I. Well I feel great. Been kick'in ass around here." In reality, the extent of his exhaustion paralleled any doctor pulling an all-nighter in the ER. Top that off with cramping muscles and a headache.

"Coffee?" Piper asked.

She appeared out of nowhere and startled Tarian to the point of a slight yelp. He cut off the sound escaping from his mouth before he looked too foolish, but he still caught Audrey snickering.

"Thank you, Piper." He took the cup of steaming black liquid. "I knew it. We are in both Headquarters and the training facility. Aren't we?"

"Something like that." Piper zestfully raised her shoulders.

"You see --" Audrey began to explain.

"Never mind, I don't want to know." Tarian interrupted sighing and shaking his head.

"You sit there." Piper pointed to a seat with the name First Born attached to it.

Eight oversized, pliable leather reclining chairs waited for readers. Each chair had an accompanying table with a stack of books. Labels pinned to each chair listed the eight nicknames given by the Commander over the past week. Since the end of the game, he had only been training with seven other people.

Tarian took his cup of coffee and went to sit in his designated chair. A surge of rebellion struck his core, and he decided he would rather sit next to Audrey in Sparkplug's chair. He had a few questions he wanted to ask her, but the obedient

120

First Born by Janelle Gabay

student in him dragged his feet back to the chair labeled First Born.

"Chicken." Audrey watched him play musical chairs.

"Yeah, well, have you seen the size of the Commander?" Tarian asked.

She laughed. "Oh, I thought you were more scared of Maria." Sparkplug was Maria's given nickname.

Tarian sneered at her then sunk into the comfort of the chair and let its soft hide embrace his sore backside. It felt like sinking into a cloud. He closed his eyes and exhaled ecstatically.

"You know this does not mean the end of physical training," Audrey said.

"Shhhh! Don't ruin my heavenly moment," he said without opening his eyes.

"Haven't you been to the therapy room yet?" Piper asked.

"No." He opened his brown eyes wide at this new and appealing information.

"I'll take you later," Audrey offered. "First, I'll put you in the hyperbaric oxygen chamber. Second, I'll squeeze you into the compression suit." As she said the words, her mouth curled wickedly.

The weight of her playfully sinister gaze rested on him. He wasn't sure he liked the idea of her enclosing him inside of something or squeezing him into anything, but his stinging calf muscles and burning shoulders insisted he allow it. For now, he tilted his head back onto the cozy leather again and stole a few minutes of relaxation before the remaining trainees filled the room.

First Born by Janelle Gabay

The smell of used antique leather against the tangent aroma of printed ink on paper brought back memories of high school nights spent studying with Delia in the Eastwood Estate's vast library. They would escape their homework and the harsh computer monitor light to treasure hunt through the delicate vellum of centuries old books stacked on rows of shelves. Scavenging to find the oldest book or personal journal became a competition that led to a game of imagination. They loved history, and these books brought them back in time to foreign and fascinating places. Hours would pass, and their homework would remain undone. Thinking back, Tarian wondered how he ever passed any of his subjects while he lived in the house with Delia.

The old and new books sitting next to him on the table would be studied in conjunction with virtual learning. The next phase of training dealt with the government, culture, geography, language and history of the Guardians, the Entente and the Prevallers. Not an easy task.

On the second day of their library assignment, a note slipped into Tarian's *Phosphorus Phacts* textbook read: *In ten minutes, meet me in classroom 12-C. Audrey.*

With some difficulty, he found room 12-C. It was an old and forgotten classroom packed full of wooden desks and one antique chalkboard. A thick layer of dust gathered on the furniture, and most of the light bulbs did not work.

Audrey sat in the back corner of the dimly lit room with a thin, portable laptop. She appeared ghostly as the blue monitor light hit her face.

"What are you doing?" he asked.

First Born by Janelle Gabay

"I've found something interesting," she answered. "I wasn't honest with you about Margaret's and my conversation during the game."

"I knew it," he spat. "And you should also admit you weren't very friendly to me either."

She raised an eyebrow at him and did not smile. He sat next to her.

"I wasn't sure who the blogger was back then, but I had my suspicions. I'm not positive what it means or if it's connected to the murders. And I'm not telling anyone. Got it!"

"Doesn't Margaret know?" he asked.

"No, she handed the investigation over to me over a week ago when it was still ambiguous."

"What did you find?" Tarian asked.

"Your girlfriend's anonymous blog page."

"What?"

She nodded her head.

"Is it current?" he asked.

"I have about six years worth. They change servers twice a year, April and October. She also deletes entries, so it's difficult but not impossible to find them. The past three months are still missing," she said. "The first four years are very basic, kids' stuff. Most of her blogs are school related or generic, but in the past few months, her voice has changed."

"How?"

"It's almost like a depression fell upon her or--"

"How did you find out?" He interrupted. "You said she wrote them anonymously. I know Delia. She's thorough. She wouldn't have blogged lightly. Not now, maybe when she was

123

First Born by Janelle Gabay

fourteen, but definitely not now. And what could she have possibly written?"

"Her blog was flagged because she writes about the Prevallers."

"Why?" he said but he knew the answer. She was a conspiracy nut. He could only imagine what she wrote under the guise of anonymity.

"She is one of millions of bloggers around the world carelessly dropping flagged words, but I happened to notice some other statements. My instinct triggered, and link onto her site. The more I researched, the more I believed blogger Ebony6 was actually Delia Eastwood."

He did not like the suspicious tone in her voice nor the dark look in her eyes. Delia was on trial, and he would defend her to the death.

"Exactly what are you accusing her of?"

"Nothing," she said. "I brought you here to have you read them for yourself. You know her. You can help me figure out some of the most encrypted blogs. Here's one from a year and a half ago after Beast and just before your first year at EMA."

August 15
Today I get to see T for the first time in
7 weeks. I'm nervous. We will only have a
couple of hours so I cannot discuss serious
topics. I will have to force myself to
keep the conversation light. I do not want
to burden him with my suspicions. I want
to kiss him. I want to hold him close to

124

First Born by Janelle Gabay

me. I miss him more than I ever thought
possible. It's like having a hole in my
chest. Yes, that's it. I'm not whole when
I'm not with him. I'm broken, incomplete.
But I am torn. Does he have a right to
know? But there is nothing he can do while
he is at TGL. And it really does not prove
anything. What is it really? I don't have
all of the facts yet. I will wait. Once I
know more, I will tell him. I will get my
car in the next couple months and drive up
to tell him. I cannot believe I waited so
long to get a driving permit. What was I
thinking? I guess I took driving for
granted, always having a driver and my
brother around. Why do you need a permit
anyway, the car basically drives itself.
Permits are simply a way for the government
to keep track of us and charge us fees.
But the vial of her blood in that package
to Father! It has to mean something... but
what? Why did he need a vial of T's
mother's blood? Oh, have to go. It's time
to leave for TGL. Until tomorrow.

Fortis est veritas
Ebony6

Comment: XOXO25
You have to tell him. You love him.
He's a good guy. It's his mom.

First Born by Janelle Gabay

> *Ebony6*
> *Love you XOXO25, you are always*
> *rooting for him. I'll see.*
>
> *Comment: Zigler88*
> *Come on! Dad is obvs connected!*
>
> *Ebony6*
> *Shut up Zigler88! We've discussed this*
> *already.*

"I'm T, I guess," he observed.

"I'm assuming so," she responded. "And TGL is The Gray Line, an old reference to the army academy."

"She never mentioned a vial of my mom's blood. Maybe there was a logical explanation that she found out later. Knowing her, it has to do with her illness that she will not discuss with me. Everyone says she is fine, but I'm worried about it. Maybe she needed my mom's blood…" he rambled then drifted off in thought. The information inside this blog left him terrified and uneasy. "You said that was almost two years ago."

"A year and a half."

"Okay. After that blog I spent all Christmas and summer with her and she never mentioned it and seemed fine. Her health had significantly improved," he said. He knew she was not truly well. He often thought her cocoa complexion dipped into a gray zone and her slender frame too thin. He worried about eating disorders, but she dismissed his questions. She once ate an entire

First Born by Janelle Gabay

banana split in front of his face just to prove she was not
anorexic.

"I know it's not definite. Here is one from this
September, on her eighteenth birthday. I checked Harvard
records. She did miss two weeks of classes."

September 30th
I woke up in a pile of my own vomit again.
What a way to begin my eighteenth year! I
felt miserable all day. Happy Birthday to
me! I've been through three prescriptions
of medicine and nothing is working. This
is the weakest I've felt in a long time. I
do not understand why the doctor cannot
figure out what is wrong with me. Mother is
beside herself with anxiety, but I cannot
hide my symptoms. I've tried to vomit
quietly without her knowing, but she
doesn't leave my side. I'm so thankful for
her care, but it's breaking my heart to see
her suffer. We are both at our wits end
with frustration. Mother is worried they
are going to quarantine me soon and forbid
me to go back to College. It's obviously
not contagious or I would have already
gotten someone else in my home sick, and no
one is showing symptoms but me. I'm going
to begin my own research today. I need to
get myself healthy before holiday break. I
cannot let T see me like this.

First Born by Janelle Gabay

On a more interesting note, Biggie went
west again. If I were the Prevallers I'd
hit the West first. I think Biggie is in
charge of border security. Also, his weird
North pole friend visited the house again.
I was too sick to eavesdrop this time.
　　　Fortis est veritas
　　　Ebony6

　　　Comment: SkyEartHater
　　　Attacking from the West is beneficial.
　　　It's the Energy District. They will
　　　attack big! The Prevallers' objective
　　　is to terrorize.

　　　Ebony6
　　　They are after something. You said
　　　yourself there is a reason SkyEarth is
　　　investing heavily from Flagstaff to
　　　Dallas.

　　　Comment: Jugular8
　　　Boron you morons!! Oh and feel better
　　　Ebony6

　　　Ebony6
　　　Thanks Jugular8

　　　Comment: Jugular8
　　　Got rid of T yet? Let's do dinner.

First Born by Janelle Gabay

> *Ebony6*
> *Goodnight!*

"Who is Jugular8?" Tarian asked with no attempt to disguise his jealousy.

"That's not important," she stated.

"Who is Biggie?" Tarian asked, anger still present in his tone.

"I don't know yet," she responded. Her look suggested she had an opinion but refused to divulge her suspicion until she had all the facts, or maybe she was waiting for his input.

"What's out West?" His voice now even.

"Our Fusion Power Plant, our Wind-Solar Tower, and like Jugular8 says, the craters produced by the meteor storm, but he shouldn't know that. The craters are confidential and very well guarded."

"Why are the Prevallers after the craters?" he asked.

"The craters are an abundant source of pure chemical element Boron. But not just that, Scientists are discovering things inside the connecting cavern system that do not exist here on Earth, not only is it valuable, but it's dangerous. There is energy down there that will control the world: volatile lithium, unstable nuclear activity, much, much more. And we have not even reached the bottom yet."

"What? I didn't know they were that deep?"

"It's classified, but the meteors impact created mines as well as caverns. It's an explorers dream. I think Ebony6 and her blogging buddies are all well-connected teenagers."

First Born by Janelle Gabay

"What do you mean?"

"I mean the sons and daughters of Senators and Generals. Suspicious kids who snoop in their parents' offices."

"Is Biggie on our side?"

"It's not clear," she responded.

"I can ask her. She tells me everything."

"Does she?" Her hard eyes and doubtful mouth crushed his confidence. If Delia was Ebony6, she was obviously not confiding in him.

"This is teenage social networking. It means nothing," he protested, mostly to himself.

"Agreed. Listen, I'll give you this laptop. Read them. There are hundreds. She blogs at least three times a week, sometimes every day, and yes, most of them are totally meaningless. Weed through them yourself. We'll talk later."

First Born by Janelle Gabay

SEVENTEEN
BIT BY THE FAMILY DOG

Tarian did not know what to expect on day twenty-one. He wore the last article of clothing inside his closet. Today's minimal itinerary included eat, run, library, eat and conference room. Everyone assumed they would be given their mission in the conference room.

An elongated, shiny metal table sat in the center of the room covered with blue prints of buildings. Holographic images of weapons and persons of interest hovered over the table. Tarian's team flipped through the papers and studied the images. No one looked pleased. It was real now, the commencement of their official assignment.

In the company assembled for this mission were three centuries old Guardian warriors, Audrey, John and Warren, and two Central Intelligent Agents, Sophie and Keegan. Together they possessed exceptional knowledge and because of this fact were given rare, unlimited authority. As for Gabe and Maria, they had simply been in the right place at the right time. If they had not sat next to Tarian in the mess hall the first day of Beast Barracks, they would probably be home right now, uneventfully waiting for the restart of their second year at EMA.

"I see all of these papers and images but no plan of action Commander," John stated.

131

First Born by Janelle Gabay

The Commander grunted and continued to shuffle around the data like Tarot Cards, but unlike the cards, he could not flip one over to find mystic answers.

"Commander?" Audrey probed. Her jaw set with disapproval.

"We do not have our target," the Commander stated. He had no other option but to tell his soldiers the truth. Failure did not flatter him.

"For three weeks we've prepared. We've helped you to educate and train Tarian, Gabe and Maria under the impression that we were creating an elite reconnaissance team to find the double agent. Now you are telling me, not only do you not know who he is but you don't know where he is?" Sophie questioned, slamming her hands onto the table of data.

Tarian could tell the others felt deceived. Perturbation bubbled over as the group of veterans began to complain and argue amongst themselves. These people were not used to losing. Their loved ones had died, and the lack of progress was infuriating and unacceptable. The room burst with turbulent hand gestures and angry overlapping voices.

As if on cue, Eleanor walked into the conference room. In seconds, her presence silenced the stormy chaos. She pulled Commander General Smith aside for discussion, showing him something on her slender notepad. The ever-present tablet never left her side. Tarian imagined it held centuries of world secrets that other nations would kill to get their hands on.

"Hello everyone. We have our assassin," she said with a look of delightful satisfaction.

First Born by Janelle Gabay

One flick of Eleanor's wrist produced a light field image of a three dimensional man's face. Tarian recognized him immediately. A stab of pain wrenched through his heart as if the family dog had just turned on him. He stood face to face with his dad's law partner and friend, Roman Feng.

"Roman Feng is the man who killed Joseph Prescott, our friend and a Guardian of Dare. He is the Prevallers' hitman and guilty of at least six of the thirteen murders. We have reason to suspect he is also the developer of the serum. He is a Xia," she said matter-of-factly.

What was so special about the Xia's? Tarian knew them only as a highly intelligent and extremely secretive community of people that lived mainly in the Technology District.

"Our sources are working diligently to extract as much information as possible on this man," Eleanor concluded.

Tarian's body urged him to sprint out of the room. Run far and fast. He had spent nineteen years in an isolated dome of privilege and naivety only to have it crash down upon him. He laughed out loud considering his so-called superior private school education with its fancy professors. *What had it taught him? Lies!* In twenty-five days inside a magical village and strange training facility he had found truthful learning. All of the Entente's secrets had been dumped upon him. All of his family secrets had been dumped upon him. He shrunk under its weight.

"It can't be Roman," Tarian said.

"I'm sorry Tarian. I know it is difficult to ingest all of this in the short period of time you have, but the success of this mission will depend on the eight of you being able to do just that. You are the lucky, or maybe unlucky, few that are privileged, or

First Born by Janelle Gabay

shall I say, cursed with this classified information. The eight of you have been purposefully trained these past three weeks in our most lethal simulators to find this man and to defend the Entente. You must find Roman Feng and bring him to us alive. He *must* be alive," she said and looked directly at Tarian.

His irritated expression only grew with this news. This loathsome man befriended his father and now Tarian could not kill him.

Commander General Smith brought up holographic renderings of the blue prints of Entente Government buildings. They studied the Capitol where they would soon work, and the office building that housed Feng's law offices, Tarian's father's old firm. As a team they thoroughly examined the inner workings of the buildings.

"Tarian, Audrey, Maria and Gabe are here to lure Feng out of hiding. It would be perfectly normal for the four of you to remain together after the attack on EMA. You have been allotted an internship under EMA alumni until you can return to your schooling. This should not raise suspicion. Our goal is to appear organic. The four of you can interact in public without a problem. The rest of you must only acknowledge each other in private. Outside you are no more than work related acquaintances. Roman Feng has been untraceable and out of his office for weeks, but we have reason to believe he is returning to Boston quite soon. Our agents believe that his orders are to kidnap Tarian," Eleanor explained.

"Not kill?" Audrey asked.

"No. Study. We have evidence that the Prevallers attempted to exhume Joe's body for study, but we were one step

134

First Born by Janelle Gabay

ahead of them. His body is not in his grave," Eleanor said, with a look of sympathy towards Tarian. "We are a mystery even to ourselves, so I understand the value of studying our kind. The Entente has performed several studies on us with our permission, but if we fall into the hands of the Prevallers, the tests may become cruel under the guise of scientific advancement."

"Tarian is the most valuable of us all," Audrey said in a whisper, contrary to her character. Louder, she continued, "Isn't he?"

Tarian's gut flinched with pleasure at her concern for his wellbeing. She meant more to him than just a compatriot. Their friendship had matured, and he knew he would protect her with his life as she would him.

"Of course, he is the First Born," Eleanor said.

First Born by Janelle Gabay

EIGHTEEN
BITTERSWEET HOMECOMING

The frigid wind kissed Tarian's face as he descended the private jet's staircase. He inhaled a lung full of the familiar city air and grinned. The smell of fuel and deep-fried food mixed with the hint of evergreen and harbor sea life flooded his senses with nostalgic memories. He was home.

On the tarmac, two four-passenger sized green hovercrafts waited for them. Tarian, Maria, Gabe and Audrey slid into one. It flew them to the rooftop of the Towers of Longfellow. Meanwhile, John, Warren, Sophie and Keegan took off for the Leverett Saltonstall Building, the building Tarian's father used to work in, the building where Tarian had grown up. Could he go back to that place?

"You okay," Maria asked placing a hand on Tarian's shoulder.

"Yeah, I'll be fine. This place just brings back a lot of memories," Tarian explained never removing his focus from the scenery outside the window. He had never ridden in a machine like this before. He had seen them, but their use remained strictly for top government officials.

The apartments were true to Guardian form, eerily accurate. Unrivaled attention to detail met Tarian's sight with every turn of a corner and open of a door. He slid the refrigerator door open to grab his favorite drink, orange soda. He knew it

136

First Born by Janelle Gabay

would be there, just as he knew size 12 shoes would sit neatly in a row on the floor of his closet.

"Did you see the closet?" Gabe asked from his bedroom.

"I know," Tarian responded.

"Did you see it!" Gabe shouted enthusiastically. "Even my drawers are filled with socks, underwear, everything!"

"What's your favorite drink?" Tarian asked him with a smirk.

"Personally, I enjoy a nice peach tea," Gabe said, head held high, proud and unashamed of his choice of beverage.

"Yep, I remember. Look in the fridge."

Gabe looked at him suspiciously. He walked to the fridge, opened the door and gasped. Six bottles of peach tea sat next to Tarian's orange soda. "Who are these people?"

"They're very thorough."

"Let's go to the girls apartment," Gabe said. "I want to see how perfect their fridge is. I'm going to give Maria two days before she has it out with Audrey."

"I give it five." Tarian placed his bet.

"Come on." Gabe motioned a wave of his hand as he went for the door.

"No man, you go. I'm tired. I'll see their place tomorrow." Tarian was not tired at all, but he felt the need to be alone. Gabe nodded and walked into the hall.

Tarian sat on the saddle brown leather couch, propped his feet on the glass coffee table and stared up at the vaulted ceiling and angled walls. The room was spacious and airy. Two ceiling fans dangled above him, and a modern fireplace stood grandly in the corner. He finished his soda and stood to recycle the bottle

137

First Born by Janelle Gabay

but instead decided to walk out onto the balcony. Again the chilly air felt invigorating.

The ink black night lit with a thin crescent moon and a few scattered stars entranced him. The skyline sparkled with infinite city lights. Tarian looked down from the thirty-fifth floor and reminisced about the days when his feet walked the very pavement below with his father. Memories flooded his mind, filling him with a bittersweet homecoming. Breathing in one last whiff of Boston air chased with a lump of grief, Tarian retired to his bed and drifted into dreamless sleep.

Seven-thirty in the morning, Gabe and Tarian entered The Wicked Good Coffee Shop. The little store was jammed with patrons. Visiting this place, they assumed, would be a normal morning ritual, and they wanted to appear as ordinary as possible. Tarian needed to show himself at all the local hot spots to attract Feng.

Gabe and Tarian entered the facility first and proceeded to join the winding line of twenty to thirty-year-old young executives. Audrey and Maria came in two minutes later and landed ten spots behind them. The girl behind the counter was a sliver of a human being, a phantom in her black uniform. However, her rough voice and strong presence emitted the strength of a person three times her size.

She glared at Tarian as he fumbled through his order. Many of the loyal customers knew her, and she whipped through their orders at lightning speed causing the long line to move forward smoothly. But he was unfamiliar with the extensive menu of morning energy drinks. Coffees, teas, vitamin shots, enhancers and concoctions combining all ingredients with the

First Born by Janelle Gabay

choice of ingesting them via traditional liquid or the alternative vapor distracted and confused his thought process. Tarian's indecision provoked a revolution of angry coffee consuming regulars. He finally chose a drink and chose it quickly.

"Black coffee," he blurted out.

Phantom Girl laughed in his face. Too much hesitation for a cup of black coffee! Gabe asked for The Wicked Good Special: a triple grande latte with maple-honey. He ordered with incredible ease, and Phantom Girl smirked approvingly as if to say, *I can't believe the two of you are friends*. He had only seen Gabe drink coffee at EMA's mess hall, and he always took it black. Tarian reconsidered his order. Gabe's drink sounded delicious, but he figured Phantom Girl would bite his head off, so he took his boring black coffee and retreated to a table.

The four of them sat at a small high top barely large enough to contain the three coffees, one tea and four breakfast sandwiches. They felt very anonymous in the crowded back corner of the establishment, yet they did not chance a conversation that was anything more than shallow gossip.

"I can't believe I'm going to say this, but I miss Piper," Audrey confessed.

"Yeah, she brought me my coffee every morning when we were in the library. It was always perfectly brewed." Tarian's face softened with the memory.

"Such a boy," Maria said, and Audrey agreed.

"No, she is very sweet unlike Phantom Girl over there," Tarian said casting his eyes in the barista's direction. Phantom Girl caught his look and narrowed her gaze at him. He looked away quickly. "Did you see that? She hates me."

First Born by Janelle Gabay

"Yeah, I think she does." Audrey laughed.

They left the busy coffee shop and joined the hundreds of common staffers marching swiftly onward until they all piled up at the entrance of the Entente Government Capitol. The front of the building sprawled an entire city block. The steel and glass monstrosity stretched its body tall reaching the blue of the sky. Security had been increased after the EMA attack. Only one set of doors out of a dozen were now permissible causing an impatient traffic-jam.

Mumbles of complaints bounced around the crowd: "I've worked here for a decade." "This is crazy." "Why am I subject such harassment?" "I have to get up an hour earlier now."

Plenty of expletives could be heard as everyone entered in a single file line then spread out to pass through intimidating security machines. Giant-sized, unattractive men sat in high official's chairs peering down at those who entered, daring them to set off the alarm. Their faces were full of boredom as their bodies became larger the more they sat. Their need for an outlet was obvious, and the poor soul who tried to slip a pocketknife through the machine was destined for a good old-fashioned beat down full of pent-up perturbation.

As Tarian looked into the eyes of his watcher while he passed through the terrifying machine, a bead of sweat gingerly rolled down the back of his neck, luckily hidden out of view. He hoped the machines weren't sensitive to sweat. Just then he noticed the screen in front of his onlooker revealed body heat. Tarian forced himself to remain calm. His body heat glared bright red causing the observer to take a second glance at him, but the husky man did not pounce.

First Born by Janelle Gabay

Tarian kept a steady pace, and the four slipped through the scanners unnoticed. Under their clothing, they hid weapons designed by the Guardians and guaranteed undetectable by the Entente. They had been instructed to carry them at all times, even inside their apartments.

Once inside the establishment and after several attempts to find his station, Tarian found his office space. The horror stories he had heard were true. Rows upon rows of robotic people stuffed into tiny cubicles inside noisy, gray office domes. At least he had adequate desk space that faced Audrey.

The surrealness of holding a position inside the Entente Government Capitol did not escape him. A month ago he never would have predicted his life would end up here under such outlandish circumstances, surrounded by so many influential decision-makers. Tarian felt both pride and terror at secretly being the most important person inside the room, a person whose pure existence could spark an attack.

The Prevallers would soon ignite a Border War. Tarian knew what the past war had done to the old capital cities, and he did not want the same fate for Boston. Decades ago the Entente War destroyed Washington District of Columbia and Ottawa City. The disabled governments transitioned to Boston while the expensive and time-consuming reconstruction replicated the spectacle of these historic places. Boston became temporary housing for government officials. After reconstruction, the new government had no desire to return to the old, showboat ways and coveted a practical, more effective space for business. The old Capitol buildings turned into historic museums for tourists to observe, and Boston became the permanent Government District.

First Born by Janelle Gabay

Tarian's cover job was simple data processing, and he did, in fact, become bored fast. As time passed, the glamour of working inside the prestigious walls of the Government Capitol became commonplace and uninspiring. He missed the rugged running trails of the EMA and the challenging professors and classes. He missed the thrill of the game and the ever-changing trials of the simulations. As he looked around to watch the employees, he wondered how they could be content with such a monotonous job. Fortunately for him, he had Audrey to joke around with. They played laser tag between cubicles and exchanged messages. Unfortunately for him, the days rolled on slowly as they waited for more instructions. Day in and day out, they marched in formation into the gray government building and sat behind their efficient computers and trudged through their daily work. No new information from the Guardians came.

He knew Eleanor was plotting the capture carefully and that it had to be executed with precision, but the delay tortured him. Not being able to communicate with his family made him feel as if he had been sent to prison. With every passing day, he felt the growing distance separating him from Delia. He had read through the one thousand three hundred and twelve blogs Delia had written over the past six years, but it did not cure his need to converse with her in person.

At first it was comical to delve into the mind of a young teenage girl. As she grew older, she and her blog mates began to discuss more intimate and uncomfortable topics of a sexual nature. While he was intrigued, he was also aware of the horror she would feel knowing he had read her young intimate discoveries. Instead of bringing him closer to her, the blogs

First Born by Janelle Gabay

invaded his heart like enemy soldiers of betrayal and corruption. He became jealous of these anonymous friends that seemed to know more about her than he did. He resented Audrey for giving him another secret that he had to hide from his girlfriend. It terrified him to think he might accidentally mention a detail from one of these blogs one day. He knew Delia would never forgive his trespassing.

Discussing the blogs with Audrey made it worse. Laughing at his girlfriend's expense with another woman felt wrong, but growing up could be a funny adventure especially in retrospect from a mature perspective. Audrey continually pressed him to read more. She insisted that even the tiniest clues were vital.

He justified his snooping by reassuring himself that searching for clues dropped by teenagers of influential parents insured national security, but it felt like infidelity. Leaning on Audrey's shoulder when the burden of his girlfriend and family's protection became overwhelming. Spending hours speculating over his girlfriend's loyalties. Defending his girlfriend's treacherous words to Audrey, an Entente loyalist. It polluted his mind and did not make sense.

Tonight he read October through December. Audrey had just located the blog page only to find she had deleted her most recent entries, so January was still missing. The last entry sent a chill down his spine.

December 27
I left today. I couldn't get away fast enough from this strange, seemingly

First Born by Janelle Gabay

innocent town. I wrote my mother a sincere note of apology but not him. After what I have discovered, I am ashamed. He let my brother go back to university but not me. I had to leave secretly. I cannot live in a house of lies any longer. He still has not admitted he knows anything about T. The government would not trust T with a secret mission. He's too young. Everyone is accusing me of being crazy, but I'm not crazy. Everyone around me is crazy. I followed him and I saw where the colorful people work. It's not normal. I don't think he's even human. None of this makes sense. I'm going to X.

    Fortis est veritas
    Ebony6

    Fantastic5
    The government is doing strange things right now. Maybe he is telling you the truth about T.

    Ebony6
    Even if he is, he is putting him in grave danger.

    Fantasic5
    You should see the massive security around this place. It takes me an hour to

First Born by Janelle Gabay

```
leave the mines.  I have to go through six
security checks coming in and going out.

     Jugular8
     You left the North Pole?

     Ebony6
     Yes

     Jugular8
     Come stay with me!

     Ebony6
     I might just take you up on that.

     Jugular8
     You know how I feel about you.  You're
always welcome.

     Ebony6
     Thanks ☺
```

Tarian's blood boiled after reading Jugular 8's advances. He was seriously concerned. He wondered why the Senator would not have contacted him. *Did he know where she was now?* Desperation washed over him along with an urgency to read the most recent blogs, but Audrey had not recovered the deleted entries yet. *Where had she gone after Christmas?*

145

First Born by Janelle Gabay

He cursed Audrey for finding these blogs. He could have spent his evenings reading a good book and not these torturous paragraphs. *What did it matter anyway?*

As if she had leaped out of his mind, Audrey marched into his bedroom unannounced and plopped herself next to him on his bed.

"I'm amazing," she boasted.

"You found them?"

"I found this year's blogs and recovered the deleted entries. It took me a while but I did it. They're clever, but I'm smarter. Anyway, read this." She shoved her laptop in his face.

"Okay, have you read this?" He shoved his at her.

She glanced at the date and said, "Yes."

He glared at her. Of course, she had read ahead of him. He should have known. She had this evidence before he did.

January 15
I'm feeling a lot better. The office work
has been educational and needed to keep my
mind off of reality. X is the most amazing
person I have ever met. His medical
background from the West and the papers
from his partner have helped him to create
an antibiotic for my mysterious disease. I
hate Biggie. He has used me as a pawn in
his game for the last time. X and I will
make him pay for what he has done to me. X
has a plan. And we will find T. My work
with X is the only thing keeping me sane.
He's the only person in my life who is

First Born by Janelle Gabay

telling me the truth. I have learned more
from him in these last three weeks than my
six months at university.
    Fortis est veritas
    Ebony6

    XOXO25
    I can't believe T lied to you.

    Ebony6
    I know XO. You always liked him. I
don't think he understands it all. I don't
blame him.

    Jugular8
    Miss you. Glad you are better. You
looked pretty weak.

    Ebony6
    Cannot repay you enough Jugular8.
Thanks for your hospitality.

    Julgular8
    Anytime! Wish I could have been more
hospitable.

    Ebony6
    Don't ruin this moment with your
perverted thoughts.

First Born by Janelle Gabay

```
Jugular8
Sorry, can't help it.
```

"What does this mean?" Tarian asked Audrey.

"I won't know until I know who X is, but I do think she is here, in Boston," she said.

"What?"

"Yes. I know she left the North Pole which we already had figured out was the Guardian Village. She stayed with Jugular8 who is Jack Silsbury."

"Who?"

"Jugular8 is Senator Daniel Silsbury's son, Jack. Daniel is a Guardian. He was very close to both Joe and Zachary. Jack lives and works in Boston. Jack's older than Delia, but I know he was good friends with her brother, George."

"Okay, that makes sense. Fantastic5 is definitely a government employee at the Boron mines. And there is a lot of activity going on around there. Hasn't Eleanor told you anything about that?" Tarian asked.

"No. She is being extremely vague and has kept me in the dark. It's frustrating."

"She doesn't trust anyone," he said thinking out loud. "This is bad."

"I know, but it'll be fine," she said.

He heard the trepidation in her voice. He reached for her hand and she took it. If a woman who had lived centuries was concerned, he was petrified.

"I think Biggie is her father," Tarian said.

"I agree," she said.

First Born by Janelle Gabay

"Who is X?"

"I don't know. I tried again today to contact Eleanor and I'll try tomorrow."

"She still is not returning your calls, your texts, anything?" Tarian asked.

"No."

"Have you spoken to John and Warren? Have they heard from Eleanor?"

"I talked with them yesterday. They are in the dark just as much as we are. We just have to keep waiting. It's important to keep the chain-of-command intact."

"Let's go to Jack Silsbury's place tomorrow," Tarian advised. He wanted to meet the man who was flirting with his girlfriend. He was over dealing with the chain-of-command. The chain was broken.

"That's a possibility," she hesitated. "Or maybe I'll contact his father."

Tarian turned his head to look at her. He watched her taut face and fierce eyes stare at the ceiling. Her chest heaved up and down to a methodic rhythm. *Was she willing to go against orders?* He knew she had been a maverick in the past, he needed her to be one now. The waiting had taken its toll on him and he could not continue to sit still doing nothing, maybe she was feeling the same way.

Together, they conspired for another hour to awake in the morning still on top of the denim blue bedspread with their laptops sprawled across their chests.

First Born by Janelle Gabay

NINETEEN
WATER FALLS

January 29, lunchtime. Tarian had attempted to write down places Delia may be working in the city, but now, looking at his notepad, he saw only scribbles and the phrase *needle in a haystack*. Boston was a tremendous city, its tentacles stretching far in all directions, an overpopulated metropolis that could hide anyone.

"I didn't know you were an artist," Audrey snickered at the doodle drawings on his notepad.

"Frustration and boredom at its finest." He leveled his gaze at her without a smile.

"I know, but this is part of it. Soldiers wait for orders, soldiers follow –"

"The chain of command," he concluded her sentence. He had heard the speech a hundred times before.

"She said she'd be in touch soon."

"That was four days ago," he argued.

She sighed in response. He watched her shoulders sag, and her eyes fall. Her belief in the system was breaking down, and he would use this to his advantage.

"Are you hungry?" he asked.

"Starved," she answered.

"Mel's?"

"Sure."

150

First Born by Janelle Gabay

Lunch at Mel's was quick and cheap: burgers and fries, the kind of meal Tarian loved but made Delia cringe. He thought of her as he watched Audrey devour her greasy beef. A river of ketchup and mustard flowed out of the burger and onto the plate with a few remnants left at the corners of her mouth. She rubbed the evidence away with the back of her hand.

"I guess we don't have to worry about clogged coronary arteries," Tarian said.

"Nope," she laughed.

A twinge of guilt caught in his thoughts. *Is Delia eating well? Is she healthy? She claimed in her blog that X had the ability to make her better. Could he?*

"Maybe X is a doctor's office or rehab center," Tarian said.

"Possibly, but I still think it's a business or law office."

"Maybe we should have Gabe and Maria read the blogs," Tarian pondered some more out loud. Before, he had not wanted his girlfriend's deepest thoughts on display, but now, he would risk anything to find her.

"No," Audrey snapped.

She had always agreed that no one else should know of the blog's existence. They had alienated Gabe and Maria from all discussions about Delia and her possible link to the Prevallers. Luckily, Sophie had them working surveillance. This week they were tucked in an alley behind a Chinese restaurant called Wok Out. According to an anonymous informant, Wok Out was Feng's favorite take-out food restaurant.

First Born by Janelle Gabay

"Let's walk around a bit," he said, putting his plan in motion. "We don't really have to be at our jobs," he said the words as an inside joke.

"Actually, yes, we do have to be at our jobs," she said.

"Okay fine, but we can extend our lunch break a little longer since we finished eating so quickly. It's a nice day to be outside. The snow has stopped."

It was actually bitterly cold, but that was no deterrent for a gifted Purple Person like Audrey.

"Don't think you're fooling me, Tarian."

He flashed her a foxy grin and kept walking. She followed. Audrey struggled to keep pace with him, swearing at her uncomfortable shoes with every step. He knew she preferred her EMA combat boots or all-terrain sneakers to these classic dress heels. Luckily for her feet, they ventured only two more blocks. Tarian left the busy sidewalk and ducked into an alley, walked another three-quarters of a block to a hidden door.

He pulled and jerked the handle then looked at Audrey. "It still works."

"We can't go in there. We don't have our orders yet," she complained.

"Screw the orders," he said, in a tone more suited for Maria.

"Maria is rubbing off on you," she jabbed.

He knew it was true, but he did not mind. A lot had changed. The naïve boy from Salem Prep did not exist anymore.

"No, then I would have said something much worse.'" He smiled without teeth.

First Born by Janelle Gabay

The exterior door shut eclipsing the bright sunshine. They started clumsily as it took awhile for their eyes to adjust to the severe darkness. Tarian guided her down a long, cold hallway. She shivered as the exposed water pipes and A/C corridors made the air damp, cold and musty. She clutched his sleeve and pointed to a camera with a look of panic and concern on her face.

Shaking his head, he whispered, "Hasn't worked since I was ten."

She reluctantly let go of him and cautiously continued in his shadow taking off her heels to silence the hollow clicking noises. He did not remember the corridor being this long. Finally, he heard the sound of water, lots of water. As the path brightened, he became more excited.

Audrey pointed to the light and whispered, "Too visible."

She grabbed him again, slowed his pace, but he jerked her forward like a stubborn dog on a leash. Then they saw it: a gigantic blanket of cascading water, blue and green and gold glistening reflections of millions of twinkling prisms.

"It's beautiful," she said loudly. Her volume muted by the noise of the liquid pounding onto the pool of water. They stood behind a giant waterfall.

"I know," he said contentedly.

He watched her eyes soften as she looked at the movement of the mesmerizing liquid, her vice grip still wrapped around his forearm. She had a habit of grabbing onto him, usually due to her impatience. Now that she could let go, she didn't.

First Born by Janelle Gabay

This was no ordinary place for Tarian, and he felt blessed to be back here again. "I used to come here all the time. Whenever my dad took me into the office, and I disappeared, he knew exactly where I was, and I knew he would find me. He always did," he said as a tear formed in the corner of his eye. He forced it to stop. He would not cry. "He'd have chocolate or an ice cream cone. He'd have two, one for me and one for him, and we'd stay here long enough to eat our treats. We wouldn't talk. We'd just stare at the magnificence of something as trivial as water and eat."

"That sounds like Joe. He was always the strong, silent type," she said with a lost look of admiration.

Audrey's reminiscent gaze triggered a whip of jealousy that struck him at his core. His heart stopped and his muscles clenched. He did not want to ruin this intimate moment. He did not want her to witness his envy, so he forced his body to stand still and remain quiet. It was not her fault she had lived by Dad's side for many years and shared centuries of memories. Then uncertainty struck him, his path of jealousy led to Dad and not to Audrey. His agony did not stem from lost memories with his father but from the desire to know her as deeply as his father had.

He let the thick smoke of silence and inner reflection linger before he spoke. "You can see people through the water, but they can't see you. That always intrigued me as a boy. Why was the water a one-way mirror? I think there're two reasons. One, the light is on that side of the water and two, others are moving while we are standing still."

"Yes, I guess so," she said and laughed softly. "You're so observant. I love that about you."

First Born by Janelle Gabay

Her expression was as unguarded as he had ever seen it. He had to look away refocusing his energy onto the waterfall to avoid falling victim to her raw beauty.

"I watched you intently at EMA."

She hesitated to say more, but he had already pieced the puzzle together. It was not a coincidence that she had been assigned to be his Cadet Sergeant. She had been sent to spy on him a long time ago.

She continued, "I noticed your eyes were always twitching, but you would stay perfectly still. I realized it was your way of taking everything in, logging all details of what you saw and whom you met. You live in the moment. That's a good thing; as an immortal that is a necessary quality. For too many years, I lived in the past while trying too hard to meet the future, but to live in the moment is the key to an immortal's happiness. It took most of us hundreds of years to master that. Except for Eleanor, she has lived in the moment for as long as I've known her. Zachary is still searching, and your dad was finally at peace because of you."

A woman appeared on the other side of the waterfall and broke their tranquil moment. Tarian shot a couple of steps to the right and startled Audrey. He listened intently. He could not be positive that it was her that he saw through the obscurity of the waves of liquid.

"Tarian! Stop!" she yelled.

He halted but so did the woman on the other side. Audrey had yelled his name too loudly. The woman had heard them. Audrey and Tarian stood petrified as Delia walked closer towards the cascading wall of water. Delia reached her hand up to touch

First Born by Janelle Gabay

the waterfall, but the stream was so thick, her hand did not penetrate to the other side. Audrey saw Tarian raise his hand to the spot where Delia's hand was. Audrey tugged on his shirt. Delia shook her head, then lowered her hand and strode away. Tarian's hand remained outstretched until Audrey gently pushed it down.

Tarian sprinted down the hall in the opposite direction of the exit. Audrey yelled to him to turn back, to leave the building, to retreat, but he ignored her. Instinct took over, and he no longer thought about orders or the chain-of-command. He needed to see her. He would go against all protocol. He would break all the regulations ingrained into his being over two years of intense training just to hold her. He had found her.

Audrey saw his complete shift from obedient soldier to emotional boyfriend and ran after him. Tarian knew this building like the back of his hand unlike her, and her missteps had her inches behind him. She had studied the architectural plans, but nothing beat hands-on experience, especially that of a curious little boy in Daddy's office. He knew the alleys, short cuts and secret hallways that did not show up on written plans. He reached a cut off; he opened a door, and led her into an ordinary hallway covered in generic brown carpet with walls painted a basic tan. This could have been any one of the twenty-two floors of the building, but Tarian knew exactly where he was. He spotted the plaque labeled Feng and Justice, Attorneys at Law. He had his mark!

Tarian never made it to the door. With brute force, Audrey tackled him. They rolled onto the ground arms and legs

First Born by Janelle Gabay

banging against the walls. The noise was sure to attract curious workers.

"Dammit, Tarian. What are you doing?" Audrey said in an unfamiliar, burdened tone that snapped him out of his recklessness.

Audrey's disturbed composure announced he had gone too far. Tarian had disjointed the one person in this world he could count on to keep him in line.

Suddenly, the two of them heard voices coming from around the corner. Audrey grabbed his elbow and dragged him away. Tarian forced her back and detoured into the men's bathroom. He pulled her into a stall, their mouths inches apart, and their bodies wedged together. They stayed motionless and silent for minutes. Their two adrenaline filled bodies moist from the sweat of fear remained anchored stationary by dread. The intimate position went unnoticed until the voices disappeared, and they exhaled.

Tarian regained his senses; he released his hands that gripped her tightly. He waited there as time stood still, staring into her crystal blue eyes. He leaned in with an urge to kiss her, but she shoved him backward. Before he knew what had happened, she had his hands pinned against the wall of the stall and her knee threatening his manhood. She had the strength of ten men; however, he had grown stronger. He shoved her back into a powerless position that she was not accustomed to. She squirmed and thrashed against him in the tight space. Suddenly their force burst the stall door open, and they spilled out gasping for breath.

First Born by Janelle Gabay

"Let's go now," she demanded, annoyed by his boyish hormones.

He would've been mortified with embarrassment, had he the luxury of time. He surrendered to her, and with precise accuracy, she led them back underground behind the waterfall and into the alley. Her faultless memory and on point sense of direction impressed him.

Once out of the building, they blended in with other pedestrians hoping no one noticed their stressed faces or wet armpits. She did not speak a word. The heat of her anger scorched his body. He had crossed a line in their job and their relationship. The split second urge to kiss her was merely a by-product of exhilarated adrenaline. Nothing more. *Could it have been anyone? It meant nothing. I'm an idiot! Anyone would have tried it.* He rationalized.

He shook his head to clear his thoughts and banish his guilt. Now, separated from the intensity of the previous bathroom scene and thinking plainly, Tarian realized his girlfriend worked for a killer. X was Feng. His mind reeled as he tried to configure what this meant for Delia. Delia may know things she was not supposed to know that could put her life in danger. *What did she know?* He pressed his eyelids together and prayed she had not stepped too deeply into the hornet's nest.

They did not return to work. Instead, they walked directly to their apartments. Tarian opened his door but turned back to look at Audrey before he entered. He caught her glance back at him as well. She flashed him a small smile, and he felt the wash of relief cover his body. He grinned back and shut the door.

158

First Born by Janelle Gabay

TWENTY
THE BAR
AUDREY

Never before had information on a mission been withheld from Audrey. Her assignment to safeguard Tarian compromised without all of the facts, and this terrified her. Her repeated unanswered calls to Eleanor were infuriating. Tonight she vowed to find answers.

The celebration of Entente Victor's day incited the noisy bar. She watched the crowd of people get increasingly more and more intoxicated by the hour. Waves of loud cheers swooped through the bar when the Boston Bruins scored a goal against the Montreal Canadiens. The historic sports rivalry always played on Entente Victor's Day. The entire city awash in alcoholic revelry made for the perfect night to seek out Zachary.

Audrey flagged him down as he forcefully navigated himself through the people standing and dancing in his path. He wore a scowl of distaste on his face, and Audrey wondered when he had lost his sense of adventure. This used to be the kind of place Zachary, Joe and she would hang out. Now they were too serious saving the mortals from their own destruction and paying a fatal price for it.

He caught her waving arm in the air with his eyes and swiftly pushed his way past the drunks to seat himself. As usual he wore a designer suit and looked like a politician. He always

159

First Born by Janelle Gabay

had a well-tailored, professional style even before his personality got so uptight, but now it really fit him.

"Grant's on the rocks, and I'll have a Harp," she said aloud as she placed her order on the touchscreen display, ignoring his disapproving gaze.

"Why did you call me here," he asked.

"Delia is here," she said, getting right to the point. Without Joe, she did not enjoy conversing with Zachary. Joe could bring out his dry sense of humor, making him more entertaining.

"Yes, I know," he said slowly.

She wondered if he was hesitating to give up this information or surprised she had found out.

"What's going on? I have never been kept out of the loop this long," she said.

The server brought the two drinks and a small bowl of peanuts. She glanced at Audrey for confirmation of the order's accuracy.

"Thank you," Audrey said to the young woman.

"Is this your first beer?" he asked after the server retreated, but she did not answer. She was thrown back in time by the appearance of his antique Pierre-Frédéric Ingold watch. As he reached for his glass, the watch peeked out from beneath his sleeve. The woman who had given him that watch so many years ago was the love of his life. Now Audrey remembered the Zachary she used to enjoy so much, the Zachary pre-lost love. After Cecilia's death in 1856, Zachary had changed. At that point in time, he and Audrey had found a common companionship of depression. She had already suffered the loss

First Born by Janelle Gabay

of her greatest love. Together they drifted into the dark abyss of grief. For years, Joe had to deal with two intoxicated immortals spiraling out of control leaving a path of destruction in their wake. Joe had not found his intense love until much later when he met Carolyn, Tarian's mother. He would not have suffered as they did. He would have had Tarian to ease him out of his grieving.

During these dark days of inner turmoil, Zachary and Audrey had found themselves in many seedy bars only to have Joe rescue them before the wrath of Eleanor came down. Zachary had crawled his way out of the pit sooner than she did, but it cost him. He created another family and then another, but he never allowed himself to venture back to the intimate place where Cecilia would forever inhabit. That part of his soul was secured shut by a thick, iron bolt. Encased with her love was the part of his personality that enjoyed living. Audrey felt he became less and less human as the span of time from Cecilia's death became greater. He had wives to provide for and children to educate, but his compassion for their mortal struggle diminished.

"Audrey?" he asked.

She looked up still uncomprehending his words. *He still wears that watch,* she thought. *She is still drinking too much*, he thought. He was incorrect. She had not had a drink in a long time, and when she did, she enjoyed a nice wine with dinner or glass of ale at a pub with a friend, nothing more.

"Something is wrong, Zach. I feel it," she said. The words came from her heart. She confided in her old friend. She wanted him back. No, she wanted the good ole' days back.

161

First Born by Janelle Gabay

"There is nothing to worry about. Eleanor and I have the situation under control. It will not be long now."

"Where's Feng?" Her blunt question caught him off guard.

"We had a lead." Zachary swirled the copper liquid around in his glass.

Audrey considered his words then slowly drank her beer before speaking. *Did he mean that stupid Wok Out Restaurant that Gabe and Maria had staked out? No. No*, she pondered shaking her head ever so slightly.

"Had? What happened?" she asked. Her knuckles went white as she gripped the beer bottle, becoming greedy for answers.

"A lot is confidential right now," he said, his face expressionless.

She realized she had been put on a need-to-know basis. She never operated on a need-to-know. She was always the one to be privy to all information.

Her stare became a dagger aimed for his head, so he continued. "You must understand. Every minor detail must be calculated, or the Guardian's existence is at stake."

"I know this," she said. She took a long, hard swig of her beer. Her patience worn, she concluded he was not going to provide her with any insight. She had been downgraded.

"Dammit, Audrey! Don't make me feel guilty! You chose your position. And if you ask me, you are getting a little too close to Joe's son," he spat the accusation at her.

She flinched. "Joe's son? Fuck you, Zachary!"

162

First Born by Janelle Gabay

"Look out there," he said pointing to the few screens surrounding the bar without the hockey game.

Images of fire and destruction, along with captions across the bottom tallying the death toll caused by the Prevallers' attacks were being broadcast on local news stations. She knew the situation had escalated in the past few days. Innocent people were under fire while they sat in a bar drinking and watching hockey. The Entente was a vast portion of land, but soon the violence would reach them. It was only a matter of time until the attacks evolved into a war. She knew this and resented him for pointing it out.

"Exactly! We are running out of time," she said.

"No, we are cautious. You need to remember who you are and who Tarian is."

"What's that suppose to mean?"

"You are getting too close to him. Your awareness is clouded by feelings of…" he hesitated.

Audrey jumped all over him with words of defense, yet she worried he was right.

She had been assigned to Tarian for two years now. She had kept him safe. She had groomed him into a top notch, fighting machine. He had come to the EMA as a clumsy, confused teenager, and she gave him his strength without him even knowing it. She lurked in his shadows protecting him from his enemies. During drills and training, she pushed him beyond his limits without him ever suspecting her attention was fully focused on him and only him. She slyly set up the friendship with Gabe and Maria, knowing he would need a small but strong

163

First Born by Janelle Gabay

support system. She cared for him deeply but as what? A friend? A brother? Or more? She could not fall in love with Joe's son.

"I want to talk with Eleanor. Tell her if I do not hear from her by noon tomorrow, I'm taking Tarian and heading back to the village. Got it!" she demanded.

"Got it." He took one last sip of his scotch and removed himself sophisticatedly from the unrefined chaos of the bar.

After he had left, she noticed a hundred dollar credit on the table. Furious at this she ordered another beer and a round for the four, good looking young men gathered at a high top five feet away from her. Had he thought she had been sitting in the bar drinking for hours before he got there? The nerve!

Her reckless idea to order those men drinks now dogged her. They huddled around her table with bad intentions. She was about to give them her last polite excuse before she kicked the leader in his balls when Tarian approached. The men begrudgingly returned to their high top, disappointed.

"How'd you find me? Guardian mobiles are untraceable."

"The tracking unit in your jacket," he sarcastically reminded her as he sat down uninvited.

I must be losing it, she thought. Of course he, could track her every move as she could his.

"Ebony6 just posted a new blog."

"Show me," Audrey reached for his tablet.

January 30
Today was my last day at the office. The virus is spreading again and X insists I need to rest. I have to agree with him. I

164

First Born by Janelle Gabay

think I'm beginning to hallucinate. I
thought I heard T's name today. I felt his
presence but I know he's somewhere far
away. Probably defending the useless
Entente. I worry for him every day. X and
I are going somewhere safe. His life is in
danger. He has been careful but I fear
they want him dead. Soon the war will be
here and we will all have to flee. It is
better we hide now. I put my trust in X.
He has advanced information and only he can
cure me of this poison inside my body. I
know he can. I'm too tired to continue
writing.

 All my love to you guys. Be careful!

 Fortis est veritas
 Ebony6

 Jugular8
 I'm coming to see you. Message me
where you are.

 XOXO25
 Love you girl!

 Jugular8
 My dad can help. You know he can.
Let him try.

First Born by Janelle Gabay

```
SkyEartHater
Good luck!

Fantastic5
I agree with you.  Two more arrests
today.  They are dropping like flies around
here.

Jugular8
Answer me!  I'm giving you two days
but that's all.

Zigler88
Hang tight!
```

"She just signed off. What if we don't' find her again?
What if he hurts her? I knew I should have talked to her today."
His words filled with regret.

"No, we did the right thing," she encouraged.

"How can you say that? She was our only lead and she
just checked out," he snapped.

"They have leads. Trust me!"

"I do trust you," he exhaled and paused, exhausted. "She
didn't respond to her blog mates. She never does that."

"I know. Makes me think this is the last blog. She and
Feng are up to something," Audrey said.

"What are you doing in this bar anyway?"

"I met with Zachary."

"What'd he say?" Tarian blurted before she had a chance
to explain.

First Born by Janelle Gabay

"He told me nothing. Said they were close and we would hear soon."

"Did he know about Delia? She's here, possibly in danger." The urgency in his voice was palpable.

"Yes."

"Bastard!"

"You have to understand Zachary. His mind operates on the grand plane, not on the finer details."

"Oh, that's right. I forgot, just another mortal to have to die. Oh well," he said.

"It's not like that," she explained, but she knew his portrayal of the Senator was accurate.

"Why would Zachary put his own daughter at risk?" he asked.

"I don't have the strength to answer that question right now."

"You don't have a choice," he ordered, loudly attracting the attention of the men he had warded off only minutes ago. "I didn't ask to be invited to this party late, but now that I'm here I deserve to know what I've missed."

"I don't doubt that he loves her, but he would risk her life for the benefit of the greater good. He's a politician and a soldier. Zachary has married six times. Six times he has watched his family die while he lived on. Honestly, I find it repulsive," she paused. She did not say anything for a long time. She did find it abhorrible, but she could not blame him for erecting his wall of indifference. She too had powerful walls erected for emotional protection. At some point during their drunken rehabilitation, he had withdrawn to an almost robotic

First Born by Janelle Gabay

resemblance of himself while she had advanced towards the affinity for others. Her loss had given her an insight to others' suffering, but his loss had brought a haze of inevitable doom.

"I know it's difficult but," Tarian said cutting the silence then paused. He opened his mouth, and then closed it.

He focused intently on her with his warm brown eyes. He looked so young, she thought, but appeared more and more wise with every secret she revealed to him. Now she felt she owed him one of her secrets.

"After losing my first family and discovering what I was, I did meet a man that I fell in love with," she paused. She resumed her story hesitantly. "He was Italian with the face of a God, absolutely impossibly good looking. We shared one beautiful daughter and a long happy life together but when they died, I died too. I disappeared, away from the Guardians and spent most of my time drinking in bars. I attempted suicide." She laughed out loud at the absurdity of an immortal's suicide. "I did not eat. Eleanor and Joe tried everything to help me get past my grief. Then Zachary lost Cecelia and succumbed to a life of depression with me." She paused to recall a distant amusing memory. "Zachary and I actually had some funny episodes. We were quite a motley crew. Zachary's grief for Cecelia was real unlike his other losses, but he grieved with sophistication. When he drank, he never got messy. I drank myself into a coma." The brief levity she had felt and the smile she had shown to Tarian faded into a hauntingly absent stare.

"I'm sorry." His lineless and sincere face soothed her.

"Life was cruel. The seasons continued; the snow fell. Then the sun shown, over and over again, but I was alive and

First Born by Janelle Gabay

well," she said. Dewy moisture built in her eyes, but she was too stubborn to cry. Maybe she had already cried all her tears a long time ago. "I came back home to my family of Guardians and devoted my life to the protection of mortal people, vowing never to fall in love with any of them again."

"I understand," he said.

She knew he was being polite. She feared he truly would understand the pain of immortality some day.

"But Zachary is different. He needs the company of mortals. He needs a wife and children, but I don't think he's capable of true love, true compassion, not after Cecilia's death. I think he has a God-like complex and considers himself superior to mere mortals. He feels their death is plausible, and his continued life is a blessing from the divine. He has always treated his wives and children with the utmost respect. In the past and present, he has been a good provider, a good father, but a lousy caregiver. If Delia is useful to the operation today, and she's going to die anyway tomorrow, of course he would use her."

This last sentence widened Tarian's eyes.

"Okay," he said, moving the conversation out of the past and into the future. "Delia went to work at Feng's office. X is Feng. Zachary used this opportunity. He has a team spying on her, and Eleanor is waiting to see how this all plays out. Is that correct?" he asked, and she nodded. "Delia can get a hold of this elusive killer but the Guardians can't?"

"Sounds wrong, doesn't it?"

"Yes," he said.

"Because it is," she said.

First Born by Janelle Gabay

TWENTY-ONE
TAXI

The noise of the crowded, rowdy bar faded as Audrey and Tarian walked back to their apartment building under dim, flickering street lamps. In the distance, another couple stumbled to their car. The man did not look drunk, but the woman could barely stand. He laid her down onto the backseat of his car. Just as he entered the driver's seat, he turned his head to face Audrey and Tarian.

"Feng," Audrey said.

"Delia," Tarian said, as the car drove away.

They sprinted back to the front of the bar where several taxicabs sat. Throwing open a door, Tarian told the driver to head down Cambridge Street towards Congress.

"Just enter your location," the cab driver stated.

"No, just drive!" Tarian shouted.

"Listen, that's how it works. You enter the location, and the car takes us to it," grumbled the wrinkled faced cab driver.

"I know, but not this time. I don't know where I'm going, and you're wasting my time."

The taxi stood still. Audrey flashed a hundred-dollar credit. The cab driver grabbed the money out of her hands. The taxi sped away.

On Congress, they spotted the dark blue, four-door Mercedes and told the driver to follow it at a safe distance. Audrey looked at the secure mobile on her wrist, debating

First Born by Janelle Gabay

whether or not to call Eleanor or Zachary. They both decided against it. They could not risk tipping off Feng, unsure of whom to trust. The Mercedes stopped at what appeared to be an abandoned fishery in the seaport district. The sedan pulled into a garage and as the taxi drove by, the garage door shut.

"Drop us off here," she said, handing the cab driver another hundred-dollar credit for a thirty-dollar ride. "There's another hundred in it for you if you pick us up here in forty minutes. And give me your jacket," she said.

He scoffed but finally removed his jacket after she handed him another hundred.

"Okay," the small, elderly cab driver said. He did not smile nor did he ask questions. He left.

Tarian and Audrey looked doubtful at each other wondering if he would return even for another hundred-dollar credit. She slung on his jacket. The polyester blend stunk of a long hard day's work. He probably did not shower that morning, but it was black and exactly what was needed to cover up her cream colored sweater. She had to vanish in the night. She thrust her hands under Tarian's sweater, startling him, but he did not pull away. She lifted the fabric up to find what she was looking for, a black, long-sleeve undershirt. Then she forcibly ripped the sweater from his body and looked at him with a satisfied grin. The dark camouflage would work fine for hiding in the black of night.

Looking through the ground level windows, they saw nothing but Feng's empty vehicle. They walked down a dark, narrow alley where a raggedy old woman lay asleep against the wall. She was partially covered by a ripped, dirt-covered blanket

171

First Born by Janelle Gabay

and her shopping cart, filled with empty cans and bottles, stood beside her. The woman opened one eye but shut it immediately. Audrey did not take any chances and smashed one of the bottles over the woman's head. She slouched against the wall, her blanket tucked under her legs. Audrey hesitated to see if anyone heard the noise of the bottle. Silence. She tucked a hundred-dollar credit inside the woman's clenched fist.

"At this rate, I'll be broke by morning," she muttered under her breath.

Tarian stood still observing the actions of Audrey. This was his first in-the-field operation. In a simulation, he also would have acted quickly to silence the woman, yet here, in real life, he froze not thinking on his feet as Audrey had. They had come here unprepared. All of the state-of-the-art devices were back at the apartment. They had to use their instincts and surroundings. She did that well, and he took note to learn such valuable hands-on techniques from an experienced fighter. All the simulations in the world did not compare to life experience. He was now worried that he would fail her. He was too green. He needed to pay close attention. He would not screw this up and put her life or Delia's in danger.

They proceeded up the catwalk, Audrey in front, to a narrow ledge they could stealthily walk across. Her cat-like feet never made a sound unlike his. She gave him an irritated look, and he walked more lightly, but he could not silence his one hundred and eighty-five pounds on metal. She had worn sneakers to the bar and not high heels. She had looked frumpy and out of place then, but now she looked and sounded perfect. They passed several small windows that looked down onto a

First Born by Janelle Gabay

warehouse-type space but saw no movement. Then they heard a door slam shut and waited in stillness for several minutes.

"We should have informed someone of our whereabouts," she murmured. She looked nervous.

"The cab driver knows where we are," he said, trying to reassure her.

"All he can do is identify our dead bodies," she said.

He knew with the death of his dad; this was a new and unsettling reality for her.

Scurrying a little further on the ledge, they found a window partially opened and climbed into a room. She leaped quietly from the ledge outside to the inside floor, making a hint of a sound. Her landing was a little off balance, and she grabbed the ledge of a desk. Dust scattered like tiny fairies as she wrapped her fingers around its edge. This place must have been abandoned for years. Tarian followed her but lacked her grace and stumbled. Luckily she caught him, and he recovered. He stifled a sneeze, burning the insides of his sinuses. Dust filled his nose, as did the unmistakable rancid odor of a rotting animal.

They were inside an abandoned executive office where time had trapped the aromas of decay within its four walls. This particular office was untouched, but Tarian figured there must be more office spaces, and one held Delia.

Audrey glanced at her watch. "Twenty minutes," she whispered to him. "We only have another twenty if we want to have a safe ride home."

"I'm not leaving here without Delia," he whispered.

She gave him a look of impatience. "Look Tarian, it's important you follow my lead. Right now you have to be

First Born by Janelle Gabay

impartial; you have to be a soldier. Emotions have no place here and can get us killed."

He knew she was right, and he would truly try to treat this as any other mission, but he was worried about Delia's safety. The palpitations of his heart beat irregularly.

The door to the office was shut and opening it would be an extreme risk; therefore, he let Audrey's more delicate hands try to unlatch the lock. Turning the knob with a steady rotation, she paused, then pulled millimeter by millimeter. Success. She did it. Still no person in sight. *Where the hell was Feng*? Then he heard the clang of sharp objects, and cold fear slithered up his spine.

Following the sound, they located Feng. The room looked like a makeshift dentist office. Delia was propped in a firm chair, her blouse off with electrodes strategically placed around her chest and in her hair. Tarian saw screens monitoring her heartbeat while a mask covered her mouth and a tank nearby administered gas to make her sleep he presumed. Several syringes filled with different colored liquids lay on a table next to the chair. Feng hummed to himself and ate noodles out of a Chinese restaurant carton marked Wok Out. Tarian wondered if he was waiting for someone else. All they could do was wait and watch, hoping to catch a glimpse of his accomplice, but no one came.

Tarian felt worthless. He had no weapon. He had unprofessionally left his apartment without it. Delia was lying a few feet away from him, unconscious, and he could not save her. The unbearable anxiety built in his body, and he attempted to hold steady. He must have triggered a response in Audrey

174

First Born by Janelle Gabay

because she put a calming hand on his thigh. She patted him like a child. It soothed his angst. She made him feel like she knew exactly what she was doing, and he prayed she did.

Once he relaxed a bit, he was able to think clearer. *What were the facts? Her heartbeat was steady. She was not dead. Feng seemed calm. He was using her for testing, not murdering her. That meant she was valuable. He would not or may not kill her,* Tarian hoped.

A horn blared and interrupted his thoughts. It was the cab. The old man had come back and was repeatedly honking. He wanted his hundred-dollar credit. The horn also startled Feng whose jump to his feet was loud enough to mask the noise caused by Tarian's surprise. Delia, however, did not move. She was definitely sedated. Feng left her. He ran down the hall, cursing the cab driver. Audrey and Tarian saw him open a drawer at the last minute and pull out a Glock pistol. Tarian silently prayed for the life of the small, elderly cab driver.

Audrey saw this distraction as an opportunity to enter Delia's holding room, and Tarian followed her. He saw tiny, scared track marks on her arms and realized this must not have been the first time Feng had brought her here. He also saw a fresh prick mark and an empty syringe. Audrey surveyed the room for a container and found several inside the cabinet. Snatching two she put a few droplets of liquid from the syringes into them. Audrey shoved the two containers into the jacket pockets. Feeling a resistance in one from a vapor stick, she pushed hard, and the stick broke, scattering waxy liquid everywhere. Tarian gave her a nervous look. Quickly, Audrey wiped up the fluid, but the pungent aroma still filled the air.

First Born by Janelle Gabay

Desperate, Tarian grabbed more containers. He wanted samples of them all. He had to get everything including Delia too, but he knew he did not have time. He froze over Delia's body. He stroked her now short, espresso hair. She looked different, gaunt and ghostly, and she had cut her beautiful locks. Audrey pulled his arm away, but his feet remained planted.

"We have to leave her," she said.

Feng had not returned but the honking went on relentlessly. So far no gunshot was heard.

"I can't," he told her.

"Dammit, Tarian! We are not prepared or equipped to take her. I promise we will come back tomorrow with a plan of action. Look at her arms. He needs her. I guarantee she will be here tomorrow," she pleaded with him.

He knew she was right. They had no plan, inadequate weapons, and no reliable information as to what was really going on.

They left her still, helpless body in the chair and went back to the dusty room they had entered from and peered down at the street below. They could see the bright lights of the taxi and a shadowy figure hobbling toward it. Out of the dark stumbled the old woman Audrey had hit over the head with the bottle.

Delusional, she yelled, "Oh my darling, you've come back. Take me. Take me away."

The cab driver looked at her crossly, but as she waived the one hundred dollar credit Audrey had given her, he simply said, "Get in, Lady."

As the cab sped away, Feng looked around confused. He reentered the building, and Tarian and Audrey swiftly exited the

First Born by Janelle Gabay

window, crossed the edge and descended the catwalk. Their ride
was gone, but Feng had no idea they had been there tonight.
Together Audrey and Tarian slipped undetected down another
vagrant-filled alley and headed in the direction of Congress
Street.

First Born by Janelle Gabay

TWENTY-TWO
TEAMMATE

The next morning Maria arrived at the Wicked Good Coffee Shop without Audrey. Immediately Tarian asked, "Where's Audrey?"

"And a good morning to you too," Maria replied with a roll of her eyes.

Today was a crucial day. Last night Tarian and Audrey had agreed to start the morning as ordinarily as possible. "Sorry. Good morning Maria. I was just wondering why Audrey was not with you."

"She's sick," Maria explained.

"Oh," Tarian said. He attempted a smile, but debilitating suspicion took over his senses. *She is planning to leave me behind.*

As he looked around the crowded coffee shop routing his exit, he noticed many sick people. Most looked hung-over from last night's Victor's celebration, and he wondered if Audrey could be hung-over. But she had been alert and sober at the warehouse. His thoughts were once again booming inside his head, but Gabe and Maria seemed oblivious. They were engrossed in their own conversation, one that he had not heard a word.

To his surprise the table felt wrong without Audrey. The chair next to him remained vacant as Gabe and Maria sat next to one another holding hands. Their conversation was no different

178

First Born by Janelle Gabay

without Audrey. The same topics discussed: weather, basketball, hockey. They went on about the lack of orders from Headquarters, their boring jobs, EMA and how much they missed it, and so on and so forth. Even though the conversation was the same, Tarian felt disconnected without her. He thought of the many topics he would rather be discussing with Audrey right now. He realized the four of them had become two teams, and he missed his teammate.

"Earth to Tarian," Maria said to him and slapped his hand.

"Oh sorry," he mumbled.

"You look a little sick too," Gabe added.

Tarian decided to use those words to his advantage. "You know, I do feel tired and have the chills." He would fake illness to excuse his absence from work today.

"You and Audrey sick. Hmm! Were you swapping fluids last night?" Maria said bluntly.

"No," Tarian said, stiffening his shoulders and trying to appear offended.

"Maria, he has a girlfriend," Gabe argued.

"Yeah right! A woman he hasn't talked to in weeks," she said.

"That's not his fault," Gabe defended.

"Thank you, Gabe," Tarian said.

"Oh, come on, Audrey is beautiful, and the two of you spend a hell of a lot of time together," she cross-examined him.

"It's our job! And I could say the same about the two of you. Suddenly, I am feeling very sick." Tarian pushed his chair away from the table.

First Born by Janelle Gabay

"Where are you going? To check on your other half," Maria joked.

"Ha, ha. I think I will go home and rest, and yes, I will check in on Audrey," he said.

Maria's devilish smile infuriated him. At least she and Gabe were on the wrong track as to why they were missing work today. If Gabe and Maria thought he was having an affair with Audrey, then so be it. That's a great cover.

Tarian opened the door to Audrey's apartment after she failed to answer the door after several knocks.

"It's me," Tarian said in a panic after hearing her chamber a weapon.

"Tarian!" she screamed. "I almost shot you!"

"It's okay. I'm sure I would have survived," he said with a chuckle. Then he noticed she was half dressed and turned around. "So are you really sick or is that our reason for skipping work today?"

"So you think us immortals can survive a gunshot yet still contract the common cold?" she said, securing her weapon and placing it on the end table. She walked into her closet to find a pair of pants.

"Actually, I thought you were hung-over."

"It takes a lot more than three beers to get me hung-over."

"So we don't get viruses?" he asked.

"No. Our bodies feel pain and fatigue. We will sneeze or cough due to the elements, but that's it. We are immune to all infection. That's why the Sanoxine made you sick. Your body rejects any antibody because it does not need it."

180

First Born by Janelle Gabay

"What is our plan?" he asked her. The yearning to return to the warehouse began to stir in his gut.

"I need to eat. Do you want anything?"

"No."

Tarian watched her as she busied herself around the kitchen making breakfast. He paced. His anxiety building until her shoulders slumped, and she set the box of cereal down on the counter. She turned around so he could see her face, and the beauty that shown through her vulnerability struck him. She had always looked so fierce and assured. It made her face hard. The beautiful angles and features were sharp as a blade, and he had envisioned her slicing up her lover as they kissed. Now, with her wet hair, make-up free face, bare feet and pale blue tee-shirt, her beauty exposed soft and accessible. His anxiety shifted to fear. She was his rock in this chaos. If she let her guard down now, then things would go terribly wrong. He trusted the six hundred years of experience behind her twenty-year-old face. He did not know how to react to this emotion. He went to touch her, but she withdrew, and the hardness came back. She erected her spine and broadened her shoulders.

"Listen Tarian, I was up all night trying to put the pieces of this puzzle together and nothing makes sense," she said. "People I have trusted for years, I don't trust anymore, but yet, I know in my gut I still should. They just seem so damn suspicious."

"Who?"

"Everyone – Zach, Eleanor, plenty of others too, even Joe. I can come up with a million different scenarios, and all of them seem plausible and at the same time ludicrous."

First Born by Janelle Gabay

"I know, but together we can make sense out of it," he said. "I realized something when you weren't at the coffee shop this morning."

"What?" she asked.

"That we are a team, you and I. That I was glad you were with me yesterday when I saw Delia. I was glad I showed you my secret boyhood hiding place. I also realized that this weird bond we share feels a lot like the bond I shared with my father. It's very strange as I look back on my life with him now knowing what I am, what he was. I do think we had a different connection than just son and father. I can't explain it. It's just a feeling, and I feel it when I'm with you too. A trust, an unbreakable trust. The weird thing is I felt it when I first met you. When you were my Cadet Sergeant, and I had no reason to trust you," he explained as he paced the floor.

"Do you feel the same with Delia?" she asked.

"No." He stopped pacing. He trusted Delia but he never felt comfortable around her. He had a hunger for her that he did not have with Audrey. It was a romantic connection with Delia, but he hesitated to share those thoughts with Audrey.

"Do you think she is immortal?" Audrey asked.

"What?" he said.

"Has she ever been in any accident where she healed quickly?" she asked.

"Oh my God, could she be?" he questioned with audible happiness.

"Well, Feng was running tests on her last night."

First Born by Janelle Gabay

"But Senator Eastwood would have kept her close to him. Eleanor would know. Zachary wouldn't just let her wander around knowing of her valuable existence."

"There's a lot you don't know about Zachary. And actually he's the one I'm concerned with. If it were just his allowing Delia to be in the line of danger, I'd get it. He's not the most compassionate person. He's very logical, and he's seen a lot of his loved ones pass on and he accepts it. But the fact that he claims not to know where Feng is, and he's right here in Boston, that's not adding up," she said.

"But she has been sick a lot," he said. "You just told me immortals don't get sick."

"What do you know about this illness?"

"Not much except what I've read in her blog. She kept it from me," Tarian admitted.

"If the 'Biggie' in her blog is Zachary and Delia does not trust him. She does not trust her own father," she said, still working all the information over in her mind.

"So, she doesn't trust a lot of people. My dad trusted him with everything, with his family. There's no way," Tarian said. The thought of the Senator being involved in his dad's murder was too much for Tarian to comprehend. It did not fit, but then again, what did?

"Me too. He's been an officer for the Guardians from the beginning. I'm sure there is a logical explanation."

"Delia never fully believed anything her dad told her," he said, giving Audrey a wondering glance.

"Well, he was lying about a great deal in his life. I'm sure she picked up on that," she said.

183

First Born by Janelle Gabay

"Yes, that's true. What should we do now? I want to get Delia out of there as soon as possible. Who knows what chemicals he is pumping into her body."

"I'm still not comfortable acting without Eleanor's approval," Audrey said.

"I'm going to the warehouse now, with or without you. You made me leave her there with a murderer." Tarian whipped the accusation at her.

Audrey threw up her hands. "We did not have a choice. We could not risk detection. Delia is of some value to him." She closed her eyes, swallowed hard then added, "She's not dead."

"Yet! She's not dead yet. Isn't that what you meant to say? Where is your compassion? I guess you've gotten numb to death too." He moved closer to her.

"Do not assume that because you have known me for a few months that you know my life and my beliefs. You don't know me at all," she said, her body still and her eyes never leaving his.

He could not look away but refused to apologize. He felt terrible about what had transpired. He was hurt, and the pain was too stubborn. Silent tension lingered in the air for several minutes.

Tarian ran a hand through his thick hair and said, "Let's go. If she is still there, she may be in danger. We need to watch them, gather evidence. We need to do something!"

"Okay, we will go there first," she said, her speech ending but he could see her mind still turning.

First Born by Janelle Gabay

TWENTY-THREE
BETRAYED

Clothed in dark field pants, sneakers and a charcoal, long-sleeve shirt with a tight fitting, but stretchable black jacket, Tarian and Audrey began their mission. The Guardian issued clothes hid a multitude of tiny but lethal weapons and a tracking device. Audrey purposefully removed the trackers from their jackets.

"What are you doing?" Tarian looked at her with suspicion.

"We don't need anyone finding us as easily as you found me in the bar last night," Audrey said.

"Let's hope we don't need finding." He raised an eyebrow.

Once again they took a taxicab across town and over the bridge to the seaport district; however, once there, they had difficulty recognizing the building. It had been dark the previous night, and all the buildings looked dilapidated and abandoned. She asked the driver to maneuver slowly past each alley as they looked for the vagrant woman's shopping cart, but there were many carts. They strained their eyes trying to recognize the fire escape they had climbed, but a fresh layer of snow hid recognizable details.

"That's it," she said pointing to her left. "Stop right here." She told the cab driver.

185

First Born by Janelle Gabay

Once more, Tarian followed Audrey up the fire escape and in through the broken window they had entered last night. The filthy window smeared with dead insects showed a hint of blood along one edge of the shredded glass. Fearing it was his blood, Tarian pulled out a small device. He showed the light over the blood and watched it disappear. DNA erased.

With the cloak of darkness removed and daylight shining in, the room's grotesqueness could not be masked. Thick, avocado green dust covered everything except Audrey's slender handprint indented in the grime on top of the desk where she had placed it to gain her balance last night. She wiped it clean.

"We were sloppy last night," Audrey said as she rubbed the entire desk clean.

Tarian watched as she proceeded to clean all of the office equipment. He wondered if all this cleaning was smart, but she moved determinedly. To his relief, the creature responsible for the foul odor remained at large. Tarian figured it had died confined inside the walls.

The door into the hall was open. He remembered it had been shut last night, but recalled they had opened it. Another sloppy move. He prayed their trespassing was still unknown, and Feng had not suspected the cab last night had been intended for them.

They heard soft voices. Who they belonged to or how many voices were incomprehensible. No fear and anger were present, just normal conversation.

Audrey and Tarian crept down the hall, hugging it and staying far away from the railing that looked down into the warehouse. Last night Tarian had glanced into its depths to a

First Born by Janelle Gabay

black hole. Today, filtered light shone through windows made opaque from dirt. He could make out cement flooring several feet below along with old, forgotten machinery but saw no people. For a split second, the diffused sunshine tricked him, and he thought the building had electricity. However, he had misjudged it. Only the small dentist-like room held power via some generator. Feng was using this building illegally. There would be no trail of electric invoices to prove his existence.

They reached the room where Delia had been unconsciously experimented upon, but she was no longer there. Panic froze Tarian, and then a wash of relief brought warmth back to his limbs. Nothing had been removed from the empty room, suggesting it would be used again. He wondered if Feng had even noticed the stolen containers. Tarian removed an entire syringe and shoved it into his jacket. His desperation to know what they contained overwhelmed him. There were several more, so he felt sure Feng would not notice. He took another one.

In the vacant room, no sign of a struggle was present. *He hadn't killed her, he thought.* Once again the rush of desperation consumed him. Then his heart sank as the realization of an empty room meant uncertainty. *What was better, finding her dead or unconscious in a torture chair or not finding her at all? Answer: None of the above!*

The voices floated on the air and into the room. Suddenly, the empty room seemed irrelevant. He needed to find the people behind the voices. He motioned to Audrey to leave the room. She took the lead.

First Born by Janelle Gabay

Faint whispers lured them deeper down the hallway but still they found no one. Tricky echoes bounced from upstairs to downstairs, from left to right. The sounds skipped jauntily around an unending carnival maze of metal warehouse walls and tinny staircases. Tarian closed his eyes to stop the maddening disorientation of his thoughts. He concentrated on a female voice muffled inside a distant room, and with his eyes closed he could more clearly identify its location.

Walking with eyes shut, the voices guided him towards an office that sat halfway between the warehouse floor and the upper story. The room hung in the air with a staircase connecting it to the downstairs, but no visible stairway led upwards to where he and Audrey stood. Now having pinpointed the voices he opened his eyes and inched closer, carefully hugging the wall, following Audrey. She stopped, and Tarian bumped into her. He glared at her but she returned his stare with unblinking, wide, worried eyes, and he saw her throat's heavy swallow. He snapped his head around to gaze inside the office. What he saw froze every muscle in his body to rigid stone.

He heard Delia's laughter then he saw her teeth filled mouth. Her head tossed back, her long neck exposed until she whipped it back into place with another joyous release of laughter. Her face filled with expressions of glee. Her ocean eyes twinkled as she looked into the yellow eyes of Feng. Then she kissed him, and his hands left his side to find the small of her back and the crook in her neck. Their embrace was passionate, and the sight of it pierced Tarian's heart. The scene today was entirely opposite from that of last night, and it sent waves of shock pulsating through Tarian's veins. He had rehearsed how

First Born by Janelle Gabay

he would remain professional at the sight of her tortured body or even her death, but the sight of her in Feng's arms never occurred to him. He had no practiced response to cling to. He felt the floor under his feet disappear. He leaned against the wall for support.

Audrey turned and pushed Tarian's bulk backward towards the escape route, but he was an immovable brick wall. She persisted. He looked at her bewildered.

She gently whispered, "The first betrayal always hurts the worst."

Her words were not comforting; they were cynical, cold but true. He guessed after living as many years as she had lived the heartbreaks were still painful, but unfortunately, expected. He was defeated, stunned, immobile.

Audrey managed to hedge him in the right direction, but he had not fully committed to leaving. She delicately slipped her hand in his, linked his fingers to hers and dragged him away as gently as a lover drags her man into her bed. It worked. He retreated.

Careful to crawl back out the same window, she inspected it for traces of their blood or clothing but saw none. She guided him down the fire escape and a safe couple of blocks east of the building then she ordered another cab.

The drive back felt like hours. They no longer held hands; in fact, they sat at opposite ends of the back seat, not touching or looking at each other. Even the driver could sense the thorny silence as he attempted small talk about the weather. The cold but sunny day only dampened Tarian's mood as it mocked his heartbreak.

First Born by Janelle Gabay

Once at the apartment, he plodded straight to Audrey's balcony, and she followed. She assisted him into a chair. She released a sigh of relief when he sat.

Did she think I was going to jump off the building? He was not that desperate, yet. This life had not worn him down to that point. He only felt sadness and more confusion.

"I don't know what to say, Tarian," she said, a long paused followed. "We knew she admired him. She said as much in her blog."

"I know," he responded in a whisper.

Just then, the door swung open. Both Audrey and Tarian were on their feet reaching inside their jackets for a weapon when they heard laughter. Maria and Gabe had sneaked home from work to check on them. They were laughing as always and carrying sandwiches. They were the most in-love couple Tarian had ever met. They cursed and insulted each other like siblings, but it was all teasing.

"What the hell, You Two!" Maria said. "We have all the boring work, and you don't. Spill!"

Maria knew they were up to something, but it was Gabe who noticed Tarian's distraught face. Maria had been too preoccupied with her accusations and suspicions to see Tarian's exasperation.

"You ok, Man?" Gabe asked.

"Oh my God, Tarian. You look horrible!" Maria finally noticed his irritated eyes and red dotted face.

"Last night we saw Delia," Audrey told the story from the blogs, to the waterfall, to the bar, to the kiss.

"Tarian's Delia from home?" Maria asked.

190

First Born by Janelle Gabay

"Yes," Audrey continued. She recanted the entire day to night, to day activity.

"Harsh man. I'm so sorry," Gabe said and placed a thick hand on the back of Tarian's shoulder.

If Tarian had any feeling coursing through his body, Gabe's bear-sized hand would have consoled him.

"Well, what do we do now? What does this mean?" Maria asked. Visibly angered by Delia's betrayal of her best friend, Maria punched her palm with her fist. Like the rest of them, she was going stir crazy from the weeks of sitting behind the bland cubicle looking at fake pictures of fake people in their fake lives at their fake jobs. Excited for action, Maria tried to disguise it so as not to look indifferent to Tarian's suffering.

Tarian had remained silent for almost an hour while his friends tossed words around. The silence concerned them. Tarian seemed to be the calm before the storm, and they expected him to become a hurricane at any moment.

"Delia must be involved," Tarian finally said but remained still.

"I'm afraid I agree," Audrey said.

"She never trusted her father. She always spied on him and questioned him. She must have found out the truth of his immortality. Maybe she got angry. Maybe she learned I was immortal and got angry. She knew something at the village," Tarian said to Audrey.

"I don't know. It's hard to say. I felt a sense of envy as if she did not like you going off on a mission without her," Audrey commented.

"Or with *you*," Maria stated.

First Born by Janelle Gabay

Audrey jerked her head around towards Maria in objection to the comment.

"Yes, I felt it too," Tarian averted, ignoring the overreaction of Audrey. "I knew she was uneasy. I just thought she was worried about me. It still makes no sense. I spent an entire year with her after my father died. I know she knew nothing then. She couldn't have had anything to do with my father's death. It doesn't fit." Thoughts mixed like indecisive weather patterns. The rain stopped, the clouds parted, and clear skies formed only to be darkened again with more rain and clouds. More questions.

"No, I don't think her involvement happened until after your father's death. I agree with you. Maybe after you went to EMA, she felt isolated or left behind," Audrey said.

"Like she felt now when you left with Audrey on this mission?" Gabe commented with a mouth full of sandwich. He was on his lunch break.

"Or somehow Feng got to her. Who knows what lies he's told her? Let's give her the benefit of the doubt. She's a young woman. You abandoned her in a sense," Audrey said glancing back and forth from Tarian to Maria. "I mean EMA does not permit much communication. You had two weeks over Christmas, and then a few weeks over summer, then the attack. Now you've vanished. You're asking her to wait. That's tough."

"I know you're trying to make her look less guilty, but she's very intelligent. I've always sensed a distance between her and her father that did not exist with her mother or brother. And as much as I love her, she has a spiteful side. Knowing others are

First Born by Janelle Gabay

immortal, and she isn't could piss her off," he said still outwardly calm but inwardly chaotic.

"Knowing you are immortal," Maria added emphasizing the word 'you.'

"Yeah, but her involvement came later. I'm sure you are right about that. We were inseparable that year. I would have seen something or sensed something, but the blogs. It's all right there. What I've read, the hidden codes. I see it now," he said to Audrey. She was the only other person that had read all of the blogs. The pieces of the blog puzzle that did not make sense were now crystal clear.

"What does it matter *when* she got involved? She's involved, and we need to tell Eleanor. Let's go," Maria said, bouncing on her toes.

"Yes, let's go," Audrey conceded. "I have to get this evidence to Headquarters." She was turning the vials over and over in her hands, mesmerized by their content. "And we need surveillance on Delia and Feng."

"You can't reach Eleanor," Tarian reminded Audrey.

"It's okay. I'll be able to soon. We just need to get to the train before we get caught."

Audrey took charge of the group. "Maria, you and Gabe go straight to see John. Explain to him what has happened. Tell him we need a tail on Feng and Delia 24/7. Got it. Take shifts. If Zachary shows up, tail him also."

"Got it," Maria said.

"And these are Eleanor's orders. Understand," Audrey leveled her gaze square into Maria's hazel eyes.

"Yes," Maria responded.

193

First Born by Janelle Gabay

"No. We can't lie to our team," Tarian protested.

"I agree with Audrey," Maria said.

"Tarian, we've waited long enough. Something's not right," Gabe said.

"I don't like it. I don't like any of it. I don't want to leave you guys behind," Tarian said.

"We have to get the information to Headquarters in person as fast as possible, and we need people here we can trust. Who can we trust more than Gabe and Maria?" Audrey asked.

"Go Tarian. I got your back," Gabe said.

Maria shoved Audrey and Tarian out of the door and reassured them several times that they had it all under control.

Audrey and Tarian caught the northbound train with the evidence tucked safely inside her jacket pockets. In a few hours, they would board the tiltrotor that would bring them back to Quebec City, then the car to Guardian Headquarters. He had four hours sitting next to Audrey, trapped in a passenger car, scattered with worn out people. He felt the two of them had gone over every possible explanation, yet nothing was solved.

Tarian turned his head away from Audrey and toward the window to watch the buildings roll by faster and faster. His anxiety mounted the further away he got from his friends and Delia. His forehead leaned into the window. The cold glass bit him. Icy shivers rippled through his body and covered his heart, but his mind was hot and active. Memories of his dad's funeral flooded into view, and he tried to remember the entire event, to piece any clues together. He scoured his memory for even the tiniest of details to find a more reasonable solution than what he

First Born by Janelle Gabay

had seen with his own eyes. Every fiber inside his body yearned to talk with his father, to know what he had known.

He was tired, and sleep stole him without warning. His forehead remaining stuck to the window, pulsating clouds from his breath growing and shrinking on the glass. Audrey gently placed a pillow between his face and the window then attempted to sleep as well.

First Born by Janelle Gabay

TWENTY-FOUR
DREAM TARIAN

Tarian's smudgy, faded dream body stood over an empty hole where his father would be laid to rest. Unlike the real hole that Tarian's conscious mind remembered, this dream hole dove down for miles, deep enough to stack a hundred bodies one on top of the other. It felt strange to be dreaming while being aware of dreaming.

Tarian glanced around the cemetery and spotted a true memory exaggerated by dream enhancements. The green of the leaves gleamed an unnatural margarita hue, and the branches swirled fantastically until they reached the curling pink clouds of the sapphire sky. Day was night and night was day - a place without time.

Even though the ground he stood on and the sky he looked at seemed impossible, his thoughts remained logical. He thought just as he had the day of his dad's burial, focusing on the irony of an estate attorney not having a life insurance policy. That was Dad's job: planning peoples' lives so they could keep their money for the future or their children's future. Tarian guessed that his father was too busy planning others peoples' lives and falsely assumed he had more time to plan his own.

Tarian had a flashback inside a flashback, which mocked his conscious mind, yet he still did not wake. As he teetered on the edge of the hole, he remembered his teenage years spent at the law offices. He recalled his father's first law partner, the

First Born by Janelle Gabay

ancient Mr. Jones, who walked with a cane. Mr. Jones materialized and hobbled over to peer down into the pit. Mr. Jones ignored Tarian. Tarian reached out to touch his elderly, translucent skin.

"Stop it, boy," Mr. Jones said, spittle flying from his lips. Tarian retracted his arm.

"I told you not to go behind the waterfall. I told you Zachary's girl was no good for you," Mr. Jones spat.

The spit wet Tarian's face, but he did not wipe it away. Tarian tilted his head, furrowed his brow and said, "This did not happen before. You never said anything like that."

"What?" Mr. Jones yelled.

Tarian said nothing. He knew Mr. Jones would not hear him. Mr. Jones' ears were filled with plastic that did not aid his hearing. He did, however, still have his hair and a great deal at that. A thick nest of hair perched itself on top of his head, white as copy paper. Then his hair became paper banners.

Banners that read, "Enjoy your retirement Mr. Jones," flew like birds across the dream sky. The banners circled around Tarian's head like snakes in flight then dropped into the hole disappearing into the blackness of its depth.

The image of Mr. Jones evaporated. In his place floated the smiling, young face of Roman Feng. Roman had no body just a giant, friendly face. Tarian laughed with Roman, just as he had in the past. Tarian remembered how happy he was when Roman replaced Mr. Jones.

The dream shifted direction. The scenery remained the same, but the events changed from funeral to retirement party to a

First Born by Janelle Gabay

celebration for Roman. A man stood behind a podium and began to recount all of Roman's accomplishments.

"Roman Feng graduated from Stanford Law School at age twenty-four. Roman landed the most high-profile, lucrative case inside the Industrial Science District. He won Xia Technologies Inc. vs. Marybeth Feng. His aunt netted twenty million dollars, and he became the most sought after attorney in the Entente. Somehow Joe got him to leave the Xia community and work for Prescott and Jones, PA." The man's voiced boomed without a microphone.

The crowd roared with applause.

The mobile on Tarian's wrist buzzed just as it had two years and eight months ago. His brother, Charlie, messaged him to come inside the den of the funeral home. Charlie was handling the well-wishers with ease and charm, but now it was Tarian's turn. Tarian observed the reception, his back against the wall. He watched his mom accept the many hugs doled upon her: big bear embraces, small gentle hugs and formal cheek kisses.

All the caring people turned to stare at Tarian. They wore sympathetic looks and spoke kind words, but each word floated through the air and morphed into tiny hornets that stung him. The poison swelled into tiny bumps, but he did not care. He studied each face. He recognized all of the faces, whereas before when he was seventeen, he had not known these people. All the faces belonged to Guardians he had recently met in person or seen in photographs. Once again his conscious filtered into his dream, yet he remained asleep.

First Born by Janelle Gabay

In an instant, Tarian stood at the edge of the gaping hole again. His father's casket lowered into the bottomless black space. Once the casket disappeared all the guests vanished.

"No!" Tarian yelled. He paced the edge of the hole. Threw his hands in the air. He turned to see only his family remained. He looked into his mother's eyes and said, "I saw him."

"Saw whom?" Carolyn asked.

"Dad's killer."

Tarian's family, along with Roman, circled the gaping pit holding hands. Without warning they all jumped, forcefully hurling Tarian in with them. Fear flashed through him causing his body outside of his dream to jump, but his mind remained asleep. He fell into pure darkness and came out into the yellow light of the kitchen inside his childhood home.

Without reason or logical explanation, he sat with his family at the table. The fact that the violent leap into the hole took them to the serene chairs at the breakfast table seemed perfectly reasonable to everyone, including Tarian. Again Roman's presence brought warmth and peace.

Exactly as it had happened two years and eight months ago, Joe's will was read, and the memorandums handed out. Tarian received Dad's favorite novel *The American* by Henry James. Tarian had read the book and didn't like the ending at all. He never really understood why Dad liked it so much, but he was grateful to have it. His father had written in the margins and dog-eared some pages. Even a chocolate stain smudged page one hundred and five. Tarian ran a finger across the brown mark.

First Born by Janelle Gabay

Charlie got Dad's first law book that also had little characteristics of Dad's personality hidden throughout the pages. Teresa, the sister born after Tarian, got a very old, gold and emerald ring that had been in Dad's family since the 1500's. To Tarian the ring looked like a wedding band, but Dad never spoke of it. He just kept it securely in his bedside table drawer.

Chloe, Tarian's youngest and closest sister, who was sitting patiently on pins and needles for her momentum, received the Teddy Bear. She knew she would get the bear and could not wait to hold it. Roman gently handed it to her with a wink. In her seven-year-old mind, Daddy was up in heaven with Trigger, their Labrador, and they were playing fetch like they always had.

Roman handed Joe Jr. a beautifully gilded knight's sword from Queen Elizabeth's court. The sword usually hung in Dad's office.

Soon the ordinariness of what transpired inside Tarian's dream turned abstract again. The kitchen table became a flying, circling merry-go-round. They each sat atop a life-size teddy bear, whirling and bouncing. Tarian's book *The American* and Joe Jr.'s sword glowed neon yellow and levitated in the air inside the spinning ride.

The carousel jerked to a halt when Audrey appeared. She had stabbed the heart of the machine with Dad's sword. Charlie leaped from his teddy bear to take Audrey's vacant arm, and together they strolled down a sidewalk. The family and Roman followed. Charlie and Audrey were engaged in an intimate conversation, faces locked on one another and bright cherry mouths hovered mere millimeters apart, as they lead the group back into Tarian's childhood home.

First Born by Janelle Gabay

Tarian stood heavy and mute while his other family members appeared carefree and floatable.

"Go to your room," ordered Charlie.

Tarian went and sat in solidarity for what felt like hours. Every person and every thing inside his dream vanished. He lay on the black comforter covering his bed, alone and tired.

Tarian's mother faded in and out until she materialized in his room. She sat next to him on his bed. She spoke in her real voice and existed without dream alterations of color and substance.

"Your Dad has special plans for you and Charlie. Plans I was not even aware of," she said. Her makeup smudged around her eyes as they puffed with tears.

"What kind of plans?" Tarian asked, but he knew the answer. He had already had this conversation with his mother the night of the funeral.

"He arranged for you and Charlie to live with Senator Eastwood and his family," she said.

"No," Tarian stated.

"That was my immediate reaction too, but your father's wishes are quite clear."

She handed Tarian two handwritten notes one addressed to Tarian, and one addressed to Charlie both signed by Dad. His intentions and reasons were plainly stated and hard to contest. Official, typed legal documents followed his dad's note, and it was clear, his dad thought it best for the family. He trusted his dad more than anyone. Dad never made a move without thinking it through. Tarian refused to play chess with him after he turned twelve because he never won and knew he never would.

201

First Born by Janelle Gabay

"I read through everything, and I feel the Eastwood's can give you a lot more than I can at this time. He is a very powerful man, and he was one of your dad's closest friends. Plus, you and Delia are very close, and Charlie practically lives over there with George anyway. Luckily, I finally got my real estate license last year, and now I can put it to good use. I have enough money saved up to work from home. Once I sell a couple of houses, it will be fine. Without you boys, my grocery bill will be a lot less." She babbled on, trying to convince herself she was doing the right thing. However, with the last sentence the tears came back.

The tears brought the abstract back into his dream. Carolyn's teardrops became a river that swept Tarian away from her.

He screamed as he floated on the swift current, "It's going to be okay. I'll go live with the Senator. It'll all be fine!"

Terror struck Tarian as the waves crashed into his back causing his sleeping body to jump. Inside his dream, he tumbled somersaults in the water. The violent force of the flow poured Tarian onto a gigantic chessboard. He was dry and on the board in the position of the pawn directly in front of the queen. Queen Audrey and her king, Charlie, stood behind him. Mother and Teresa set in the bishop positions, and Chloe and Joe Jr. were Rooks. Gabe and Maria sat on top of bucking black stallions. On the opposing side stood Senator Eastwood's family. Zachary and his wife occupied the king and queen squares while Delia and her brother George posed as bishops. Strangers sat upon the white horses. The end rooks, Roman and Dad, stared him down.

First Born by Janelle Gabay

Tarian shot two spaces forward. He wore his EMA gray jacket with black collar, as did the pawn directly across the board from him. The game began and pieces whizzed passed him at lightning speed.

Soon his father knocked him over and screamed at him "Get out of here! Don't trust the babies!"

"What?" Tarian asked, still down on the floor and completely confused.

The pawns had morphed into crawling infants. Adorable big round eyes and plump bodies inched towards him, and he wondered what he had to be fearful of until blood red droplets dripped from their fanged teeth. A scarlet pool rolled toward him, covering the black and white checkered spaces on the chessboard, spilling over the sides like a wicked crimson waterfall.

"Get some rest Tarian," his mother said, no longer standing as the queen on the chessboard.

Ferociously looking around, Tarian saw that he was back in his childhood bedroom, nightmare to dream just like that. No blood. No babies. Everything was as he had remembered the night of the funeral.

"I plan on sleeping in and doing absolutely nothing tomorrow," his mother said with a small smile. "This is yours."

She handed him EMA paperwork, dad's handwritten note about his future at EMA and the nomination letter obtained from Senator Eastwood to endorse his application. All the other requirements and forms nestled in a file, neatly organized.

Tarian pulled several unfamiliar photographs from the file. A piece of white paper with his father's writing stuck to the

203

First Born by Janelle Gabay

photos. It had an equation on it. The numbers and letters would not stay still. They danced across the page.

"Stop!" Tarian ordered.

****

The train stopped. Tarian awoke. The haze of temporary amnesia set in, filling his brain where his past thoughts had just been. He desperately scrambled to recollect the images. The faces he had so easily recognized were now mere shadows. He had seen some clues in his subconscious, but now they had disappeared. All that lingered were eerie feelings of mixed emotions.

"Oh, you're awake," Audrey said as she entered the cabin. She carried two bottles of water and an assortment of nutrition bars. "It's important we hydrate, and I thought we should eat a little something."

Tarian's thoughts shot to the Guardian Headquarters' kitchen upon seeing the unsatisfying bars of food. His stomach growled.

"Damn it," he said.

"What is it Tarian?" she asked.

"It's gone, and I can't get it back. Now I'm focused on food," he grunted, discouraged, his stomach rumbling.

"What's gone?" She had no idea what he was talking about.

"Why are we stopped?" he asked, noticing the absence of the train's vibration.

204

First Born by Janelle Gabay

"We are at a station. It's not our stop yet, though," she explained.

"How much farther?" He gulped the water.

"We're the next stop. What's gone?" she asked again.

"My dream," he sighed.

"Oh," she murmured, turning to face forward and unwrap her bar.

"No, it's not just any dream. It was like a vision. I was back at my father's funeral, and it did not make sense. It made sense to me in the dream. It was clear who the killer was, and it wasn't Roman, but now it's vague," he rambled.

"Roman? You've never called him Roman before. In your dream was he your friend." She nitpicked details like a veteran detective.

"Yes, no, I mean he's better than dad's old partner, Mr. Jones. Roman's young, energetic and very intelligent."

"Smart enough to create Death Serum."

"Perhaps, but that was not the feeling I got. It was all so clear while I was asleep."

"You said you knew who the killer was?" she asked, leaning in.

"Yes and no. I just remember seeing his face at the funeral reception, and I knew he was guilty. But now I only have the feeling, not the face." He slumped back into his seat.

"You can't force it out of your subconscious. Relax. It may come back to you."

The familiar and oppressive energy that had burdened him for so long after the funeral returned to his shoulders. The revisited past slid under his skin weighting him to the ground like

First Born by Janelle Gabay

an unwanted spirit. He closed his eyes, rested his head against
the bench and waited for the ride to end.

First Born by Janelle Gabay

TWENTY-FIVE
HISTORY

The tiltrotor descended onto the blanket of freshly fallen snow covering Battlefield's Park. Tarian tightened his grip on the handle above his head and steadied his breathing in an attempt to regain stability inside his stomach. Audrey, not holding onto anything, glanced at him and smiled. Feeling humiliated, he let go of the above handle. Seconds later, after a rather turbulent shift of the aircraft, his hand shot back to the trusty grip. Tarian saw Audrey's shoulders bounce and knew she was laughing.

The same dark green, unmarked sedan sat empty and frigid as the three entered it, and again, the engine started after a little encouragement. Thoughts of his last trip into the village washed through him. He had discovered unbelievable facts about himself and the secret society of immortals he belonged to. What mind-blowing information would he learn today about Delia?

The familiar roads now narrower with more snow squeezing the banks closer together wound around the city just as he remembered. He recognized storefronts and predicted the winding turns before they tossed him to one side or the other. The sedan crossed the threshold into the quaint magical village and zipped inside the mouth of Guardian Headquarters' garage.

Two female Guardians dressed in green uniforms awaited as they exited. The two women hugged Audrey and shook

First Born by Janelle Gabay

Tarian's hand. "Welcome back, so good to see you. Come, come, Eleanor is waiting," said the blonde haired lady.

The brunette's hand pressed on Tarian's back, gave a slight shove, and moved him forward into the elevator. She pressed button six. The elevator doors opened to find Eleanor standing stiffly in front of them. Her boney shoulders acted as precise hangers for her pristine white lab coat covering her thin frame. Her long, gloved hands took the vials of evidence Audrey and Tarian carried. Without words, she turned on her heels.

Inside the lab equipment waited for the testing. Droplets of the liquid inside the vials were fastidiously placed on small slides of glass and investigated through microscopes of all sizes. More droplets dribbled into test tubes immediately transforming from clear to a rainbow of colors. A human test subject sat in a sterile chair awaiting injection if necessary. Eleanor and her staff worked like buzzing bees but made no sound. Tarian looked questioningly at Audrey but she wore a blank face. They waited and waited and waited.

Finally, Eleanor walked toward them with her tablet. She showed them the encrypted codes, which meant nothing to the unskilled eye.

Eleanor quickly explained. "None of the vials of solution are Death Serum or any sort of antidote. It is also not like our immortal DNA of any kind," she said with a straight face.

Tarian's interior jumped with joy but his exterior remained as calm as Eleanor. He hoped this meant Delia had zero involvement with the murders.

"Then what is it?" Audrey asked.

First Born by Janelle Gabay

"One seems to be some sort of painkiller but unlike any common analgesic. This particular painkiller is highly complex. It seems to repair cells, reduce inflammation, and sedate the mind all in one. In my opinion, this pharmaceutical is used after being injected with the first vial. The first vial is still evasive to our tests but when mixed with sample DNA, it rips it apart."

"Is it a virus?" Tarian asked.

"No. It's synthetic, man-made. I don't think it has been perfected either. It does not fix, repair, change the DNA, but it does add biomarkers tags to the nucleotides. Further study will be necessary. So far the test results are inconclusive," she said.

"You've only mentioned two. What about the rest?" Tarian asked. He looked at Eleanor hoping to gage some sort of indication of her true suspicions, but her icy expression revealed nothing.

"Patrick, any change in J or K yet?" Eleanor called over her shoulder to her lab assistant.

"No," Patrick responded.

"Inconclusive." Disappointment at her failure crossed her pale face.

"What does this mean? What are Roman and Delia up to?" asked Tarian.

Before Eleanor could answer, a man walked into the lab to announce the arrival of Senator Zachary Eastwood. Audrey looked at Tarian. This was it, time to discuss their findings with him. Audrey had already lectured Tarian to treat this as any other investigation and warned not to make it personal on any level.

After Eleanor spoke to Patrick, she removed her lab coat and with a flick of her telekinetic wrist, it obediently placed itself

209

First Born by Janelle Gabay

on its designated hook. She wore her deep violet pantsuit and stiletto heels. Her respectable attire reflected her power as Chancellor.

They met Senator Eastwood one floor below in a plainly decorated conference room. Eleanor showed him the lab reports. He was in a navy business suit making Tarian's field clothes look ignoble. As Tarian watched Audrey take control of the debriefing, he felt proud of these field clothes. The Field Clothes had done the dirty work while the Suits sat behind desks. Soon Tarian's confidences out numbered his insecurities.

"As I told you before, Audrey, I have not had contact with my daughter since she left. She is an angry teenage girl who lashed out. She probably has no idea what she has gotten herself into," Zachary explained.

Audrey glared at him. The air inside the small room grew heavy. Without releasing Zachary from her stare she continued, "I still don't understand why the location of Feng was an issue." She turned towards Eleanor stretching herself tall, but dwarfed by Eleanor's height in heels. "Eleanor, you have people in the field and you could not locate Feng? Meanwhile, Delia waltzes into his office and not only gets a job but some weird relationship with him." Audrey's strong and insinuating voice made up for her petite size.

"Audrey, our people are spread thin. The Guardian's survival is top priority, but I also have the Prevallers to contend with. Your team of eight is large. Most of the missions are limited to two and are spread from the cavern system to the fusion power plants to foreign targets overseas." She closed her eyes and released a brief sigh. She continued, "Nothing

First Born by Janelle Gabay

suspicious has occurred. We know their cause but the true leader has not surfaced yet. These are terrorists we are dealing with, cowardly phantoms. The actual leaders of the Prevallers are still just a long list of possible suspects. Our information is not reliable. The duplicity of this situation travels far."

"You know who they are," Audrey said with a strong jaw and piercing eyes.

The muscles around Eleanor's mouth tightened a fraction of a millimeter, and for only a brief second, but it was a tell. Zachary saw it too.

Audrey's body emanated high heat, and Tarian took two steps away from her. He had never felt her release such intense heat before, but then again, he had never seen her lose control. Her stance and voice displayed a confident, self-restrained Audrey, but inwardly she was breaking down.

"Eleanor, if you have information, the government must be informed. We are being attacked and a full-scale war is eminent. We have to work together. We cannot repeat the past," Zachary demanded. His mobile flipped over and over in the palm of his hands.

"What?" Tarian blurted out. "Eleanor, you are withholding information from the Senator? And Audrey could not contact you?"

Eleanor pivoted in the direction of the door. "Tarian, Zachary, Audrey," she addressed them in precise, punctuated breaths. "I assure you I have every intention of working with the Entente, but I have nothing to share at this time. I'm needed back at the lab. Everyone get a good night's rest. We will adjourn this meeting after breakfast tomorrow." She left without even a nod.

211

First Born by Janelle Gabay

Audrey's shoulders slumped and she looked exhausted. Zachary folded his arms around her for as long as he could stand the heat. Tarian studied this embrace. Audrey did not welcome it. It seemed like a gesture made out of habit rather than out of genuine concern and affection.

"Audrey, I know what you are worried about, but it is different this time. What happened *then* will not happen again?" Zachary said. He stood tall over her and his tone was condescending.

"What happened before?" Tarian demanded. He was sick of being uninformed. He was tired of the Senator's superiority. He wanted answers.

"War of course! That's all mortals do. Kill each other."

"Stop it Zachary, there's a lot more to it," Audrey said.

Zachary smirked and began to leave the room.

"Wait a minute. I have a right to know. And I also want to know why you are so flippant about your daughter being involved with Roman," Tarian ordered. Nerves trembled inside his gut, but he forced his body not to shake. He refused to be intimidated anymore.

Zachary halted mid step. He turned to face Tarian. Slowly walking forward, he spoke. "Year after year, century after century, I have protected this great nation. I helped build the Entente after the war. Piece by piece, the Guardians helped the people of North America unite, close the borders and become financially independent and productively resourceful. No little girl, not even my brilliant daughter, can bring down my success. Ludicrous! I'm wasting time explaining myself to you. If you need answers go to the damn library." Zachary did not wait for

First Born by Janelle Gabay

anyone to respond to his words. The door slammed shut behind him.

Audrey sunk into a chair and covered her head with her hands.

"We have learned nothing!" Tarian blurted then noticed Audrey. "What is it Audrey? What are you thinking?"

She said nothing. He placed a supportive hand upon her shoulder, but she pushed it away. Standing next to her for several minutes, he felt helpless and angry. He silently slipped out of the room.

Tarian tromped through the crooked halls, walked down two flights of stairs. He entered the library intent on finding more answers. The familiar chill mixed with the tranquility of people silently reading comforted him. The busy laboratory combined with the whirlwind of the last few days had caught up to him. All he wanted to do now was search for Piper and relax in the cozy chair by the fireplace.

He trudged the long corridor to his destination but did not see Piper anywhere. "Piper," he whispered. "Piper!"

"Tarian," Piper squealed, appearing from nowhere as usual.

She wrapped her arms around him, hugging him with such force that he felt pain.

"Hi," he said. He hugged her back but was now prying her off of him.

"You're back. I missed you. How was it? What happened? Do you want coffee?" She disappeared again before he had a chance to answer any of her questions. Reappearing

213

First Born by Janelle Gabay

seconds later with a steaming cup of coffee, she shoved the cup into his hands.

"Thank you," he said. He sat in the big, leather chair and set his coffee on the table.

Piper did not sit. She stood pulsing with energy watching him.

"Please sit down Piper. You're making me nervous."

"Oh, sorry." She obediently sat, legs crossed, in the giant chair, rocking back and forth.

"Our mission was a success," he lied.

"Where is he? The Killer?" she asked.

"Well, we are watching him." He paused, gathered his thoughts then asked. "Piper can you please explain to me what happened during the Entente War."

Piper's perpetual movement suddenly stilled, and she focused on Tarian. He had never noticed the lavender color of her eyes before. He wondered just how powerful she was.

"I'm sorry Piper, but I need to know the truth, not what I learned in my history books at school. I need the Guardian's version of history."

"Okay," she said back to her perky self. Again she was gone, then back with a stack of books two feet high. "Here, everything you need to know."

Tarian thumbed through a book entitled *The Mind Ring*. The stack in front of him would take him days to read.

"Piper can you please summarize for me what these books say?" Tarian asked using his best puppy dog eyes.

First Born by Janelle Gabay

Piper jumped to her feet visually stressed. She was like an exploding firecracker shooting around the room. Then she stopped.

"Oh, Tarian. It was a horrible time, horrible. Blood, lots of blood. Frankie." Piper began to cry.

"Was Frankie a friend of yours?"

"Yes. We lost so many friends."

"It's okay. I'll read the books."

"No, I can do it. I want to tell you. Well, first off we have come so far since then, so far. The United States government was bad, very, very bad. It had taken over completely. All the states of the United States no longer had rights. The federal government controlled everything, like a dictator. It pushed us away. The Guardians had always been there to help, to give advice, but the government had turned into a giant monster that listened to no one. Whatever it said was the law, no questions asked. No Congress, no free will, no checks and balances, no different branches, just one big tree!" She had been still for her entire speech, but it seemed to be too much for her. Now she needed to move. She zipped up and down the corridors asking all library patrons if they needed anything.

Tarian realized Piper was incapable of long periods of serious conversation. He began to read. Four chapters later, she reappeared ready to relate more historic facts to him.

"It was years and years of oppression," she continued.

Tarian had to refocus his brain to keep up with her.

"Four presidents came and went. We, the Guardians, became neutral observers for many, many years, but we had

First Born by Janelle Gabay

critical information. Eleanor, she wouldn't get involved. No, no. She was so mad." She rocked some more.

Piper's eyes were not present. She looked at something unseen, a memory, Tarian guessed.

"And…" he coaxed.

"And the United States government had become corrupt. Elections were corrupt. No diversion of ideas. Every aspect of life from education to healthcare to sports was federally controlled. The continent's resources were not being used. Awful, awful, awful," Piper shook her head violently.

"It's okay, Piper. You've told me enough. I can read the books."

She smiled a very mature and un-Piper-like smile. "No, I have to tell you. It's my job. We were making nothing. No industry…this vast land… brilliant people… everything was being imported… inflated prices," she paused, breathless. She looked as if she would explode if she had to say one more word.

Audrey's voice took over the conversation. "The government lobbyist had thwarted all rational and profitable uses of our resources. Everything was being imported and heavily taxed."

"And it wasn't as if these imports were superior. No, no. Everything was worse than before and cost more money," Piper interjected.

Audrey continued, "Yes, Piper's right. Finally, the states and people had had enough, and an uprising was inevitable. In fear of losing control, the government created a mind control ring. A striking piece of jewelry that had been disguised as a badge of honor and to be worn strictly by the highest ranking

First Born by Janelle Gabay

members of all of the United States military branches," Audrey said. She held up the book on the top of Tarian's stack, *The Mind Ring*.

"And the Guardians knew about this ring?" Tarian asked.

"We did," she said, with a sigh of hindsight knowledge.

"We more than knew," Piper said.

"So the government turned its military on its people," Tarian added.

"Yes, but humans are clever. They evolve and adapt and become suspicious. The most brilliant minds of the United States and Canada fought back. Other nations stepped in to help and began gathering territories. Too many lives were lost and too much progress destroyed before the Guardians finally stepped in," Audrey paused and her gaze dropped to the floor. "The violent deaths I witnessed haunted me for many years."

"It was our fault. We did it." Piper's hand flew to her mouth. She had told him a secret.

Audrey glared at her.

"I get it. The Guardians created those rings, didn't they?" Tarian asked.

"And they stole them from us," Piper said.

"Yes, we created the rings, and now we had to destroy them. We had followed this evolution and knew whom we wanted. We knew whose capable minds we needed to put an end to this war."

"An end to the government dictatorship," Piper interrupted.

"Yes, to end the government that had grown too large and uncontrollable and start new."

First Born by Janelle Gabay

"We closed our borders," Piper once again interrupted.

"We secured our natural resources. We put people back in charge of their lives. We gave them their independence back. We formed the Entente of Nations with Canada, creating a solid and united continent. The people owe their prosperity to us, the Guardians."

"But we waited too long," Piper said eyes downcast, voice soft.

"Maybe we did," Audrey agreed.

"What do you mean?" Tarian asked.

"Since we had waited so long to interfere, the war got severely out of control. It took several more years to retrieve every ring, and we had to kill almost every government official."

"We killed Frankie," Piper said now rocking violently back and forth.

Audrey paused, and smiled softly at Piper. Piper's rocking slowed and Audrey continued. "The rebuilding of the Entente took decades and now to see it threatened. You see, the people have forgotten. The men and women of that generation have either died, or they're way too old to remember. But we can't die, and we don't forget!"

"It's a curse," Tarian whispered.

"No, don't say that," Piper gasped.

"The secrecy and Eleanor's aloofness is concerning," Audrey added. "I went back to the lab, and Eleanor wasn't there. She and Patrick were somewhere else. I just don't know where. They are up to something."

218

First Born by Janelle Gabay

"I've been thinking about what she said about the vials. It's like medicine. It must have to do with Delia's illness. I know it's connected, but how?" Tarian pondered.

"I agree. But Delia is still working with our lead suspect. She is guilty of something."

"She's only eighteen."

"It's the young that are impressionable," Audrey said.

"And recruitable," Piper added.

First Born by Janelle Gabay

TWENTY-SIX
WAITING

Six o' clock the next morning, Audrey and Tarian sat at the breakfast table in Headquarters' charming eatery with mounds of fluffy pancakes stacked high, bulging with blueberries and oozing pure maple syrup. Tarian had not touched his food; instead he thumbed through the pages of the book his dad had left for him after his death. He concentrated on the writings in the margins but had come up with no hint of condemnation of Roman, nothing to secure his guilty verdict. His flashback on the train still haunted him. He could not shake the feeling that Roman was a good guy, but a good guy would not kiss a girl, fourteen years his junior. He shook his head trying to remain objective, but the beast of rage and jealousy would not be tamed.

Eleanor had not given an exact time for their meeting, but Tarian knew when Eleanor showed up, he had better be well fed, well groomed, and ready to meet. Tarian reorganized the food on his plate, swirling his fork in the sticky syrup, taking few bites. Unfortunately, he could not enjoy the fresh fruit nor the hearty pancakes. However, the warmth of the coffee satisfied his senses. Audrey glanced over at him as she, too, attempted to eat as the time slowly trickled by.

Eleanor still had not arrived, and the six a.m. breakfast became a leisurely one. They had managed to eat all of the pancakes over the course of an hour and a half. Now they sipped on coffee and reminisced about EMA, which had oddly enough

First Born by Janelle Gabay

become their home of the good ol' days. Tarian began to wish he had more of a past to share with her. His curiosity about her past grew, and he wanted her to tell him everything.

"Are you reading *The American*?" Audrey asked.

"Yes, Dad gave it to me. It was his."

"Where did you get it?" she asked.

"I sent someone to the Inn to fetch it for me," he said.

"Why didn't you get it yourself?" she questioned.

"I don't know," he sighed. He had slept in one of the empty rooms at Headquarters. He hadn't found the strength to visit his mother yet.

"I lived it," she said with a chuckle.

"What?"

"The book. It's your father's adventures. Joe was the hero of the story. He's Christopher Newman," she said.

"No way!" Tarian gasped.

"Yes," she laughed.

"Tell me about it."

"Good morning kids. I see you've been here awhile. Did you enjoy breakfast?" Chef Richard boomed after he slapped a friendly hand on Tarian's shoulder.

"Yes, excellent," Tarian and Audrey said in unison.

"You know your dad was a great cook. Use to come in my kitchen, and we'd cook for hours. He could make a mean spaghetti sauce. Would stink up my kitchen with garlic for days. And all without magic."

"Yeah, he did make great spaghetti. Sunday nights were always spaghetti night." Tarian smiled broadly.

First Born by Janelle Gabay

"*The American*, oh my goodness," Chef Richard laughed noticing the book on the table. "Do you know Henry James wrote that book about your father?" He began to laugh uncontrollably. It was infectious and soon both Audrey and Tarian were chuckling.

"Ok, I need to know the story," Tarian said.

"You tell him, Audrey."

"Well, Joe had gone gallivanting through Paris, and Henry got wind of the failed marriage proposal by eavesdropping on London gossip. Your dad first read about his horrible misadventures back here in Boston. Articles about 'The American' were being published in the Atlantic Monthly."

"Joe was so angry, salt in his wound," Chef Richard interjected.

"So he went straight to London to put a stop to this Henry James person who was capitalizing on his grief," Audrey continued. "Before long, Joe was feeding Henry's imagination, and the two were creating a novel together."

"That's unbelievable," Tarian said, grinning widely.

"We had so much fun that year in London. I hadn't been back since I was born," she reminisced.

"You were there," he asked.

"No," responded Chef Richard.

"Of course," said Audrey, "Zachary too. We were not about to let Joe go off to Europe alone again. Not after the catastrophe of his first trip."

"So it's all true?" Tarian asked.

"Well, it's elaborated."

First Born by Janelle Gabay

"But the old woman, the mother, she'd rather her daughter go in the nunnery than marry Dad?"

"Yes, she was a horrible woman," Chef Richard added.

"She suffered for it, as she should," Audrey said.

"Died alone," Chef Richard whispered, drawing about the syllables for effect.

"It was rumored her ostentatious eldest son poisoned her just as she had poisoned her husband. It was a bad time for Joe. She broke his heart. What was her name?" Audrey thought.

"Madame de Cintre," Tarian answered.

"Yes, but that wasn't her real name," she paused in thought, looked at Chef Richard for help but no name came to either of them. "I told him she was not the right woman for him. I told him Jeannette Renault was a hell of a lot more fun."

"Who?"

"Miss Noemie, her real name was Jeannette Renault. She had a zest for life but Joe was too proper, and she was too modern for her time."

"Wasn't she a prostitute?" Tarian asked.

"No, is that how you read it?" she asked.

Tarian nodded.

"No, she was a poor, socially ambitious girl that lacked all sense of appropriate behavior for her time," Audrey said, and Chef Richard nodded.

"Oh, I see."

"Excuse me, I can't leave Ralph alone in the kitchen for too long. I think I smell smoke," Chef Richard left the table in a flash.

First Born by Janelle Gabay

Tarian and Audrey exchanged a look and a laugh. Tarian had actually relaxed, forgotten Delia and had an enjoyable breakfast.

"Why do you have it now?" she asked.

"Not sure, really, but it was in my dream, and it seemed important. Luckily, Mom brought it when she was forced to evacuate Salem to come here. She brought all of my dad's momentums." While he spoke, he rolled the book around in his hands and flipped the pages like a magician shuffling cards. "Dad wrote in the margins. I wondered if he left me a clue. I guess he was just sharing a part of his life with me. He probably expected you or the Senator to explain it all," Tarian said with obvious disappointment.

"I'm not sure. What did he write in the margins?"

"Not much. The only thing that may be a clue is a bank account number." He flipped to the page with the *Bank of Boston: 511-6298-2803-37*, written on it.

"Let's check it out," she said beginning to enter the information into her mobile. Then she grabbed his arm and led him out of the kitchen.

He quickly snatched his warm mug of coffee before she whisked him away from the table and into the lounge area. Together they sat in front of a large computer. As she began to speak the banking number, Tarian noticed a large gathering of purple and green suits around the television. A very scared and beat up news reporter broadcast from the center of a city under attack. The reporter's hair pushed back by one too many swipes of his hand. His cheek had dark red rake marks that went from his mouth to his temple, and he was covered in a thick gray ash

First Born by Janelle Gabay

that could only mean buildings were collapsing. It took Audrey and Tarian seconds to recognize the city. Boston. Those were the streets they had walked only yesterday.

Audrey firmly clutched his forearm and jerked him toward the exit. The two of them ran full speed towards the stairs, climbed the flights two steps at a time, raced down the hall, burst through the doors on the left into the reception area, then flung open the solid oak doors without knocking. Eleanor sat behind her computer and looked as if she had not slept at all. The stress of dealing with the Prevallers's allusiveness, the emerging war, and the Guardians' mysterious traitor invaded her psyche withering away her beauty.

"Eleanor!" Audrey yelled. "Oh my God! Thank God you are okay!" She spat the words between gasps for air. "I saw the pictures! And you were late! You're never late! And none of this is making sense. What's going on?"

Audrey was the most in-shape person he knew, so her exhaustion was clearly from fear.

"I'm sorry, Audrey. Tarian. I've had to keep you uninformed because I did not know whom to trust. Yes, it is bad. The Prevallers have attacked the government building in Boston. The city is destroyed, and many of the Entente's Congressmen are missing. I do not know who is dead and who is alive. One thing I do know is Delia and Roman Feng are alive. They have not left the vacant seaport building."

"They must have known about the attack, so they stayed out of the city," Tarian thought aloud.

"Is our team safe?" Audrey asked.

225

First Born by Janelle Gabay

"John, Warren, Sophie and Keegan are all accounted for, but we still have not had correspondence with Gabe and Maria. They were surveilling the office buildings. I'm sorry Tarian," Eleanor said.

"What?" Quick, sharp breaths took over Tarian's lungs causing a dizzying effect. "No! I can't lose them again!"

Zachary flung the door open in mid-sentence, "There's been another killing. Death serum. Daniel Silsbury, he's gone." He looked distraught beyond compare.

"That means Delia and Feng were not the assassins," Audrey said, keeping a clear head about her.

Jugular8's dad had been murdered. Delia had stayed with him. There had to be a connection. Tarian's mind wandered.

"Yes," Zachary said, looking at Audrey.

The Senator gave Audrey an interesting look that Tarian could not read. *Was he angry for her lack of concern over Daniel? Was he aware that he had not thought of his daughter? Do I want to be immortal, to live through years of this turmoil and death, to become callous to the human struggle?*

"Audrey, get them here now," Eleanor ordered.

Audrey left the room. Tarian stood in place awaiting his instructions.

Eleanor yelled, "Go!"

Tarian ran down the hall catching up with Audrey. The two of them leapt up one flight of stairs to the communications room. She linked her secure mobile to the appropriate source and found the location of John, Warren, Sophie and Keegan. She

First Born by Janelle Gabay

ordered them to capture Jack Silsbury, Delia and Feng and return them to Headquarters as soon as possible.

"Do you think Eleanor knows about Jugular8?" Tarian asked.

"I don't know, but his dad's death is no coincidence. All of Joe's closest friends are being murdered. All of the people he entrusted with the secret of your birth. It's not random. Joe was up to something. What?"

Tarian had no answers to give her.

After several long minutes, Audrey was still working hard at the computer. Urgently speaking her demands and swiping her fingers across the screen as she released sighs of exasperation. She attempted communication with Maria and Gabe, but the signal never attached. The haunting sound of a single dead note crossed the line. It was loud and vicious, an in-your-face assault on the acoustics. NO ONE AVAILABLE!

Tarian crumpled into a chair. Audrey turned toward him, concern on her face.

"Are you going to be alright?" she asked.

"I don't really have a choice," he said.

"I know." Her voice was sympathetic.

"Do you have another request?" the computer asked.

"Keep searching," Audrey stated.

"As you wish," responded the computer.

They were playing a game of hurry-up-and-wait. They sat in the sterile, gray room lit with glaring, benevolent, overhead lighting. Soulless liquid crystal and curved glass screens smudged with dirty fingerprints surrounded them. Misty images danced in the air revealing maps and places where Gabe and

227

First Born by Janelle Gabay

Maria should be, but even the latest tracking technology could not find them. They had simply vanished. Their bodies dead or alive were gone.

The minutes turned to hours, and Tarian's stomach began to growl.

"You need food. We still have a couple of hours, and then I'm not sure Eleanor will let us interrogate them immediately."

"I know, but if I eat, I'll vomit."

"No you won't unless you want me to give you Sanoxine," she said with a smile.

"Uh no. Never again," he said, then grabbed her petite body into a headlock and gave her a noogie. Under his stronghold, she could not move. Finally, his immortal strength matched hers. She was no longer dominant over him. This minor act of camaraderie felt nice. For a brief moment, the chaos surrounding them was forgotten.

228

First Born by Janelle Gabay

TWENTY-SEVEN
THE TRUTH

Time snared in molasses for the next two hours. Audrey sat behind an intricately carved, antique desk in her room while Tarian attempted not to pace the rug in front of her. During their wait they journeyed through the clues they recalled from Delia's blogs. They also flipped through the pages of *The American,* searching for any missing information. The bank account that matched the numbers in the margin of the book belonged to a Christopher Newman and had been closed after Joe's death.

"On the train, in my dream I remembered all the items Dad left us. It was very vivid, especially the teddy bear, Chloe's teddy bear. Also, the faces I saw on the guests at Dad's funeral were those of the murdered Guardians. I'm sure of it," Tarian recounted. Parts of his dream came back to him in pieces. "Yes, the many people hugging my mom were all Guardians." Tarian eyes shut in concentration.

"That's good, Tarian. Focus."

"If all of Dad's confidants were targeted by the traitor, who's next?"

"Me probably or Zachary. Maybe even Eleanor," Audrey said. She dropped her head to her desktop.

"Why weren't you at the funeral?" Tarian asked.

She lifted her head. " I was. I just kept well hidden. Zachary forbade me to go; he said it would interfere with his

229

First Born by Janelle Gabay

future plans for you at EMA. I didn't know the plans at the time. He snuck me into the academy that year."

"Of course he did," Tarian said with a wrinkled brow. "In the dream, I remember being surprised at my father's ill-planning just as I had been on the day of his real funeral. Now that I know he was immortal, I guess he never planned on his death. It just wasn't like him not to plan for the future. He over planned everything."

"Yes he did," she said. "Annoyingly organized."

"I don't understand. Where's all of his money?"

"What do you mean?" she asked.

"We were sent to live with the Senator because we had no money."

"That's false," Audrey said.

Shaking his head he continued, "I think Dad and the Senator were in on this together. They were planning something," Tarian said, his eyes jumping with memory.

Margaret stepped into the room through the open door and interrupted their conversation.

"They're here. You need to come at once," Margaret ordered.

"Thank you Margaret." Audrey jumped to her feet, hitting her knee on the edge of her desk. "Dammit, ouch!"

Together, they rushed downstairs to the fifth floor into a darkly lit room that felt more like a closet. Here they viewed Delia behind a one-way mirror. She sat alone and looked terrified. Tarian's heart skipped as it always did when he saw her beautiful face, but he did not like the look he saw in her eyes. She wore the active eyes of a trapped dog. She shivered as she

230

First Born by Janelle Gabay

crossed her arms and rocked back and forth in her chair. Her hair was cropped short to her scalp, several inches shorter than her normal length. It appeared even shorter than it had when he saw her sedated and strapped to the chair in the warehouse.

He recalled her morning ritual before school. Awakening, she would pull up her gorgeous straight hair into a ponytail. Disappearing into the bathroom, she would emerge, hair down, breathtakingly beautiful. He wasn't sure what she did behind that bathroom door, but her hair would be fuller and bouncier with a slight curl at the end. The waves swayed mesmerizingly as she walked. He remembered wanting to stare at the back of her head all day. That luscious hair was gone now.

Her once slender, regal frame downsized to sickly skin on bones. The circles under her eyes matched the circles under his, and he wondered if her sleep had been riddled with nightmares too.

Finally, someone brought Delia a cup of hot coffee and a blanket. She flashed her killer smile, and Tarian found himself smiling back at her. He had drifted away encased in his own presence; he had forgotten the other team members in the room. They were evaluating her movements and appearance. Discussing what she had said and done on the trip to Headquarters, but he had heard only muffled sounds that had no meaning, belonged to no one.

"Tarian!" Audrey said for the fourth time. She shook his shoulders. "Did you hear what Sophie said?"

"No," he said, his eyes regaining focus and his mind settling back to the present.

First Born by Janelle Gabay

"Delia is still sick, very sick but she will not talk to anyone. Feng isn't talking either."

Audrey pushed Tarian ten feet to the right where he could peer into Feng's room. Roman had lost weight as well, but carried a healthy complexion and stood strong. He did not seem scared; instead, he looked defiant and determined.

Eleanor walked into the small room and gestured for Audrey and Tarian to follow her. She escorted them into the elevator where she used a special key to unlock the keypad. After entering a number, and having her face scanned, Tarian felt the elevator jerk and drop further than expected. They stopped far underground. Tarian followed Eleanor and Audrey through the damp cave-like hallway into a windowless room that had strange soundproofing materials on the walls, floor and ceiling. The cushiony floor felt fun under his feet. On top of the cushion a haze of fog lingered hiding his steps inside rippling rings of milky clouds. Tarian had never seen anything like it before. Eleanor left the room and locked the door.

"She just locked us in here," he said, with a hint of panic in his voice.

"It's okay," Audrey said. "This is the only place that's one hundred percent secure, silent and magic free. We call it the Dead Zone."

"Well, that's comforting," he snapped.

"Look at your mobile." She waited for him as he tapped, swiped and shook it. "See?"

The device was dead. He could not turn it on, none of the control functions worked. He had used the mobile just a half an

First Born by Janelle Gabay

hour ago in the hopes of receiving information about Gabe and Maria's whereabouts.

"Okay. What does this mean?" he asked.

"I don't know," she answered. "All I know is that I completely trust Eleanor. If she is the traitor behind all of this, then I'd rather be dead."

"I don't think it's her. I know I don't know her very well. It's just my gut trusts her. It's just a feeling."

"I think she wants us to talk to Delia and Feng in here. I believe Eleanor knows who she can't trust but will not leak that information to anyone yet."

The click of the lock shot through the room like a hollow thump. Its usual, clinky echo thwarted by the weird, chevron wallpaper that melted onto the walls. All sounds were harsh and flat. He braced himself for whatever walked through that door. *Was someone coming to kill them with Death Serum? Were they trapped? No!* He shook away those paranoid ideas and prepared himself to face Delia and Roman. He wanted to be strong and calm.

Tarian first saw the familiar blackberry suit and confident stride of Eleanor Dare. Behind her, barely visible, shuffled a bulky figure with Delia's short dark hair. Delia still had the blanket wrapped around her and hung her head low. Eleanor locked the door behind them, and Delia jumped, looking at her with distrust. Roman did not accompany them. Tarian's shoulders fell to rest back into their natural position releasing the knotted tension caused by the mounting anticipation of confronting Roman.

First Born by Janelle Gabay

Delia began to lower her head again, but then she looked up. Tarian saw the strength return to her as she stood taller, straightened her shoulders, and forced her head up. But it was her eyes that broke him. Those giant ocean eyes were dark and stormy, reflecting not evil, but despair, and they pulled him in like the voice of a Siren. His one step forward was enough movement to drop her blanket. She looked as if she wanted something from Tarian, but what? She teetered on the cushiony floor, but she did not seem unbalanced only unsure. Tarian tilted his head and took another step forward. Confused, he could not comprehend her involvement with Roman, but he saw her suffering.

She slowly walked toward him but Tarian stood still. She kept walking and embraced him. His mind screamed with anger but his body refused to push her away. He breathed in the sweetness of her sweat and began to feel muscle memories from a time of happiness. She burst into uncontrollable tears and her body jerked with her sobs. Instinctively, he held her tighter. His arms had tripled in size since their first intimate hug over two years ago. In their past, she had been the one to comfort him. She had been the solid rock of security he needed after losing his father. Now it had all changed. He had become a substantial man, a man that could fight, and a man that could encircle her inside arms of protection.

Eleanor cleared her throat loudly. Tarian faced her and she looked as if she was about to physically pry them apart so he let go of Delia. The release felt more than just physical to Tarian, it felt personally freeing. Suddenly his love for her had changed, as if the part of his soul she had kept, but no longer deserved,

First Born by Janelle Gabay

ripped away from him once he let her go. She would always have his past, but she no longer had his future.

"Delia, it's time to talk!" Eleanor stated.

"I don't trust you," she said, her eyes darting back and forth between Eleanor and Audrey. She turned to Tarian. "They've been spying on us. Testing on us!" Her eyes were searching Tarian's for signs of damage.

"No one has been testing on me Delia." Tarian reassured her.

"He has," she said.

"He who? Roman?" Tarian asked.

"No!" She stated firmly and looked surprised.

"Roman killed my father," he said.

"Is that what she told you?" Delia said, looking at Eleanor. "And you. You are in on it with my father." She accused Audrey.

Delia's venomous words spewed poison all over Audrey. The hatred motivated Delia's strength, and she stepped toward Audrey, but Tarian stopped her with his grip. Delia sharply looked at him then back at Audrey, but she halted.

"No Delia, you are confused. Audrey has been with me every day for the last six weeks, and before that I saw her every day at EMA. You can trust her," he said, but Delia now looked even more malicious. "Tell us what you know about Roman," he urged her, surprised and impressed by his tranquil posture in the presence of her lethal stare. He noticed Eleanor's slight smile as she encouraged him to press further. "Roman has been making you sick."

235

First Born by Janelle Gabay

"No, no, no!" She grabbed her head and squeezed, then continued in a soft, restricted voice. "You have it all wrong. Roman is trying to make me better. Father…" She could not complete the sentence. An organ-sized lump caught in her throat, forcing her voice to deaden, and her eyes to bulge with tears.

It took a second for Tarian to register 'father' as Senator Eastwood, and then the look of terror crossed his face. He and Audrey had been suspicious of Zachary but simply could not bring themselves to convict him. The centuries of good deeds he had done with Audrey coupled with the year he took Tarian in as his own son were filled with fond memories.

"You knew," Tarian growled at Eleanor.

"Yes," Eleanor said.

"How long?" Audrey asked.

"I secured my suspicions after the team was established in Boston, but I did not have proof. I still do not know who is conspiring with him. I have told no one."

"You've always been a brick wall, Eleanor." Audrey sighed and closed her eyes. "So my meeting with him that night, did I screw it up?"

"At first I was devastated by your breach of command. You hadn't broken orders in centuries."

"What was I supposed to do? I couldn't contact you for weeks so I had to make my own plan," Audrey said then caught Tarian's face with her glance and reformed her statement. "We decided to make our own plan of action. So you did not end communications with us?"

"No, I was unaware. Zachary must have interfered with my communications. Zachary was my liaison. I trusted him

236

First Born by Janelle Gabay

completely. When there was no steady line of information coming, in fact, there was no information at all, I became suspicious. I waited. I was hoping he would make a mistake but he didn't. I was so preoccupied in the lab and with other state of affairs that I lost track of time. Time has a different feeling for me. In hind sight, I realize how the waiting for you and Tarian must have been torturous."

"Delia, what is going on?" Tarian asked. He wanted concrete facts not feelings and speculation.

She still looked hesitant.

"It's okay. You can trust us, all of us." He tried to convince her.

She hesitated but eventually began her story. "After you left, that first year, I started getting sick. Mom couldn't figure out what was wrong with me and the doctors said it was just a lingering virus. Over a year I suffered. Healthy one day, sick the next. One day when I was home from school and mom was out, I sneaked into father's office. I was looking for information about the rumors I had heard concerning a war, the Prevallers. Instead, I found a syringe and a lot of notebooks filled with scientific studies," she said then stopped. She breathed heavily and cast her eyes towards the floor.

"Okay," Tarian coaxed.

"I even found vials of blood, one drawn from Carolyn," Delia paused and looked at Tarian.

He attempted to be surprised. Her blogging was still a secret. He did not respond verbally fearing his voice would betray him.

237

First Born by Janelle Gabay

"One night, Father thought I was asleep and injected me with a syringe. At first I assumed it was a medicine to help cure my illness, but then I came to the conclusion that it was what was making me sick in the first place. My own father was testing on me." She laughed a wicked laugh of a girl who had come to the realization that her own father did not want to protect her. "It was horrible. My plan was to tell you over Christmas. Father's a powerful man. I couldn't just confront him. And I wasn't one hundred percent sure for myself. I needed you. I needed your advice. But then the attack happened," she paused from exhaustion. "Your name was on a few of the data reports. I think while you were staying with us, he tested on you."

"But I was never ill," Tarian said.

"You wouldn't be if he *took* your blood instead of injecting you with serum," Eleanor said.

"Gary," he murmured.

"Who?" Eleanor asked.

"The physical trainer Zachary hired to get me into shape for EMA. He took my blood once or twice a month. He claimed I had an iron deficiency and gave me pills."

"Your DNA is valuable, Tarian. You are the first of our kind born in over 500 years. The serum you gave me yesterday, the one that I told you was inconclusive, I decided to test it on the blood I'd gathered from you weeks ago," she said looking at Tarian. "The results were unimaginable. The serum successfully duplicated your DNA-genome."

"What is Roman doing with a serum like that?" Tarian asked.

"He copied it from your dad's notes," Delia said.

First Born by Janelle Gabay

"What?" Tarian asked.

"Joe was trying to understand why or how you exist," Eleanor explained.

"Roman was trying to help me," Delia said.

"Zachary is trying to duplicate the process that produced your birth," Eleanor explained.

"We don't need more immortals." Audrey paused glancing at Tarian. "Think of it. An army of immortals would be impossible to fight."

"Unless you had a Death Serum," Tarian said. "Do you think my dad created the Death Serum? Maybe he suspected Zachary."

"Roman found a secret vault with a lot of documents and studies that your dad had kept. He and I have been studying these together. That's when I learned what my father was and what you are," Delia said staring at Tarian. "At first I was furious, I couldn't bear the thought of growing old and you remaining young and handsome. The life I desired and dreamed to have with you had vanished. We couldn't get married and have children. How would that work? How did my father do it? He was going to leave us all, maybe divorce, maybe fake death, or maybe he was going to kill us, say it was an accident. What do you people do anyway?" She asked Eleanor and Audrey, with the venomous tone returning to her voice.

"We are all free to live the life we choose to live. Some of us never become romantically involved with mortals, some of us do, but murder is not allowed," Eleanor said.

"Where are these papers? Half of Boston has been blown up!" Audrey said, refocusing the conversation.

First Born by Janelle Gabay

"They're not in Boston," she said. "There's a safe deposit box at Xia Bank in Los Angeles. Roman is from there. He chose to hide the papers there. He wanted them as far away from here as possible."

"What about copies? You must have made copies," Audrey demanded.

"Yes. Some. Your people have everything we kept at the warehouse. We didn't keep anything at the office for fear of…, well for fear of exactly what happened. Destruction," Delia said.

A dull thud came from behind the chevron-patterned material on the door. Eleanor answered it and brought in Roman. She also gave her assistant strict orders to arrest Zachary Eastwood. None of her devices worked in this room, so she only knew of his last location. It happened to be upstairs in her office, around one hour ago. She had baited him with false information to ensure his cooperation and reduce the risk of him fleeing the building.

Roman rushed straight to Delia and put his arm around her. He examined Tarian with a concerned expression. His honey colored eyes softened and his strong jawline relaxed, but he did not speak and Delia lowered her head.

"So, what's this?" Tarian voiced without control. His composure had reached its breaking point. "You found out what I am and that wasn't good enough for you." The poison seeped from his words, just as it had from hers. His aching wound reopened and turned into a jealous laceration, infecting his entire being.

"I found out what you were and knew we couldn't be together," she spat back at him, just as infected.

240

First Born by Janelle Gabay

"Thank you for making that decision for us," Tarian snarled.

"You had vanished!" she reminded him. "With her," she accused, looking directly at Audrey.

Audrey took the accusation with impenetrable stoicism, Tarian noted, impressed. The only hint that the claim angered her was a slight squint of her crystal blue eyes.

"We are getting off track," Eleanor interrupted. "I'm truly sorry for this abrupt reunion. This should be a private affair, but I'm afraid time does not allow us that luxury. Roman, I need you to tell me what you know. Then we will go upstairs and review the copies that you have. I've studied your counteractant. It isn't working, is it?"

"No," Roman said. "And she is getting worse. Her father's serum is like an agglutinogen, which is a type of antigen. Her cells adhere together but none of the antibodies I've used can repair the agglutination. I thought I was approaching this all wrong and treated it as if it was cystic fibrosis because it shows similarities being that a specific chromosome pair has mutated. But I've exhausted all of my knowledge, and I'm out of favors from my physician friends. They are beginning to ask too many questions."

"I'm impressed you've gotten this far, Roman," Eleanor said.

"In my community, our school requirements include two years of medical training. Most of our inhabitants are doctors but since I chose the profession of law, my medical education was very basic. I took only the required courses that would get me into Harvard School of Law. Joe must have been a great

First Born by Janelle Gabay

scientist. His research was very well documented. It was like having the best text book to follow," Roman said. Then he stroked Delia's back and asked, "You will help her get better, right?"

The pitch in Roman's voice was that of a lover in despair, and even though Tarian was ready to except his loss of Delia, ready to move on, rage and spite uncontrollably brewed in his blood.

"I think I will be able to help her," Eleanor said. "I'm sure those papers will clear up a great deal of confusion. Did any of Joe's studies or papers include a Death Serum?"

"Yes," Roman said, and he looked as if he was betraying the confidence of his best friend. "I didn't know what to make of that. I actually wondered if the Joe I knew was not who I thought he was. I thought maybe he was murdered because he deserved it."

Roman's words took Tarian off guard. Every day for weeks, Tarian had pondered who killed his father and why? He never once considered that his father deserved to die. Now that he suspected his father to be the developer of the Death Serum, that possibility needed to be addressed. He physically shook at the thought. Audrey seemed to be the only one who noticed his shifting skin.

"You knew he was murdered? His cause of death was listed as a heart attack," Audrey added.

"I never believed that. In the days before he died, he confided some limited information to me. He left me the key to a safety deposit box at the Entente Bank of Boston listed under the name Chris Newman."

First Born by Janelle Gabay

Audrey and Tarian turned to one another in recognition of the name, the hero in the novel *The American*. They smiled and Audrey briefly touched Tarian's arm. Delia scowled at her.

Roman continued, "I was to retrieve all items from the box and tell no one about them. His instructions were for me to store the items until Tarian graduated college. I was not to look at the contents," he said turning his attention on Tarian. "I violated his request. I just felt I had to look. It certainly changed everything when I found out he was a member of a secret society of immortals."

"Exactly what is in the box?" Eleanor said.

"His Last Will and Testament, a sealed note to Tarian, only. No other family member received one, which I assumed meant something. That I did not open." Roman turned to face Tarian with an honest smile. "A ten-page document detailing how to kill an immortal. He explains why his serum works and from what I can gather, he had been attempting to develop it for a long time. Actually, at first I wondered if he used the serum on himself, committed suicide, but he loved his family too much to do that. It did not make sense and all his research seemed to allude to a greater threat. When I looked through the box, all I could sense was fear. Once I found out he was immortal, I realized whatever he had to fear must have been truly horrible."

"Why did you hide?" Eleanor asked.

"I didn't really. I had clients in Los Angeles but I did not hide. I did become somewhat of a recluse because of my suspicions. I rarely left my office. There is a hidden room where I spent most of my time. When Delia came to our office in need of an internship, I hired her immediately because I knew her

243

First Born by Janelle Gabay

father was a Guardian. The few notes on Senator Eastwood suggested Joe didn't trust him," Roman said.

"Then why did you let me and my brother go live with him?" Tarian asked.

"I didn't open the file for the first year. I tried to respect Joe's wishes, but I couldn't shake the feeling something was wrong," Roman said. "Then it took me another month to decipher all the information I was reading. There's no proof in those papers that Senator Eastwood is your dad's murderer."

"But you suspect him," Tarian stated more than asked.

"Yes, because your dad suspected he was helping the Prevallers, but it was not until Delia came to me that I realized the man is evil."

"Evil?" Audrey questioned.

Tarian knew from their previous conversations that deep inside her heart she would never believe he was truly evil, just influenced by corruption. But Tarian believed. Roman and he now had three things in common: Dad's trust, Delia's love, and abhorrence for Zachary.

"What kind of monster would poison his own daughter?" Roman said bitterly.

"I did not matter to him or I wasn't good enough because I am mortal," Delia spoke again, but this time her words were soft and weak. Delia was not easily broken, but a father's betrayal would break any daughter.

Another knock on the door brought everyone back to reality. There was a crisis going on outside of the room and they needed to address it. Delia was taken to the infirmary where Eleanor had given the doctors strict orders to keep her bedridden

First Born by Janelle Gabay

and full of fluids. Eleanor already had her scientists working on perfecting Roman's antidote. She then ordered Roman and Tarian to retrieve all of Joe's documents from the safety deposit box in Los Angeles while she and Audrey interrogated Zachary.

245

First Born by Janelle Gabay

TWENTY-EIGHT
LOS ANGELES

Besides the crew, Roman and Tarian were the only two on board the luxurious, Guardian jet. Tarian sat next to the window in the last row. Roman sat in the first row on the opposite side window seat. Tarian wondered if Roman picked the seat furthest away from him on purpose, if so, they were thinking alike. Tarian planned to gaze out the window and avoid all eye contact with Roman for the duration of the flight. The clear, brilliant blue sky and calm winds promised an uneventful flight.

Hours later, the jet began its descent. Neither one of them had moved, not even to use to the lavatory. Nor had they spoken. At one point, Tarian noticed Roman glance back at him, but Tarian made no attempt to acknowledge his effort. The heavy, awkward silence continued. During the last remaining minutes before touchdown Tarian decided to engage in minor small talk. He asked a couple of questions about the bank and avoided all mention of Delia. It wasn't much, but they both knew an amicable appearance was necessary in order to pass as business partners in this mission. When the jet landed, they were ready to act professionally and get the job done.

They landed on a private landing strip and went swiftly into an unmarked vehicle courtesy of the Guardians of Dare. The bank was not far from the airport; however, the traffic was thick and moved like sludge through the sewer pipes. The drive took

246

First Born by Janelle Gabay

over an hour to go 20 miles. Once again, Roman and Tarian remained silent and uncomfortable in one another's presence.

The exclusive trust bank stood only four stories high. A well-built, solid Spanish Baroque-influenced building, constructed over three hundred years ago during the Wild West days of horse and buggies. The exterior stucco heavily swirled, like the thick buttercream frosting of a birthday cake, and the windows were hidden behind arched portals. The Spanish influence followed to the interior as well, with catacomb-like corridors inlaid with Sevillian glazed tiles. It smelled of old clay and fresh coffee. It remained an archive of the past and stood apart from the modern Xia buildings that surrounded it. The other buildings downtown were tall, steel, glass structures that screamed Xia modernization.

Roman was not a regular here and the teller treated him like a stranger. She was a stout, older woman with a harsh face and a sickly smell of flowers and powder. Her many wrinkles made her expressions difficult to read. The wrinkles depicted a road map of a long life filled with happiness and sorrow. She welcomed the men with a smile, but her frown lines remained in place. It was a peculiar dichotomy.

"Entente registered license please," the teller said in a rough, monotonous voice. Roman produced the holographic image form his mobile. "That gentleman as well."

This made Tarian uneasy, but he produced his documentation.

Roman filled out all the paperwork to allow their joint permission into the vault where the security boxes were stacked and available. If she or anybody else in the bank had any

247

First Born by Janelle Gabay

suspicions about them, they were hiding them well. Tarian believed this was a normal procedure for this bored woman teller who had probably opened many safe deposit boxes and had asked for several identification licenses of many businesswomen and businessmen.

After the formalities, the elderly teller left her desk and unsteadily led them down a long corridor to a thick vaulted door. Her unbalanced steps on the terra cotta tiled floors caused Tarian to brace for her fall, but she miraculously walked the full distance without a misstep. Tarian watched her rickety fingers turn the old-fashioned dial in order to unlock the door. Everything seemed ordinary, but Tarian could not relax.

Inside he saw floor to ceiling rows of small cube shaped boxes, all with numbers, no names. They were little secure havens for personal and business items, and he wondered exactly what was in all of these boxes. *Jewelry? Last will and testaments? Drugs? Perhaps something as miniscule as a small figurine, a memento of someone's history to preserve the memory of a lost loved one. Why not?* In a sense, he was there to retrieve a memory of a lost loved one.

His furious joy grew knowing he would read his dad's letter, and he steeled himself to the fact that the note may be intimately personal perhaps bringing tears to his eyes. The last thing he wanted to do was cry in front of Roman. He did not want his empathy.

Roman went to box 428, one of the larger boxes among the many rows. He pulled out a bulky, legal-size file, filled three inches thick. It looked worn. Tarian envisioned his dad flipping through the many pages inside several times, trying to figure

First Born by Janelle Gabay

Tarian's existence out, trying to keep his family safe from the predators at his door. His dad must have been ecstatic to find out he would continue through the years with his son. How disappointing it must have been to be slapped with the realization that in the wrong hands, Zachary's hands, birthing immortals could be fatal to the mortal race.

The file went swiftly and directly into Roman's empty briefcase. The box obediently returned to its snug rectangular hole like a good schoolboy returning to his line. Roman controlled himself in a businesslike manner while Tarian stood immobilized by delight, grief and anger. Tarian's secret fear crept into his theories. He did not believe his father was guilty of any wrongdoing, but it was one of many possibilities. The tiny droplet of doubt about his father's innocence had a tricky way of multiplying into rivers of questionable thoughts. *Why did Dad create a lethal serum?*

With a forceful shove of the shoulder, Roman brought Tarian back to reality. He gave Tarian a look of brotherly wisdom. Suddenly Tarian's hatred for him lessened and he remembered the old Roman; he recalled the fun Roman that was like a brother to him at the law office when they pulled pranks on the office staff and made his dad swear. It was not in his father's nature to swear, so it was hysterical to hear him curse. The graphic words came out stiff and awkward.

As they exited the thick, submarine-like steel door, Tarian noticed the efficient but precarious teller discussing something with the manager in a hushed voice, and the hair on the back of his neck stood up. Something was wrong; he could feel it but he remained stoic wondering if Roman felt it too. A sideways

First Born by Janelle Gabay

glance of Roman's yellow eyes and a reach into his pocket where Tarian knew Roman's Guardian weapon hid, convinced Tarian they would need to act.

Tarian's EMA and Guardian training kicked in. The security guard stepped toward them. With one quick move, Tarian disarmed him. Before the scared old teller could press the alarm, Tarian fired a shot from his undetectable, minuscule gun. The bullet passed close enough to her hand that she rebounded it, giving Roman and him enough time to open the exit door. The teller's hasty movement caused her to collapse to the floor. Tarian resisted the temptation to help the poor woman to her feet. There was no time for chivalry.

The car waited with its alert driver and the untraceable license plate.

"Thank you," Tarian whispered to himself, grateful for Guardian precision.

The bank chaos meant something at Headquarters had gone wrong. Once safely tucked into the back seat of the vehicle, his suspicious instinct reared its ugly head with such force that he snapped on Roman. Before Roman could react, he was pinned against the back of the car seat, weapon taken, arms immovable and Tarian's forearm across his windpipe. Tarian could kill him with a quick thrust of his elbow, but instead he held just short of a life-threatening position and yelled.

"How did they know?"

"I don't know," Roman tried to say, but the compromised air in his lungs made his words barely audible.

Roman shook his head jerkily. His honey colored eyes went wide and Tarian saw their sincerity. He released him. He

First Born by Janelle Gabay

had rushed to judgment but wasn't apologetic. He needed to know beyond a shadow of doubt if he could trust him, and it felt good to bully the man who stole Delia from him.

"Dammit, Tarian!" Roman choked out. "You've made your point." He coughed and rubbed his throat. "Do you think I want to be in this situation? Your father was my mentor; he meant everything to me. He trusted me! Why can't you?"

"It's not you. I don't trust anybody anymore," he said. "Not even my dad's memories are without interrogation."

"Don't forget who he really was, Tarian," Roman encouraged.

"We need to get out of Los Angeles as fast as possible. Is the plane waiting for us?" Tarian asked the driver, not wanting to delve into his father's moral compass.

"Yes," the driver said.

The gridlock, rush-hour traffic made the hour-long trip to the airport unbearable. There were cars on all sides of them, trapping them in a mob of vehicles that together moved sluggishly forward inch by painstaking inch. Tarian felt claustrophobic.

"Can't this thing hover?" Tarian growled.

"Yes, but I have strict orders to remain on the ground," the driver answered.

"Why?" Tarian asked.

"Hovering is illegal on the freeway. Eleanor does not want any unwanted attention brought to you."

"Too late for that. Get this vehicle in the air," Tarian demanded but the wheels remained on the street.

251

First Born by Janelle Gabay

Tarian phoned Audrey twice and she assured him the jet had not been compromised, and they should be able to leave without incident. Her tone, however, was too strict, too much like Cadet Sergeant Gualtiero and he didn't trust it. He asked her several times if everything at Headquarters was all right and she quickly, too quickly, said yes. He knew she was lying. *What was it? His family? Delia? Gabe and Maria?* He hated being on the other side of the Entente.

First Born by Janelle Gabay

TWENTY-NINE
THE LETTER

As usual Audrey was true to her word. Roman and Tarian took off from the private runway without incident. The bank disturbance had not made it into the computer system of the small private airport. *Maybe, this airport was strictly used by the Guardians of Dare*, Tarian thought. He figured if these people had been around for over six hundred years, they probably owned a lot of property.

Before they were at cruising altitude, Roman and Tarian had the contents of the file on the petite conference table. The interior of the plane although vast in luxury was small in size with only twelve oversized first class chairs, one typical aircraft bathroom, a steward station, and a small conference table. The conference table's chairs held lap belts for safety, but neither he nor Roman had thought to put them on. The plane started on a steep incline and they scrambled to hold down papers, but this did not discourage them.

Roman organized the papers into piles. Scientific studies and lab reports went into one pile, while information about the Guardians went into another pile. Then specific information clearly based on some facts but mainly opinion or intuition on individuals inside the government made up another pile. Newspaper clippings form several wars throughout history and modern printouts from the Internet concerning the looming war to come created another pile. Bank statements from accounts

253

First Born by Janelle Gabay

around the world, some of which had been opened hundreds of years ago, stacked up. The rest of the items lay to the left of the stacks: several safe deposit keys that Tarian assumed held a collection of treasured possessions gathered throughout his dad's long life, along with the letter to Tarian, a paper thin, silver tablet, and finally a last will in testament he had already seen.

"Read it," Roman said. "It's not the same one I read to you on the night of the funeral."

As Tarian skimmed through it, he noticed a life insurance policy. "My dad has a seven million dollar life insurance policy?" he asked Roman.

"Yep. Kind of odd for an immortal right?" Roman said.

"Also odd that it would be kept hidden," he said, continuing to think out loud. "Unless, the Senator didn't want us to know we had money. He wanted me in his house."

"And who did Eleanor say was the latest Guardian to die?" Roman asked.

"Daniel Silsbury," he remembered.

"Daniel Silsbury," Roman repeated, as he handed Tarian one of the bank statements. It was a joint account for Daniel Silsbury and Joseph Prescott opened four years ago.

"What's on here?" Tarian questioned as he picked up the silver tablet.

"Pictures, a lot of pictures, but nothing more. I don't think your father trusted putting his ideas on anything other than paper," Roman said as he handed the sealed envelop to Tarian. "Read the note, Tarian. Maybe it will offer more information."

Roman rose from the table and sat in one of the first class chairs facing the other direction in order to give Tarian as much

254

First Born by Janelle Gabay

privacy as possible in the confined space. Tarian knew he had to do it; he had to open the envelope. Dreadful, yet excited, emotions swirled and melted inside his gut causing physical pain like the first day of middle school.

Rip. Out spilled tiny white granules and a silver bracelet. He put the bracelet on and tested the granules. Salt? Then he dove in. Three pages of continuous, uninterrupted, hand-written script awaited him. The familiar handwriting cut through his heart. Millions of individual letters could be scattered about, and Tarian would be able to choose without a doubt the one written by his dad.

Dear Tarian,

First, I must tell you that you are a true miracle. The day Carolyn gave birth to you, I knew you were going to be the one to capture my heart. You were a happy and content child and grew to be a smart young man. You are truly special. What I'm about to tell you, you may already know because if you are reading this letter, than I have failed. It is my worst fear that I leave this world before you know the truth, and I ask for your forgiveness. You are a Guardian of Dare. You are an immortal just as I am. However, no immortals have been born since 1568. I have prayed for our lives to be forever joined in this impossible immortal madness. I did not want you to go it alone. It saddens me that you are reading this. I remember when I first found out who I was. All the questions I had and no family to guide me. It is a hard journey, but just as I did, you will meet many incredible people and it will be an amazing life for you. After all, I met your mother after only a few hundred years. You will see that you can

First Born by Janelle Gabay

fall in love and people will leave you. You will wish for death but it will not come to console you. Life is your gift, enjoy it and use this precious honor wisely. I do believe we are still God's children. We are not evil creatures of darkness or the aftermath of witchcraft, as was believed centuries ago. Luckily, you are in a more accepting time of freedom of religion. A time when science and religion are working together to understand the world we live in. It will be easier for you, I hope. Of course, science is a gift and a curse. For the past eight years, I have known you were an immortal. You gave us hope for our kind to develop families, but for some, you gave us hope to populate and gain power and control over mortals. What I saw as a joyous gift, others saw as a future for dictatorship, a future with an army of immortals. I have seen many wars in my time, and I know the quest for control leads to destruction. They will cloak this desire for power under a blanket of false truths of protecting the mortals and state they are only looking out for the better interests of mankind. All wars start with good intentions. There are only 343 of us, and I always believed all 343 wanted to stay in the shadows, wanted to let the mortals live the lives God intended without interruption from us. Few mortals know of our existence, and these people are in extremely powerful positions. They need us for our knowledge and our strength. We help the good, the mortal good, and we never subject ourselves to the public because they will demand tests and services. It will become a witch-hunt or a malicious scientific experiment. Since we are stronger than mortals and cannot die, the possibilities to use us as weapons are great. We've all known this since the first days, and for that reason most of us disappeared in 1587.

First Born by Janelle Gabay

Unfortunately, since your birth I have discovered that my beliefs are not that of all of us. Some of us only remained silent because of our limited number. There are few among us who believe we are God-like and should be in control of the weak mortals. We have seen massacres and destruction caused by human ignorance, and these few believe this is mere evolution. We have lived for centuries, gathered phenomenal knowledge and an abundance of wealth. We have evolved further than mortals. Some of us even have special gifts; therefore, we should rule. But that is not what I believe. I fear a genetically created immortal army is not what God intended for us. Through science, I have created a way of killing immortals to counteract our reproduction possibilities, which, by the way, are still a mystery to me. Your birth, as far as I can tell, is a miraculous coincidence. Back in Elizabeth's England, there was a belief that the seventh son of the seventh son would have supernatural powers. I'm a seventh Joseph Prescott and you are my seventh son. These old, silly superstitious beliefs from my past I had dismissed long ago, but life is very strange and people are even stranger. I'm beginning to fear that I put my trust in the wrong individuals. Like I said previously, if you are reading this I have failed; the Death Serum I created has been used against me to silence me. Here is a list of Guardians and mortals I know you can trust:

First Born by Janelle Gabay

Eleanor Dare
Daniel Silsbury
Jonathan Ward
Thomas
Edwards
Julia Emmerson
David Smythe
Stephen Harman
Virginia Snow
Audrey Ballard
Gualtiero
Christine
Kershaw
Winston
Longhurst
Jake Aston
Lauren
Cheshire
Jason Steer
Tracy Smith
Roman Feng
Cameron Tailor
Patrick Wallace

First Born by Janelle Gabay

> *Take care of your mother. She has made this miracle, and she is the love of my life. Take care of Charlie; he is older and on a steady path. I believe he will be fine. Teresa will cling to her mother, and together, they will be a great team. I worry most for Chloe and Joe Jr. Please help them to remember me, but never tell any of them who you really are. As Guardians, we swear an oath of silence and hold a promise for public service. Once you meet Eleanor, you will see why I trust her. She is our Matriarch. She is our punisher. She is the most loyal and dedicated Guardian we have. She is also the strongest person I have ever met. Once you know who you are, you must go to Headquarters. Eleanor will be expecting you.*
>
> *1192 Rue de la Magie, Quebec*
>
> *I wish you good luck. Protect yourself. Even those born to strength must carry weapons.*
>
> *All my love,*
> *Dad*

> *"Do not tell secrets to those whose faith and silence you have not already tested." Elizabeth I*

A long pause, then a second read, another long pause. Tarian closed his eyes as his nostrils stung, his brow creased and his eyes watered. He caved into his empty chest and silently suffered. He felt tired and longed for peaceful sleep, but that was not a luxury he had time for; instead, he cleared his throat, put on a brave face, and welcomed Roman back to the table.

First Born by Janelle Gabay

"Well, my dad has a list of people I should be able to trust and you are on it. In fact, you are the only mortal on it as far as I can tell," he stated.

"Who else is on it?" Roman asked.

"Not Zachary Eastwood," he said.

"Well, that solidifies my beliefs," Roman said.

"Yes but, you, Patrick, Eleanor and Audrey are the only ones left alive. Somebody is wiping out my dad's confidants." Tarian held up the paper with the list of names on it.

"That makes me feel safe. I'm on some sort of immortal hit list."

"Yes," Tarian said, and he could not prevent the curl of his lips. "There was salt in the letter and a silver bracelet." Tarian raised his voice alluding to a question and showed Roman the fine, yet masculine, bracelet hanging from his wrist.

"Superstitions from the past. My people have some too. We believe if a dog howls for a long time late at night, someone has died or if you cut your toe nails late at night, you will invite ghosts," Roman said.

They laughed, releasing pent up stress. Tarian had a few answers now, and the sticky suspicion began to ease.

"Unfortunately, my dad does not convict Zachary of the crime of his murder. I mean he doesn't list him as a possible suspect, but he's not on the people-to-trust list either. Also, we know Zachary must have changed my dad's will and hid the life insurance policy. I will confront him at Headquarters and he better have given up several names of the conspirators," Tarian said. Three hundred and twenty-eight was not a lot of people,

First Born by Janelle Gabay

and he wondered just how many Guardians Eleanor would lose to Zachary's collaboration with the Prevallers.

The remaining hours of flight were filled with in-depth reading and analysis of all papers in the file. Eventually, the steward served a plate of roasted chicken and mashed potatoes, and they took a break. To their delight it was better than most restaurants and the two men conversed quite naturally over the meal. Neither mentioned Roman's relationship with Delia. Tarian had also checked his phone repeatedly for any transmission from Gabe and Maria. Still nothing and his dreaded worry returned. He tried Audrey, but she kept stalling and stating they would talk once he was inside the security of Headquarters. She sounded frantic. At least, he thought thankfully, she was safe.

First Born by Janelle Gabay

THIRTY
SILVER BRACELET

Once back at headquarters, Tarian and Roman split up. Roman went straight to Delia's bedside in the infirmary. Tarian went upstairs to Audrey's room to find out why she had been so evasive over the phone.

Audrey sat behind the same lion-footed desk and silver computer she used every time they had been at Headquarters. Her room was full of old and new objects. Her two worlds knitted together: immortal/mortal, old/new, magical/ordinary. He wondered how many years this had been her space. She peeked at him from behind her paper-thin screen before he called her name. She looked as if she had aged ten years.

"Tell me now! Don't dick me around," he ordered, more harshly than he intended.

"Zachary escaped," she said, putting her face in her hands then running them through her hair and dislodging her ponytail. She looked up and he knew that wasn't all. "They have Charlie, Gabe and Maria."

"Charlie?" he asked, the horror spearing his insides with acid laden darts. "What about mom and Chloe and..." he growled but she interrupted.

"They're all fine. I told you the village is impenetrable," she said with confidence.

He felt a nudge of relief as if one life replaced the other, but it only satisfied for a second.

262

First Born by Janelle Gabay

"Do you have the file?" she asked.

"Yes, I do, but we have to go. We have to go now. We have to get Charlie and Gabe and Maria. We have to go." Tarian barked the sentence over and over, but she wasn't moving.

He craved action. She was still sitting in that damn chair. Realizing she wasn't going anywhere, he pushed the chair. He shoved it harder than he had meant to, and the wheels whirled the chair across the room. Audrey hit the far wall. Her neck jerked back, then snapped forward. He ran over to her and bent down.

"I'm sorry, I'm sorry," he said, caressing her neck trying to take the pain away.

Then he fell to his knees, and his head slumped into her lap. She gently stroked his hair, and he let it go. The torture of the past two and a half years spread into her lap. She cradled his pain, making it easier for him to release his brave exterior. Salty liquid drizzled from his eyes and onto her thighs.

"It's okay," she said.

"Nothing's okay," he corrected.

"I mean I'm okay. You didn't hurt me. Yes, we will leave. We'll find them, but first things first."

"I know. What's first?" he asked, still desperately anxious for a task.

"What's this?" she asked, finding his bracelet and looping her finger through it. She smiled at him as if she knew what that bracelet meant.

"It was in the note from Dad. What does it mean?"

"Joe," she said, with a harmonious smile attached to his name. Her mind drifted far away, to a distant memory she had of his father many years ago. "He was always so superstitious.

First Born by Janelle Gabay

Silver brings good luck and I recognize this piece. It's very old. He wore that for many years in the beginning when we first came to America but then he put it away. We all have trinkets like that stashed in safe deposit boxes scattered around the world. You can collect a lot of treasured possessions in six hundred years, but it's the things we had at the beginning that mean the most, usually because back then we were all poor, uneducated, scared. These antiques are precious things we tightly held on to so that they became a part of our soul. You have your dad's soul. Right there." She gently trailed her finger around his wrist touching the silver bracelet.

Tarian enjoyed her touch. He liked her gentle side. When she shared that attribute of herself with him, he felt as if he was the only one that knew this secret tenderness of hers. She warmed him from head to toe, tickling the lining of his stomach and tingling his senses. His vision tunneled straight to her, and he could not look away. They both sat, she in the chair and he on the floor, like they knew once they stood up, this special moment would disappear like smoke, and poof, in its place chaos and fear would return. But they had to rise and carry on, and Audrey released herself first from their emotional trance.

First Born by Janelle Gabay

THIRTY-ONE
THE HIGH COUNCIL

Eleanor stood in the back of her enormous room next to the giant monitors arguing with four other Purple People while her two green-clad assistants stood next to her with remote controls in their hands. Life-size images that looked as if they belonged on the board in an advanced biology university classroom were plastered on the screens. Eleanor and her group criticized them vehemently. Tarian recognized these four people. Their pictures mounted on the wall in front of the library. Under their faces hung plaques stating their numerous achievements and awards in a range of different sciences.

"This is the High Council," Audrey whispered.

Tarian nodded, but he had already figured that one out.

The three gentlemen and one woman dressed in flowing long coats the identical blackberry hue of Eleanor's tailored suit studied the screens. They were infinitely more pale and thin than Eleanor. Tarian suspected their ghostly appearance was due to a constant existence inside classrooms. At least he hoped the lack of sunlight was the reason for their horrid appearance.

"Come in, come in," Eleanor hastily invited.

Audrey and Tarian entered the rear of the room followed by one last guest, Margaret Davenport. The eight of them gathered around a conference table, and Tarian was acutely aware of his lack of authority; yet, all eyes were upon him.

"The file, Tarian?" Eleanor asked, and the briefing began.

265

First Born by Janelle Gabay

Tarian organized the file papers into groups just as Roman had done on the plane.

"Here is the letter from my father. He explains someone is trying to create an immortal army. There is a list of people, and they are all dead except for Eleanor, Audrey and Roman…" Tarian began to read the list of names, but one of the gentlemen interrupted.

"No, no, no, son. The data on Death Serum development that's what we need. Where is it?" The gentleman began to scatter roughly Tarian's piles of papers.

"That's enough George, let the boy continue," the woman council member said.

"Here," Tarian said and slid the stack of papers that included all the pertinent information on creating a Death Serum.

George snatched the papers. The woman argued with him over his rude behavior. Soon the pages were tossed around. At which time, Eleanor and all four council members rapidly spoke and argued over Joe's theories. Tarian and Audrey no longer seemed relevant to the discussion.

Tarian watched the feeding frenzy at the table. None of the high council members except Eleanor were on Joe's trusted list, and Tarian understood why. These four Purple People were nothing more than giant brains devouring their scientific candy. Tarian hoped he had done the right thing giving them his dad's work. But someone needed to create an antidote.

Eleanor and Margaret left the busy council members and pulled Audrey and Tarian aside to talk.

"Tarian, Zachary gave us a few names before he escaped. It was not a total failure," Eleanor said.

266

First Born by Janelle Gabay

"What happened? How could he slip away?" Tarian asked.

"He got violently ill, and I sent Gregory Lycott to escort him to the infirmary while Audrey and I spoke to the President. It was a mistake. Gregory was helping Zachary all along," Eleanor admitted.

"The President's phone call was urgent and could not be ignored, Eleanor. You did the right thing. He informed us of vital intelligence concerning Zachary's suspected treasonous activities and the current negotiations being established with the leaders of the Prevallers," Audrey said, coming to Eleanor's defense.

Eleanor sighed then continued, "They poisoned the guards then disappeared. Both these men were extremely familiar with the building. They knew where the cameras were and where they weren't. They knew where each hall led and what was behind each door. It wasn't that difficult for them to escape, especially since everyone was dealing with a multitude of issues."

"Now what?" Tarian asked.

"At least, Gregory's betrayal gave us insight as to how the fifteen Guardian's had been murdered. Gregory is capable of invisibility," Margaret stated.

"So he can sneak up on people and inject them?" Tarian asked.

"Yes, but to another gifted immortal he can be seen as a shadow that is why he has not attempted to kill Eleanor or Audrey," Margaret added.

First Born by Janelle Gabay

"This is him," Audrey said showing him a picture on her mobile.

Tarian recognized his face as the rumpled meditating man in the corner of the conference room that Tarian entered on his first day at Headquarters. He remembered the disturbing qualities of the man, and the fact that no one else seemed to notice his presence.

"Gregory is a precious weapon and now he's gone," Audrey stated.

"I've seen him," Tarian said.

"Where?" Audrey asked.

"The first day, when you brought me into the room with Margaret." Tarian turned to Margaret, but she looked puzzled.

"I don't remember seeing his shadow," Audrey said.

"I saw him clearly, not as a shadow," Tarian said.

"You are very gifted, Tarian." Eleanor smiled proudly.

"What about Charlie? How are we getting my brother, Gabe and Maria?"

"They are being held at an old Coast Guard base on Mount Desert Island," Audrey informed.

"The Entente base that was recently shut down?" Tarian questioned.

"Yes, ten of our bases are now being used to house prisoners and aid the Prevallers," Eleanor exclaimed.

"Of course, shutting down those fifty bases was a stupid idea. You can't deplete your military during a time of peace. Peace is not free." Tarian threw his hands up in the air and began pacing.

First Born by Janelle Gabay

This was a hot topic for him. During his high school years, he had followed the congressional decision to close bases and voiced his opposition on social media. It was one of the many issues he and Delia disagreed on.

"I understand you are upset. Many people are extremely upset. I am now dealing with violent protests breaking out all over the nation. But the President and I have rescue teams in place for those captured."

"In place?" Tarian yelled loud enough to be heard by council members in the distance.

"Tarian I assure you we are doing everything in our power to get our men and women home safely. This is a delicate house of cards. In less than twenty-four hours, many cards have been put in place. We are dealing with numerous threats. The Prevallers have destroyed our drones and penetrated the closed borders. They are making demands and threatening war. They have an impressive army stationed and ready to attack. It's now an intense standoff with the President and Congress. Negotiations have begun, but…" Eleanor paused and glanced at the High Council.

"But what?" Tarian barked.

Audrey concluded Eleanor's explanation, "But the High Council is considering the history of events leading to this war. And the history before that. The High Council's reluctance is due to the Entente's continued dismissal of the Guardians' warnings. None of the advice given to the Entente has been utilized, and now the Entente is in a vulnerable predicament just like the past."

First Born by Janelle Gabay

"But they have to consider Zachary's role in all of this. He and his group of traitors may have been diluting the Guardian's advice," Tarian suggested.

"Yes they do," Eleanor said.

"Who does the Senator have?" Tarian asked.

"About 45 congressman and several other influential people," Eleanor answered.

"He also has his immortal army?" Tarian yelled.

"That's preposterous," George yelled back.

"What do you mean? It's in my dad's papers," Tarian returned, walking back to the table.

"Nothing has been proven. These are simply theories of mind control or cloning," George countered.

"Well, the mind control ring was invented," Tarian hissed.

"Yes…well… We have taken all precautions to prevent that from ever happening again," George said.

"What about cloning? He took my DNA. He's tested on Delia!"

"Hosh Posh! Zachary's attempt to alter Delia's DNA is unsuccessful. He has done nothing but damage her beyond cure. She is far from immortal," another gentleman council member added.

"Beyond cure?" Tarian asked; terror twisted inside his gut.

"We have not given up, Tarian. I'm still working on a few alternative medical experiments," Eleanor said, and she looked confident. "But I agree with the Council, cloning is

First Born by Janelle Gabay

impossible. We have tried in the past with nothing close to success."

"Zachary is conspiring with the Prevallers. We know this. He is not creating any army. He already has one," George spat.

"We will work on the concrete evidence, not the speculation. Joe's creation of Death Serum is our top priority. We must find an antidote. And if Zachary has done the impossible then we will be forever grateful to your father for this weapon," the female council member explained.

Tarian left the briefing feeling the puzzle was still unfinished. Haunted by the fact that he knew his dad would not have developed a Death Serum simply to prevent the Guardians defection to a new and different world leader. The High Council may not be interested in speculation, but Tarian and Audrey were very much interested in hypothesizing. They left the meeting ready to conjure their own plans but first they needed rest. Having been awake for over twenty-four hours, they couldn't think straight.

First Born by Janelle Gabay

THIRTY-TWO
CHLOE

Tarian stared at the swirls in the wood on the door before working up the nerve to knock on it. Now his family knew Delia was sick, the Senator was a traitor, and Charlie had been kidnapped. And the biggest secret remained untold.

Tarian's mom swung the door open and put her arms around him. He felt the wetness of her tears as she buried her head into his chest. The burden of responsibility lifted from his shoulders, and he sank into his mother's arms, defeated and vulnerable. They stood in the doorway hugging for seconds as he let her love engulf him until Teresa pulled her off and gave him her version of a bear hug. She was sixteen now but very petite for her age. He embraced her into his muscular chest and lifted her off of the floor. She and Tarian were the least close of the siblings, never being able to converse with ease, but all that distance disappeared with one loving embrace. They were blood, a connection that could never be broken.

Joe Jr. paid zero attention to him because the Guardians had provided him with brand new toys that were much more important to a six-year-old than hugging his big brother. He gave his brother a glance, a nod and a smile, as if Tarian had been in the living room for many days. Thank goodness for the blissful innocence of small children, it made Tarian feel comfortable and at home.

First Born by Janelle Gabay

Chloe was the one who broke his heart and took the normalcy away again. She and Tarian had always been the closest, but she shied away from him like he had a disease that she didn't want to catch.

"Hi Chloe." Tarian stepped over the threshold and into the apartment that smelled of cinnamon and warm bread. When he closed the door behind him, Chloe grabbed their mother's skirt and hid behind her.

"She knows Charlie's missing," Mom whispered.

"Are you frightened that I will get taken away like Charlie?" Tarian knelt down to be at her eye level.

She nodded and a tear rolled down her cheek. His heart broke again.

"It's okay Chloe. I know where Charlie is and I'm going to go get him. Will that make it all better?"

She nodded again, still no words. Normally a talkative child with many questions and lots of enthusiasm, her timid muteness was painful to observe.

"Hey! Look at this Chloe." He pulled the egg device out of his pocket. Tarian had on a unique Guardian uniform designed to look like a business suit, and in his pockets were several interesting gadgets. Hoping to persuade her with one, he offered her the egg.

She slowly inched away from Mom's hip, still nervous and quiet, but curious.

"You know, I'm pretty important around here," Tarian teased, touching the fancy pockets on his shirt with the Guardian emblem.

"I know. Mom said so," Chloe said.

First Born by Janelle Gabay

"Are you proud of me, Chloe?"

"Yes!" she said, coming out of her aloofness.

"Then come give me a hug."

She ran into his arms and he squeezed her tightly. He needed her approval more than anyone else. She smelled of sugary vanilla, and he sniffed her hair. She giggled.

"What are you doing, Silly?"

"You smell good enough to eat. Gobble, gobble, gobble." He tickled her and pretended to eat her up.

The sound of her laughter trailed on in his brain. Echoes of satisfaction filled his soul. His little sister had to be happy and safe at all times, in order for him to move forward.

The room at the Inn was warm and homey, even without the fresh-cut Christmas tree and twinkling lights. The dwelling sprawled out to include a spacious living room with a separate office. Here, Joe Jr. housed his many toys. Provided also were all the amenities - two televisions, two computers and a quaint dining area that seemed the most peaceful spot in the home. Mom had told him over and over she was very happy here, but he could see her vacancy. This was not her home, but then again, no place would seem like home until Charlie was safe. He had to get Charlie back as soon as possible.

"Thank you for staying here, Mom," he said as he guided his mom into the kitchen away from the children.

"Of course, I want to be here." Carolyn poured hot water for coffee.

"No, you don't," he said, and watched her eyes lower their gaze. "It helps me to know you're safe. I can concentrate on bringing Charlie home if I don't have to worry about them

First Born by Janelle Gabay

kidnapping you or Chloe, Joe or Teresa. I need to know you are secure."

"We are. We are safe and secure. Joe Jr. is ecstatic with all of his new toys. Chloe is scared since the news of Charlie. She has to be next to me every minute. Most nights she sleeps in my bed instead of with her sister. Teresa loves it here, thankfully. Eleanor has taken an interest in her. Said she is very bright. Teresa wants to go to the lab every day. I'm actually quite proud of her. She has matured greatly in this adverse environment. I never knew how strong she was until now."

"Really? I didn't know. I haven't seen Teresa around the lab." Tarian paused to comb his memory. "And what about you?"

"I'm fine," she said but her hands shook.

"Come on Mom; this is so much for you."

The rattle of the delicate china cup on its saucer told a tale of quiet suffering. Tarian wanted to reveal his secret now since his three siblings had settled in the other room with toys and television, but would the truth bring more pain than peace. Telling his family went against his father's wishes, but so much had changed since Dad's death. He had discussed this possibility with Audrey and her thoughts were divided. Together they had not come to a conclusion on the better option - truth or well-intended deception.

"I know. It does not seem real. I mean, how is any of this possible? I've been reading their history, and I guess now your history. It's a fascinating, magical phenomenon. I'm happy for you, Tarian, I really am. This is a gift. You will have a unique

First Born by Janelle Gabay

journey ahead of you." Carolyn's eyes filled with unshed tears, and she moved her shaking hands to her lap.

"What? You know the truth?" Tarian asked, not yet willing to say the word 'immortal' for fear his mother was talking about something all together different.

"Yes. I know you are an immortal and so does Teresa."

"Who told you?" he asked, feeling betrayed. *Who had the right to give away his secrets?*

"Teresa found out at the lab. Like I said, she's a very bright girl. No one told her; she became suspicious and inquisitive. Of course, at first the two of us thought it was absurd, but the innkeeper downstairs is not very good at hiding her magic."

"How can a sixteen year old comprehend such a thing?"

"Actually, she is taking it very well. Our little life here was going along splendidly until Delia arrived. What Teresa does not understand is Delia's illness. You know how close she and Delia are. She wants to help Eleanor find a cure. Delia does not like Eleanor and that is upsetting her. The two woman she admires most don't seem to like each other."

"Delia doesn't trust immortals. I can't imagine she is representing us in a very nice light."

"No, she's very hurt by her father. Teresa has a mind of her own, though. Like I said, she figured it all out on her own before she shared it with me. After she convinced me her crazy idea was true, we started our research. After Chloe falls asleep she and I sneak down to talk with Emma. She's the innkeeper, very sweet lady. She also has taken a liking to Teresa. She knew

First Born by Janelle Gabay

Joe, and of course she knows Zachary and Audrey. They seem to be a big, happy family."

"They were until the Senator decided to murder them."

His mom winced, concerned for her oldest son. Tarian felt horrible for his choice of words.

"Yes, true, but Zachary is the exception. They are a very close community. They care deeply for one another. I'm glad you have them for the rest of your long life. I just wish I could be there to see it."

He grabbed her hand and squeezed it, "Me too."

"I can't imagine what your poor father went through. I wish he would of told me. I wish I could have helped him."

"He was hoping for a different ending."

Tarian slipped the letter from his father across the table and watched his mom read her husband's words. She smiled with tear-filled eyes but did not speak. After a long pause, she spoke of Delia. He knew she could not bring herself to discuss Joe.

"When I went to visit Delia, she told me about Roman. I'm sorry Honey."

"It's okay. I just hope she gets better," he said, wondering if he would ever go visit his ex-girlfriend.

"She did not look very healthy, but Patrick seems to think she'll recover. I hope so," she said, and then paused.

"What is it Mom?" he asked.

"Whom are they sending to rescue Charlie?" she asked.

"That's still to be determined. I don't care what they decide. I'm going to go find him."

277

First Born by Janelle Gabay

"I want you to stay here," she said, with steady hands on her cup. "Delia needs you. We all need you."

"No," he pleaded.

His mother's protective instinct was strong. Her shaky hands and slumped shoulders evaporated once she feared for the loss of a second son. She would not have it.

"Chloe needs you. For the sake of your family, Tarian! What if she loses two brothers?" she asked, then lowered her head.

He could hear the stranglehold of sobs under her breath.

"I don't want to lose two of my babies," she said.

"Don't worry. They won't send me," he said, weighing his words.

He wanted to obey his mother's wishes, but he knew he couldn't stay in the village while his brother and friends suffered as prisoners. How selfish of him to take off into enemy territory, but how selfish of him to stay here to be coddled by his immortals. She had already lost her husband and her son was missing, but he could not stay here. He was of no use to anybody here. What was he going to tell her? He had to lie or he had to avoid the topic. But she would not drop the subject.

"Promise me." Carolyn grasped his face, forcing him to look at her.

"I promise." Tarian looked straight into her eyes so she would believe him.

The lie tore him apart. He wanted to stay here to take care of the ones he loved, but he was an EMA and Guardian trained soldier, and soldiers fight. Every cell in his body pulled him towards combat. He had also been trained to lie if ever taken

278

First Born by Janelle Gabay

as a prisoner of war. He never imagined he'd have to use his training on his own family.

"Thank you," Carolyn said.

"I'm going to go visit Delia now. See how she's doing," Tarian lied again and stood up. He felt a need to separate himself from the family that relied on him and go to the one he now needed, Audrey.

First Born by Janelle Gabay

THIRTY-THREE
OR ELSE

Audrey stood in the doorway as Tarian opened it to leave the apartment.

"What are you doing here?" he asked her. Then he noticed Eleanor stood behind her.

"May we come in?" Eleanor asked.

Tarian did not step aside. He did not like the look in Eleanor's eyes. To his dismay, his mom, standing directly behind him, welcomed them inside.

They gathered around the breakfast table. Tarian sat back in the same spot, and his mother warmed his cup with hot coffee. Both Audrey and Eleanor refused any beverages or food. Once the niceties concluded, Eleanor handed her small tablet over to Tarian.

"You need to see this," Eleanor said. "This broadcast has been transmitted to all immortals via their Guardian issued tablets."

The Senator's smug face appeared. Tarian turned to look at Audrey with an uneasy face.

"Watch," Audrey said, tilting her head towards him with determination displayed in her eyes.

"My fellow Guardians I have set a plan in motion." The Senator spoke in a voice that did not belong to him. He attempted to be likable, but he came across like a man who had a very indecent proposal to make. "I have a vision for the future.

280

First Born by Janelle Gabay

A future without war, with only peace, a future where everyone would be safe and would be cared for by my new government, my new military."

"Lies," Tarian growled but kept listening.

The Senator spun accusations in his eloquent speech. He charged Eleanor and the council with a lack of dedication to the mortals, putting Guardian needs first. He described a lack of empathy for mortal suffering while the immortals lived lavishly in the village and spoke of an absence of competence in governing, resulting in an inefficient and vulnerable Entente.

"None of this is true!" Tarian yelled. Tarian knew that under the Senator's well-manicured nails and powdered face laid an evil dictator trying to take all mortals' freedoms away.

"We know. It's pure propaganda but he has managed to persuade some of us. With this speech maybe more will follow. We need you to speak on our behalf. The Guardians need to hear from you, from Joe's immortal-born son. We need to give them a positive message of hope and erase this lie from their thoughts," Eleanor explained.

"He has to hear the rest, Eleanor," Audrey said.

Eleanor seemed reluctant to hit play.

"You have 48 hours to surrender the First born," the Senator's voice ended and the screen went black.

"Or else what? What are his demands?" Tarian asked.

"Tarian will not go," Carolyn ordered. "He will not go!"

Tarian slid his chair closer to his mother and held her hand.

"Or else he kills Charlie, then Gabe and then Maria," Audrey stated.

First Born by Janelle Gabay

She stared into Tarian's eyes with a look of defiance. *She had a plan.* He knew it. He also knew she was only willing to share her plan with him.

"No!" Carolyn barked, causing Chloe and Teresa to run into the kitchen.

"What's going on? Why is everyone here?" Teresa demanded.

"Hello, Teresa," Eleanor said. "Everything is going to be okay. Please take Chloe back into the living room."

Teresa did not move; she just focused on her mentor.

"Please, when we are done, I need you in the lab. I have new data for our cure for your friend," Eleanor explained.

With this, Teresa left with notable unhappiness.

"I'm going to get my brother and my friends," Tarian stated.

"We need you here. We cannot risk your life at this vulnerable time. Zachary has injected a poison into our community and you are the only antidote. I've already assembled a team to extract your brother and your friends. Without them as leverage, Zachary has nothing," Eleanor said.

"Do you have an execution team assembled? Because that is the only way to stop this man," Tarian said.

"Yes," Eleanor stated.

Eleanor wanted to have Tarian filmed in a simulated take down of Zachary and his traitors, yet he would actually remain safe and sound inside Guardian Headquarters. She was creating her own propaganda, and Tarian did not like being portrayed as something he was not. He wanted to fight in reality, not in some

First Born by Janelle Gabay

sort of commercial. Tarian began to protest but Audrey shot him another fierce glare. He remained silent.

Once Eleanor left with Teresa, Audrey and Tarian were anxious to leave as well. They politely lingered at the table to console Carolyn, but neither of them wanted to venture into a discussion about Tarian's position as the First Born icon. Neither of them wanted to lie to Carolyn. She deserved better than lies but the truth was too uncertain and death was a possibility. Audrey and Tarian wanted Carolyn to think they were content with Eleanor's plan.

The conversation kept circling and skirting Tarian and Audrey's true intentions. Tarian became guilt-ridden and Audrey became impatient.

"Let's go, Tarian." Audrey tugged on Tarian's sleeve.

Carolyn still shook, but she seemed mentally better. She was as stable as she was going to be until Charlie returned safe and sound. Carolyn looked at the two youthful faces in front of her with her own slightly lined face, and then she let go of Tarian's hand. Without a word, Carolyn stood up from the table. Her regal face bore the wrinkles of a woman whose forty-eight years of life had given her wisdom and courage. She would ask no more questions of Audrey nor would she make any more demands of Tarian. She simply grasped Audrey's hands and shook them fervently, then kissed her son's cheek. A whispered *I love you* grazed his ear. Then Carolyn left the kitchen to sit in the living room with her two youngest children.

Once out of the apartment and in the hallway, Tarian turned Audrey towards him and asked, "The tablet went black; how do you know his demands?"

283

First Born by Janelle Gabay

"All Guardian tablets went blank except Eleanor's. Her message had a photo at the end, a picture of a piece of paper with the execution information on it. It happened unexpectedly. We saw the photo; then it was gone. Luckily, Eleanor was not alone. I witnessed this along with four other Guardians, but we did not think fast enough to save it," she explained.

"Execution," he murmured. "I never thought the word execution would exist in my life." He stared once again at the swirled wood on the closed door of the apartment and prayed for the safety of his family inside.

"You can't cling to things, Tarian." Audrey placed her hand upon his shoulder and pulled him around.

"These aren't things. This is my family," he rebuffed, his stare incendiary.

"I meant ideas. As an immortal you have to accept change even when it's excruciatingly painful. Clinging to people only makes it hurt worse and devours productive energy. You have to learn to just be and to let your loved ones just be. Do you understand?" she asked.

"I get it. Believe me, I've done a lot of soul searching. Being immortal has made me very possessive of my family and even Delia. I realize that. But I can't stop. They will be gone from my life forever, how can I not cling to them? Seeing Delia in Roman's arms was like having my best…I don't know…my best car stolen." He paced struggling to find the words to describe the indescribable. "I've never felt like this before. I used to be carefree and happy."

"Reality check, most teenagers are carefree and happy, then they get older and wiser and more troubled. It's not just an

First Born by Janelle Gabay

immortal problem. It's a human problem," she exclaimed, and her kind tone was gone.

Tarian understood he was having a pity party for himself, and she would have none of it. She turned and marched on, and he hurried to catch up to her.

First Born by Janelle Gabay

THIRTY-FOUR
ROGUE

"Ready?" Audrey asked.

Tarian took her in as he walked toward her. She looked like a glorious and fearless predator, and he felt like a meager field mouse.

"No," he confessed, in a miserable tone of voice, still haunted by his mother's last kiss.

"Sucks for you," she said with a mocking smile.

They took their leave during Eleanor's meeting with the President of the Entente. Their absence would go unnoticed long enough for them to be well into enemy territory. Once Eleanor found out what they were up to, she would either offer them assistance or not.

They had begged Eleanor for the rescue mission, but she had denied them even after Tarian starred in her humiliating propaganda commercial. Luckily for Tarian, Audrey had a soldier's heart and wanted to help him. She understood and had all the contacts needed to conduct the mission rogue.

He buckled into the Guardian hover bike that was far more advanced and deadly than the one he had flown at EMA. He was basically strapped to a titanium death gun, but it flew with dauntless precision. Soon the thrill of speed engulfed him, and he felt rejuvenated.

Their mission was to land onto an Aircraft Carrier stationed off the coast close enough to the Coast Guard base for

First Born by Janelle Gabay

them to approach underwater. However, the sky gusted with brutal winds, icy rain thick as wool curtains, and vicious waves tossing spurts of salt water high into the air. Once within landing distance, Audrey turned to look at Tarian, giving him a wide grin and cocked, cheeky eyebrow then she dove her hover bike downwards.

He attempted to smile back at Audrey, but his palms sweated and his grip on the controls slipped several times. His heart pounded inside his chest cavity, and breathing inside his helmet became almost impossible. He mustered up his courage and dropped his bike down for a fast landing but failed.

On the third landing attempt, they received orders in their headsets to abort, but they refused to give up. Tarian's mind reeled. He imagined the unbearable pain to survive a fiery crash. Survival would take days of healing, time they could not afford to lose.

Tarian took one last loop around for a better angle then looked at Audrey and said, "Let's do it!"

"Yeeaahh!" Audrey yelled and flew downwards.

The city-sized, floating craft swayed so far left and right that it seemed they could end up in the hostile ocean. The bow and stern rocked like a turbulent seesaw, threatening to jam the front end of the bikes. Miraculously, Audrey landed perfectly. Tarian's landing was a bumpy, embarrassing mess.

"Smooth," Audrey teased.

"I told you to abort!" the Captain of the craft yelled. "Look at this bike."

"Sorry Captain. Don't worry, I'll take all the blame," Audrey insisted.

First Born by Janelle Gabay

"Damn right you will. This must be Tarian Prescott."

"Yes sir," Tarian answered.

"Welcome aboard."

"Thank you, sir."

Incessant pellets of rain pounded them as Captain Jeffrey escorted them under cover. Jeffrey did not stop scolding until they were standing in front of a massive map.

"Are you sure about this Audrey?" Captain Jeffrey looked long and hard at her.

Tarian got the impression they had worked together in the past. He must have owed her a favor.

"Why wouldn't I be?" Audrey smirked.

With an exhausted sigh, Captain Jeffrey offered his knowledge of the area and his newly uncovered information. Audrey had asked him to run his own surveillance operation, independent from the Guardians. She did not trust anyone.

"My men did not find your prisoners on the base with the rest. They are three and a half miles north in an underground bunker," Captain Jeffrey informed.

Audrey glanced at Tarian with raised eyebrows and a nod of her head. Deviations in missions were likely. They had expected it, but they did not like it.

Coordinates were established, and they suited up in the Entente's best SEAL suits. Captain Jeffrey did not fail them. The SEAL suit was like nothing Tarian had ever seen and would never have known existed. The material was designed to go from wet to dry in a matter of seconds. It could be worn in and out of the water without compromise. The aerodynamic suit held a

First Born by Janelle Gabay

multitude of waterproof secret compartments. They were walking/swimming toolboxes, and yet, as weightless as a feather.

Enormous waves thrashed cruelly against the vessel, rocking it uneasily and making their every movement a struggle. Audrey lost her balance while attempting to slip the Death Serum-filled needle safely into place and nearly jabbed her thigh with the point. Tarian rushed to her side in a flash, helping her up from the floor.

She accepted no help and told him, "I've got it."

He grunted at her stubbornness. "If you fall again, I'm taking it."

With assistance from Joe's notes, Eleanor had finally succeeded in duplicating the lethal serum, and now Audrey carried it. Who carried the weapon had been an ongoing argument, but Audrey had won. He was still her underling and ironically, this both infuriated and consoled him.

They plunged into the freezing waters of the Atlantic. Once submerged under the water, they felt more secure. The superb underwater propulsion devices kept them stable in the tumultuous currents. Time was the prevalent enemy. Luckily, their special suits and state-of-the-art equipment were built for speed. The accuracy of their landing location was critical. Captain Jeffrey did his best to educate them in their short period of time together. He had been stationed in this area for several years and knew its strengths and weaknesses.

The location took some delicate maneuvering to get to. The propulsion devices programmed with the coordinates guided them from the violent sea, through the narrows, and up the Somes Sound, where they entered land via an empty boathouse. For

First Born by Janelle Gabay

now, this unpopulated area of land was quiet. Audrey and Tarian knew they were borrowing time from the official attack. The theory being that Zachary would be so preoccupied fighting Eleanor's team that Tarian and Audrey could slip through unnoticed. But the team headed to the old base, not the hidden bunker. At which location Zachary lie in wait remained the mystery.

After trudging through the mountainous land for two hours, they hit upon the earth monster Captain Jeffrey had told them about. The building had been swallowed whole by dirt, ice and snow, leaving very little steel and concrete visible. Three well-armed, massive men stood alert in front of the mouth of the beast.

"It's okay, Tarian." Audrey assured when she saw his growing concern. "We knew your brother and friends were the well-guarded bait."

"They're your friends too," he stated.

"Yes, they are my friends too," she corrected softly.

He knew what she was trying to do. She was not this nice.

"I'm fine," he spat, but his frozen hands could barely grip his gun.

"Okay, that's all I needed to hear."

"Can't you warm this place up?" he questioned, giving her a wicked sideways glance to express his annoyance.

She ignored him, yet just then he felt a blast of warmth surround his frigid body.

These three thugs would not fall easily. Audrey and Tarian had to take the guards before they had time to contact

290

First Born by Janelle Gabay

Zachary. Since they had not yet been seen, Tarian and Audrey had the advantage.

Their weapons fired simultaneously, silently hitting both targets. Audrey swooped in on the third mark as graceful and quick as a lethal cheetah; however, her opponent reacted with experience. He had the ability to analyze the numerous activities and stimuli going on around him, take that information into his cerebral and find the correct solution. He thwarted her attack as he slammed his forearm into her chest, causing her neck to snap disturbingly backward. She fell onto the unforgiving ground and lay motionless.

Tarian's brain, thinking like a mortal and the shock of the kill move on his partner, sent him into a rage - a non-strategic, unprofessional rage. He created too much noise and commotion. His ridiculously obvious, civilian-like attack startled the thuggish guard. Tarian broke the guard's rhythm and looked so absurdly incapable that the guard took him for granted. Fortunately, he neglected to call for backup. The guard believed, as Tarian did, that he had killed Audrey, and that Tarian could be easily handled. So while Tarian thrashed about causing a diversion, Audrey awakened from her semiconscious state, cleared her head, and threw her steel blade directly into the center of the guard's back. He went down immediately, and she snapped his neck without hesitation. It was vicious and primal, and Tarian admired her for it.

"Seriously, Tarian," she said exasperatedly. "You have to start thinking like an immortal. Can you handle this? This is only round one, and you've failed."

First Born by Janelle Gabay

"I know, I know. I'm fine now. Just a little on edge. I got it now," he said, but she did not move. "I do, I do. Honest!"

"Grab all corresponding devices and weapons! When the other two come to, we don't want them having access to anything."

"How long have we got?" he asked

"Probably an hour until the stunners wear off."

It took them several minutes to strip the two soldiers of their clothes and weapons. Hoping to fool the surveillance, they quickly dressed in the enemy's uniform. Another challenge was finding the entrance. A thick, avocado green moss, more abundant than any he had ever seen in the woods of Salem covered the door. The overgrowth of much voluminous, thorny shrubbery had also been a deterrent while a layer of snow that padded the entrance hindered the mission even more. Nature had gone out of its way to form an unwelcoming presence, which he was sure the Senator helped along by abandoning all maintenance. Tarian expected eight, creepy, furry spider legs to curl around his bare fingers as he fumbled to find a keyhole or doorframe. Shivers ran up his spine at this thought.

Finally, Audrey found the opening. She gently put the key into the hole while he kept his back to her and his eyes toward the path. No one approached. The door opened smoothly to their surprise. With so much damp dirt and decay, he expected to hear a loud creaking noise, but they were inside without notice.

Upon entering, blinding darkness surrounded their bodies until their eyes adjusted. Every several feet there were tiny lights giving off a soft yellow glow to guide them. The hall was a long and claustrophobic underground tunnel made entirely of gray

First Born by Janelle Gabay

steel. Tarian felt the familiar strangle of an oxygen dump. He grabbed his throat and gasped for breath.

"Are you okay?" Audrey asked.

Once again, he proved to be a reject soldier. "Yes," he said and forced his breath to slow down, but he was not okay. He felt nauseous inside his gut, and his head began to ache.

"Are you sure, you don't look good?"

"I'll be fine. Just having a little trouble breathing."

"It's just like in the game. Remember?"

"Yes." His voice struggled to release words.

"Zachary has set this trap up strictly for you. Calm yourself."

"I'm going to pass out."

"It's okay, calm your breathing. You must put mind over matter. Concentrate." She looked into his concerned, brown eyes and gently rubbed his shoulders.

Her touch worked. As he looked into her stalwart iridescent eyes, his strength grew. His breathing steadied, his head became clear again, and nausea in his stomach relaxed.

"Thanks." The color in his face returned.

She gave him her affable smile, the smile he loved. The softness in her eyes made him feel content. Her eyes were brilliant, clear-cut diamonds layered with varying shades of blue and a hint of silver that sparkled. They could look extremely icy; he had been at the receiving end of those fearsome eyes way too many times. Yet, they could look dazzling and inviting. The latter softened her angular face, and when combined, her icy stare became even more intriguing.

First Born by Janelle Gabay

The hallway gradually sloped and morphed into an open space again, still resembling a submarine. It was filled with thin, glass screens monitoring inmates. The young technician watching the screens did not see the trespassers until it was too late for him. The needle from Tarian's syringe plunged into the kid's arm before he could do anything about it. He would sleep for a while and then not remember a thing once he awoke.

"Found'em," Audrey said after scavenging through a clipboard with a meal log on it. "They're scattered down different hallways."

"Charlie first," Tarian said.

"No, Maria and Gabe, they can help us fight off the guards. Your brother's in law school, not military training."

"Fine." He knew she was right.

Suspiciously, they did not find a guard stationed at any of the three cell doors. It was as easy as getting three dogs out the kennel. This baffling lack of security made them uneasy. After the ecstatic reunions filled with embraces, tears and laughter, they sat perplexed next to the young technician lying crumpled on the floor.

"What the hell, Guys!" Maria unfolded the young man's legs.

Tarian realized how much he had missed her brashness.

"You could at least lay this poor kid down nicely." Maria proceeded to turn the young man gently onto his back, cradling his head so it would not thud to the hard surface. She was a mirror of opposites. Her coarse speech and body language made her tender actions seem misplaced, but at heart she was a very nurturing person.

First Born by Janelle Gabay

"Happy?" Audrey jeered at Maria after the young man lay more comfortable.

"Yes!" she stated.

"They're not with the Prevallers," Charlie flatly stated. "I figured that out when they let me outside into the yard for some sunlight. Senator Eastwood took me to another building, a giant compound."

"What?" Audrey's head snapped around to examine Charlie.

"The Coast Guard base?" Tarian asked.

"No. At first I thought I was a political prisoner. I was beaten, tortured, starved, the whole nine yards. I assume you all were too." Charlie gestured to Gabe and Maria.

When they nodded in agreement, acid-filled vomit hit the back of Tarian's throat, but he managed to swallow it back down and cover up his guilt-ridden disgust.

"Then it stopped. It stopped abruptly. Suddenly, I was like last year's Christmas toy. They no longer had any reason to play with me, so obviously, a new toy came into town," Charlie concluded, and Gabe and Maria nodded in agreement.

"That still doesn't infer that they are not the Prevallers," Audrey said.

"No, but that along with the fact that most of these people are not military soldiers. Don't get me wrong, there are a few thugs around here, but I get the feeling most of them are scientists. I also believe that they are not as numerous as they want us to think. On several occasions, I've noticed a very limited number of guards. Always the same people. No new faces," Charlie said.

First Born by Janelle Gabay

"Maybe the Prevallers don't have as many followers as they'd like us to believe," Audrey said.

"Oh no," said Charlie, "The Prevallers' movement is huge. There will be a border war. No doubt about it. The Entente is vulnerable. I'm pro-Entente, but I do understand the motives of the Prevallers, and why they've been able to rally so many allies."

"How do you know all of this?" Tarian asked.

"I'm going to Harvard. Do you know how many Senators' sons and daughters attend this school? It's ridiculously stacked with influential people."

"It doesn't matter." Audrey shot to her feet. "We need to get you all back to Headquarters."

"Wait a minute." Tarian stood to face Audrey. "We need to find out what's really going on here."

"No," Audrey countered.

Tarian did not like her tone of voice. "You can't order me, Audrey."

"You wanted to secure your brother and friend's safety. That's our mission. Nothing more. I can't secure their safety if we go off on an AWOL mission without proper channels and information." With a rigid jaw, she growled the words at him.

Her voice discharged intensity and nastiness, but Tarian saw her eyes displayed concern. She was worried the three rescues would get killed, and Tarian would suffer.

"You're right. Let's get them home safely." Tarian gathered supplies and readied to leave.

"What?" Maria said. "I'm nobody's fucking Christmas toy. I want to know what the hell's going on."

First Born by Janelle Gabay

"Me too, Tarian," Gabe said earnestly.

Audrey paced the floor like an Alpha dog whose pack was challenging her. "What do you know of this other facility?" Audrey directed the question to Charlie.

"Well, I know this is just a mound of dirt where they hold prisoners, nothing more," he said. "I believe the main building is a few miles north. He took me to it, but I was blindfolded. I've been closely listening to the conversations of our keepers and Zachary. He has visited me several times, and I've observed him closely. I honestly think he was hoping I would cooperate with his cause, but instead, I spit in his face. SOB has some balls to think after he's beaten me, that I'd follow him. If Dad only knew what his friend was capable of!"

Tarian heard the hatred in his brother's words, stinging him to the core. Charlie did not even know the half of it. After all of this craziness, Tarian would have to tell him that Zachary murdered their father and that he was immortal. How was he going to accept all of that?

"What have you heard Zachary say exactly?" Audrey's eyes narrowed and her keen instincts heightened.

"I don't remember…but his eyes were different. They were infinitely black. He wore sunglasses the entire time I was with him, but when he took them off to wipe the sweat from his nose, I saw his eyes, strange and fascinating. Then…," Charlie hesitated. "It sounds stupid… but I think he was talking about babies."

"Babies?" Audrey's brow furrowed and her head twitched to one side. "Like children?"

"No, like newborns," he answered.

First Born by Janelle Gabay

"Tarian!" Audrey gasped, looking at him with horror-filled eyes.

Tarian saw Audrey stumble as she approached him. He positioned himself to catch her just in case she collapsed. She was so strong and virile, yet seemed fragile at this moment. He knew her very well, but sometimes, he did not know her at all. He was not unaccustomed to her moments of weakness, but they were so few and far between. He remembered the beauty of her vulnerability in the apartment in Boston just before they found Delia with Roman. He remembered how her strange and delicate face had entranced him at that moment. He felt that same pull towards her now. He believed they were meant to share the burden of this journey together, and yet, she had held the position as the leader, the rock, the alpha. Would she reject his help, his concern? Her eyes weighed upon his as if she did, in fact, want him to step up, to be an equal, so he did.

First Born by Janelle Gabay

THIRTY-FIVE
SUCKER PUNCH

"Charlie, lead the way," Tarian stated. He had to know the truth. If he died here on this frigid, rocky mountain, injected with Death Serum, at least he would know the truth.

After Audrey re-injected the technician so he would sleep longer, Charlie led them down the long, dungeon-like tunnel to exit the facility. The crisp, chilly air hit Tarian's face refreshing him, but the hard, closed-fist sucker punch that followed derailed him. Charlie caught him before his face slammed the ground, while Gabe landed a convincing punch squarely on the man's temple, knocking him out cold. Unfortunately, the other guard had enough time to contact a superior before the bullet took his life. How much information he was able to give up was unknown.

It was survival instinct for Audrey, but she lowered her head once she realized she shot him dead. This realization came rapidly as she knew the bullet had pierced his heart. She was a trained assassin and did not miss. She did not want to kill a man for doing his job, especially a young man. He looked to be about twenty-five, someone's son or grandson.

"We can't get caught," Audrey said in a ragged voice.

A stunned Charlie whispered so only Tarian could hear, "She's charming." His words were sarcastic and cynical.

Tarian looked up at him with a pounding headache. "Do you want to live or die?"

299

First Born by Janelle Gabay

"Touché little brother!"

Tarian staggered back to his feet while Gabe, Maria and Audrey gathered the guard's transmitter. The aged and tarnished machine had definitely transmitted an electromagnetic wave to someone.

"How did he have this communication device? We took all of their equipment," Tarian asked Audrey.

"I don't know. He must've left here to retrieve it or he had it hidden somewhere. He has no weapons so my guess is that they had the emergency back-up radio hidden somewhere."

"Let's move, Audrey," Maria said impatiently. "If we've been made, we need to get the hell out of here."

"Let's go, Charlie," Audrey said.

A nod from his brother reassured Charlie, and he continued moving forward. At this point, it was evident Charlie had the most knowledge of Zachary's operation. As they started north, Audrey distributed weapons to Gabe and Maria, but left out Charlie. Tarian quietly slipped him a sharp, steel blade. He knew his brother could fight, but he doubted he could shoot. A knife would be helpful in a fight, and if he came up against a gunfight, he'd be at the disadvantage with or without a gun.

Given the extensive training and weaponry on hand, they would have been at an advantage; however, the lack of proper footwear for Gabe, Maria and Charlie crippled the escape. The thick, icy jagged rocks, uneven pathways, sliced into their prison shoes. Luckily, the damaged shoes provided just enough material to prevent serious injury. But now that it was compromised, there was nothing between skin and freezing cold ground. Audrey worked her gift but she could still see their fragile feet

300

First Born by Janelle Gabay

subject to hypothermia. In true EMA fashion, this drawback did not deter them, but it slowed them down considerably.

The dense, wicked terrain reminded Tarian of the elaborate capture-the-flag game the four of them had endured during their training in the village. He saw shadows and a monkey and feared they were being tracked. No one else witnessed these creatures because everyone else gazed downward, hoping to avoid more injury to their feet. Audrey had the front, careful to guide them through areas with less ice and snow. Tarian had the rear, and felt it was his job to keep all of them safe. But he could not shake the uneasy feeling that something unwanted followed behind him. Fear tightened his abdomen and heightened his senses. Several glances backward found only an empty path, but this fact did not settle his prickly nerves.

Tarian was determined not to let his friends nor brother get captured again, but the frailty of their plan sank into his thoughts. His suspicions were secured once he saw the vastness of the facility and heard the whirling blades of many tiltrotors. Dozens of men with machine guns walking the perimeter made Tarian feel foolish. At the sight of such an intricately designed, lethal compound, Tarian knew this place held something extremely precious to Zachary. Something he would viciously protect. Looking ahead at his motley crew, he felt the weight of inadequacy. They were undersupplied. Tarian saw that Audrey knew it too. Her shifting skin, hawk-like stare and taut mouth mirrored his.

First Born by Janelle Gabay

"What the hell kind of Christmas present is in there?" Maria' eyes opened wide as she viewed the ceremony of weapons displayed around the building.

They all stood hidden by the shadows of the forest looking down onto the building from the sizable hill they had just surmounted. The tan, sharp-edged erection of concrete that sat at the bottom of the bowl-like valley looked as deadly as a scorpion in the bottom a glass container. The large hills encircling the building provided the ultimate security and conquering this place on foot would be impossible. The inner slopes of the hills were intentionally bare to make intruders highly visible. A person could easily be seen from the ground, tracking down the snow-covered slope to get in or climbing up to get out; either way the person would be a moving target. Another scan of the facility and then a glance at Audrey affixed Tarian's belief that they needed a new plan of action. He was going to have a private conversation with her, but first he needed to get Gabe, Maria and Charlie someplace safe and warm.

"What do we do now?" Gabe asked.

"We can't go down there," Maria said.

"Is there a tunnel?" Audrey asked Charlie.

"I don't know. He's definitely upped his game. I don't remember armed tiltrotors," Charlie said noticing the swirling blades getting closer to their location.

"Get down!" ordered Tarian.

They all fell flat to the ground. The pulsated wind of the tiltrotor swept passed the five of them, but they went unnoticed. The deadly bladed bird steadily flew above them then traveled out-of-sight.

First Born by Janelle Gabay

"We have to wait for nightfall." Audrey slowly stood up and wiped the dirt and snow from the front of her uniform.

"I'm about to catch frost bite and I'm starving," Maria said. "We have not eaten since breakfast, and not only is the food crap, but there is barely a mouthful of the mystery cuisine. They want to keep us weak and it's working."

"That looks like a cabin over there." Gabe pointed to a heap of logs that had been thrown together by unskilled laborers long gone.

The five of them trudged the remaining small distance to the cabin. It stood dwarfish, vacant and nonthreatening. Tarian ducked severely to squeeze his tall body inside but Audrey walked through the threshold unchallenged. Together they swept the area before the rest staggered inside.

"It will have to do," Audrey said. "But I doubt there is any food in here."

"We have rations in our suits, Audrey, remember?" Tarian told her.

Captain Jeffrey had gone over all the compartments of the land and sea combat suits, and one compartment had packages of food.

"Oh that's right," Audrey said, smiling at him. Audrey peeled off the guard's clothing covering her SEAL suit and looked down at her outfit with all of its secret compartments. She fumbled through the different pockets without success.

"This one." Tarian reached out and opened the pocket on her left thigh. Tarian felt Maria's interrogating glare on his body.

"Thanks," Audrey said, but did not look at him.

303

First Born by Janelle Gabay

"You're welcome." He enjoyed knowing something she didn't.

Again he admired her state of amenability. A creature of fierce beauty when she was strong and fighting, but the allure of her true, vulnerable self entrapped him. Knowing she would find the remark sexist, he smiled inside. *One can't fight genetics*, he thought. As a man, it was a nice feeling to be able to help her. He didn't get the opportunity very often.

"Okay, I have a package of dried something and two protein bars. What do you have?" she asked Tarian, meeting his stare.

"The same." Tarian handed her his meager rations.

Audrey proceeded to distribute the food evenly. She added a few extra pieces of protein bar to Gabe, Maria and Charlie's portions, as she figured they needed more sustenance.

The cabin's moldy smell proved it had sat empty of human life for years, but several pesky insects inhabited it. Veins of black ran horizontally through the faded rust colored wood walls. The interior throbbed with life as the millions of creepy critters crawled along these cracks. Tarian felt as if he had been consumed by the belly of the cabin and could not shake off the false feeling that tiny bugs burrowed into skin. The sensation to itch every inch of his body overwhelmed him, but he overcame it until miniscule flying black specs surrounded him. They had stirred a nest of tiny, flying nats that promptly proceeded to devour Maria and Tarian's blood. They jerked and kicked their arms and legs to deter the small but incredibly irritating pests.

Distracted and annoyed by their noise, Audrey gave Maria her shoes and ordered, "Go get water."

First Born by Janelle Gabay

"I'll go. You stay here," Tarian advised Maria looking at the barrowed shoes that were a size too small.

"No, I'll go too," Maria responded, looking at her feet as well. "Really, I'm okay now. All that flapping around raised my body temperature."

Tarian knew Audrey's gift had also helped to raise her temperature, but he hesitated to reveal this information to Maria. Uncertain which Guardian secrets mortals were allowed to know.

"You have on a survival kit. Isn't there something to repel bugs?" Maria barked.

"Yes," Tarian said, as he remembered seeing a small aerosol spray bottle. He savagely ripped at his suit, searching for the bottle he remembered. He pulled it out of its compartment with satisfaction and pushed it into Maria's face.

"That's sunscreen you idiot," she said.

"What?" he looked at the label on the bottle and saw SPF 55. "Ahhhh," he sighed loudly and Maria laughed. "Oh I'm funny, am I?" He pretended to wrestle her like his little sister. He continued to riffle through his survival suit and did, in fact, have insect repellent. They lathered every square inch of their bodies.

"So what's up with you and Audrey," Maria queried.

"Nothing," he said, surprised by her question. But he welcomed this brief distraction from their dire circumstances.

"Do I look like I'm stupid?"

"Yes," he teased.

"You are about to get slapped."

"Nothing. She's my," he said, but no words escaped him.

305

First Born by Janelle Gabay

She was his everything, but how could he explain that without sounding like he was in love with her.

"Exactly," Maria said with satisfaction.

"No, it's just that she has been there before. She knows what it's like to go from mortal to immortal. She's helped me a lot."

Maria nodded in understanding. "I get it. I feel like Gabe gets me because we are from the same community. Our families know each other. It's comforting to have an equal."

Her words were meant to be supportive, but in actuality the words highlighted the inequality of his relationship to Audrey. The fact was he knew very little of her background.

Heavy silence lingered between them for a while. Tarian fidgeted uneasily as a sense of urgency washed over him, but he realized nightfall remained an hour away. He could indulge a little longer in conversation and felt a confession on his tongue.

"I like her." Tarian started to tell her how he had dreamt about Audrey during the game, and how the dream had overheated him with pleasure and angst. But he bit the words back.

"I know," Maria replied, and she smiled a huge, toothy grin at him that warmed his soul. "I'm glad for you."

"Is it that obvious?"

"It's obvious that she likes you too."

"It is?"

"Yes, Fool!" Maria slapped the side of his head as she said the words.

First Born by Janelle Gabay

"She looks at me and sees Joe's son. I know it. I can feel it. I'm too young. She is, after all, hundreds of years older than me."

"Yes, technically she's a lot older but physically you're very close in age and physically you're a hot ass man!"

"Do you think I'm sexy?" He said in a funny accent placing his hands on his waist like a silly schoolgirl.

They both burst out raucous laughter and forgot about the irritating insect bites and their duty to get water. They forgot about the fact that they were about to delve into an intricate labyrinth created by a treacherous immortal, who may very well take any future they were dreaming about away from them.

"What about Delia?" Maria moved in the direction of water.

"Well, she doesn't understand or like the whole immortal thing and she is in love with Roman Feng." His words were bitter and dry. He sounded like a jealous boyfriend. He guessed he was a jealous ex-boyfriend. He did not mention the severity of her illness. Voicing it aloud made it too real.

"Oh I get it. She's afraid she's going to get old and you aren't." Maria knelt to scoop the running stream of water into her bottle.

"Maybe, but I think her hatred for immortals stems more from her father's abuse; he's the reason she's sick," Tarian said. Even though Maria looked stunned by his confession, he did not go into the details of how Delia's father had betrayed her. "Let's just say, Delia had plenty of time to analyze her father's bad intentions. Whether all of her accusations are true or false does not matter. What matters is how she feels as a daughter of a

First Born by Janelle Gabay

horrible father. She said things to me like 'how was he going to leave us?' 'Fake his death?' 'Murder us?' 'Disappear?' She seemed pretty hurt by the reality of an immortal parenting a mortal, and I have to agree with her."

"This whole situation is messed up." Maria tightened the cap on the bottle.

"We better get the water back before Audrey hunts us down," he said giving her a devilish grin. He could envision the look of vexation stretching across the sharp angles of Audrey's face.

First Born by Janelle Gabay

THIRTY-SIX
LIVING GARDEN

At precisely three a.m., Audrey and Tarian proceeded down the hillside leaving behind a heavily sedated Maria, Gabe and Charlie. They would not wake until the mission was completed. Audrey and Tarian had come to this agreement earlier that evening. They realized the others were still very weak from their incarceration. Plus five people entering the facility would be too noticeable. Also they lacked the support of Headquarters and had no links to the outside world, which meant a very slim chance for success. Tarian would not risk his brother's life, nor the lives of his mortal friends.

The darkness hid them but the silence was tricky, every footstep had to be calculated or else they would be heard. They treaded carefully to avoid trampling fallen tree branches and miniscule twigs. The snow blanketed the trail, hindering their speed. To their luck, the occasional rustling noise they made went undetected while the blackness of night camouflaged their approach.

Soon they met the fringe of brightness radiating from security floodlights. They had reached the concrete monstrosity unnoticed. They approached what they believed to be the correct door based on Charlie's vague recollection of the layout of the building. Audrey silently prowled up to the guard in front of the entrance and took him down before he knew what was happening. The guard was stripped of his weapons, hog-tied and

309

First Born by Janelle Gabay

gagged in a matter of seconds. Because it was the middle of the night, the halls were secluded from people but not from the watchful eyes of cameras. Audrey and Tarian had their guard uniforms on from earlier that day when they took down the guards at the prison bunker. They attempted to look official and carefully strode down the long, narrow corridor.

Once past the entrance, Tarian could not rid himself of the cancerous fear and uncertainty that spread inside him. Sweat rolled down his neck despite the frosty air. Everything about this place seemed wrong and horrible. *Wrong. Horrible.* The corridors were a labyrinth that snared them in its twisted halls and disoriented turns. They found several rooms empty of people, spotlessly clean in appearance, and filled with advanced medical equipment, dangerous weaponry and the latest information technology. None of it was set up yet, but new home anticipation hung in the air. The moving boxes were in place, piled high and waiting, but waiting for what? What did the new homeowners have in mind for such an elaborate house? Finally, they rounded the last corner and found the heart of the facility - the precious jewel Zachary coveted.

The horror went beyond Tarian's wildest imagination. Tiny hospital beds were lined up in rows upon rows and filled with infants. Crying, sleeping and curious infants were everywhere connected to strange, brand new machines. Tarian recognized the heart monitors but the other data was mysteriously confusing; however, instinctively he knew the data being collected was diabolical. Somehow the newborns' genetics were being influenced, measured and monitored. Tarian shuttered with every beep of sound or twitch of movement on the screens. The

First Born by Janelle Gabay

Senator had his army right here in this room. Charlie was correct; the Prevallers were not involved in this madness. The impending war had been the perfect distraction and the Prevallers were the ideal cover to hide the truly terrorizing operation. The Senator was a magician and like all great magic tricks, misdirection was the key.

Tarian touched one of the tiny hands as it reached upwards out of his plastic container towards nothing. Instinctively, the five little fingers curled around his one digit with amazing strength when it felt he was near. The need for human touch and interaction began at days, possibly hours old. But the touch for Tarian was electric. It coursed through his veins and froze him. He saw images of Delia and himself vividly through the touch of this newborn clone. And then, he also saw his mother.

Why are you showing this to me? He pondered. The little being twitched and kicked impulsively as all newborns do making it impossible for Tarian to tell if it felt the sensation and saw the images too.

Filtering through the air was a serene composition of symphony music, but it was not calming this little one. It was wide-awake and very interested in Tarian. It smelled of fresh laundry and sour milk, and its eyes spread wide like a night owl. The infant looked haunted and familiar.

Tarian turned to look at Audrey. His confused face starred into her horrified eyes and parted lips.

"We have to destroy them," she said, slowly and deliberately.

First Born by Janelle Gabay

"What? No!" he scowled, petrified at the idea of killing newborns.

"Tarian, these are not human babies. These are genetically mutated, immortal clones."

"No, it spoke to me," Tarian explained.

Audrey's head snapped around to face his. "It's your gift. Exactly what happened?" Her expression filled with delicate intrigue.

"When I touched it, I felt a shock or a sensation. It was weird. I don't know. Then I saw my mother's face." He explained as best he could, but there were no words to describe what he had witnessed.

"Hello, Kids." A recognizable voice said from behind them.

"Zachary! Have you gone completely insane?" Audrey's voice guttural and her eyes bulged from their sockets.

The Senator stood in front of approximately twelve armed guards. He wore a liar's face and his eyes were no longer caramel brown. Tarian wondered what had changed them to oil black. They had been naïve to assume they could waltz in here undetected. An operation of this magnitude was too valuable to be left under insufficient security. It occurred to Tarian Zachary would want them to align with him. In order to survive, Tarian and Audrey were going to have to pretend they would consider his mad scheme.

"Audrey, you have lived as long as I have. You have seen the destruction these mortals favor year after year. They continue to repeat history. They never learn. They need to be controlled

First Born by Janelle Gabay

and now we have the numbers to keep world peace," Zachary said.

The Senator drew out each syllable making it painful for Tarian to listen to him. His words reflected pure madness, yet he looked like a charming, educated congressman.

"At the expense of people's freedom of choice," Audrey argued with quick, clipped words.

"And what do they do with this freedom of choice? Dictators, under the guise of whatever idea of the century is popular, threaten this freedom, killing innocents. Then governments with good intentions end up in a useless war, accomplishing nothing. Religious crusaders will murder an entire race for their own beliefs without any scientific data to substantiate their truths. Nothing changes. This repeats again and again and again. A cyclical pattern of ignorance. I'd like to live out the rest of my immortal years in peace, wouldn't you?" Zachary's lack of anger or emotion was more frightening than anything else.

"Your ideals sound just like the 'good intentions' you just spoke of," Audrey snarled, refusing to take the arm he offered.

"No," he spit back at her, finally raising his voice and sounding a little more human.

The Senator was insulted that she turned his words against him. Tarian could see she knew he was not stable and bit back another retort knowing, as he did, that survival relied on their ability to appease him.

"Come, let me show you the product." Zachary put his arm around Tarian and gently guided him forward.

First Born by Janelle Gabay

The Senator spoke in an eerily calm and saccharine voice as he strolled further into the room. They were soon surrounded with the cloned infants and their disturbing noises. It felt like they were passing over the threshold into hell. The acrid smells of human waste inside full diapers combined with lavender scented cleaning fluids created an intoxicating potion. Innocence mixed with evil swirled and dissolved inside the room and Tarian understood Audrey's point. The little beings looked pure and harmless but were an alchemy of corrupt ingenuity designed for mass destruction.

"Your father admired my vision. His accident was a pure shame," Zachary said as he continued the tour of his hidden netherworld.

"Accident?" Tarian asked. Zachary was not making any sense.

"Yes, of course, Tarian. You didn't think I killed him on purpose. I loved him like a brother." The words flowed from Zachary's tongue like honey.

The Senator spoke with conviction and his eyes did not betray him, but his grip on Tarian's shoulder tightened as he lied. It took all of Tarian's willpower to smile and nod at his demented captor.

"Zachary, these are just newborns. You won't have soldiers for several years," Audrey stated.

Tarian saw her eyes scanning the entire facility, mapping out all persons and objects.

"That's the beauty, Audrey. I will mold them. I will train them. I can guarantee Eleanor; they will embody good values

First Born by Janelle Gabay

and fight for the Guardians' cause. Together we can accomplish great things with these tiny marvels. Where is Eleanor?"

"What do you mean?" Tarian asked.

"She is late. That's not like her," Zachary said, still possessing his serpent stride and strange cadence.

Was he expecting her? Did she know about this facility? How long had she known? Tarian thought.

As if she could read his thoughts, Audrey glanced at him with a lined forehead. This development had to be handled delicately, for they did not know what could be believed.

Zachary strolled him arm and arm through the madness inhaling deeply and gazing proudly at his work as if they were amongst rows of beautiful roses. The idea of what Tarian was witnessing finally destroyed his will. Thick breath filled his mouth and lungs leaving his brain unoxygenated. His knees began to buckle. He tried not to crumble. Successfully, he forced himself to stand tall. He would not give Zachary the satisfaction of weakness but Zachary sensed his fatigue.

"Hold on, Tarian, just a few more steps. It's all right, Son. You are home now." Zachary smiled.

"I'm not your son," Tarian affirmed, as the venom in his veins rose to the surface, breaking through his composure of false amiability.

He couldn't go along with this façade any longer, but Audrey came to his side and pulled him close to her body, stopping a further outburst. She wanted his silence, and he gave it to her hoping she had a plan to get them out of the freak show alive.

315

First Born by Janelle Gabay

"Audrey, you are so fond of him. Isn't that wonderful?" Zachary's oily black eyes narrowed and his posture stiffened. "Here, here we are."

Zachary opened a smooth, white door that loomed before them at the end of the neat rows of cloned newborns. The room turned out to be an apartment. It was floor to ceiling stark white. White painted walls, white tiled floors, white leather covered couches, and the kitchen held white cabinets and countertops, and finally, a chair with white upholstery sat in front of a window. Tarian envisioned numerous children clones with dirty handprints covering the pristine whiteness with smudges of browns, reds and yellows, and it satisfied his desire to shove this false heaven in Zachary's face. The Senator was trying to sterilize his contaminated vision, but Tarian knew it would never work.

The view from the single white chair did not look upon the outside world. Instead, it provided a focus on Zachary's obscene, living garden. He gestured for Tarian to sit in the chair and gaze upon his masterpiece. It was more than sick.

"What do you expect me to do?" Tarian asked.

"Nothing, Son. You've done so much already. I can't thank you enough. I want you to sit here and watch your children grow. You were the first. We will need to continue to monitor you in order to secure the accuracy of our children. Sit," he commanded.

Tarian did not move. He would never sit in that devil's throne. They glared at one another for several seconds.

"Sit!" Zachary bellowed.

The calm facade Zachary had displayed vanished. Irritated by Tarian's refusal, he stalked over to Audrey, fastened

First Born by Janelle Gabay

his arm around her, and said, "Audrey Darling, tell him to sit down now."

Tarian quickly sat and Zachary released her, returning to Tarian's side. With one swipe of the device in Zachary's hand, solid steel cuffs encircled Tarian wrists and ankles. Once the chair had completed the binding, he prepped Tarian for an intravenous needle.

"What are you doing to him?" Audrey asked in a rough voice filled with exhaustion and helplessness.

"He is dehydrated. He needs fluids and nutrition," Zachary said.

Audrey released a sigh of anxiety that echoed throughout the room. Her momentary relief depleted her energy, and she collapsed into the couch and crumpled. She put her head in her hands and cried and that's when Tarian knew they had been beat. Zachary had won.

"Audrey, I would never hurt you or Tarian. You must know that. You are safe now."

If Zachary's intention was to create a safe haven, he was doing a poor job. The symphonic music meant to put them at peace only sounded ominous, and his syrupy sweet voice pushed them further into the depths of despair.

"Okay, okay, I know, I know," she mumbled over and over again, trying to muffle the sounds of his voice and music. She had the Death Serum inside her pocket, but Zachary was well armed. The serum might as well have been miles away since she could not inject it.

Tarian's mind fervently thought, but everywhere he looked men and women with automatic machine guns stood

317

First Born by Janelle Gabay

guard. He could not reach his gun and he knew Audrey could not risk using hers. The rows of cloned newborns seemed endless, like looking into an infinite carnival mirror. If they started a gunfight, the newborn clones would surely get caught in the crossfire. He knew Audrey said they had to destroy them but he felt conflicted. He could not murder newborns, not even cloned ones.

As Tarian gazed out the glass at the little stringy hands, skinny fingers, tiny plump feet, and pudgy toes, he knew he could not eliminate them. Suddenly, he looked more closely at their petite round faces and gasped. These were boys *and* girls. He had assumed they were all males; no, that's not true, before he thought of them as things. He saw now they had a familiarity that tapped his soul. Once the recognition hit his brain, the monitor he was hooked up to began to beep loudly and the needle erratically swooped across the page in violent skips and leaps.

"What did you do?" Audrey screamed at Zachary.

"Nothing, he is stressed,"

Tears rolled down Tarian's face in voluminous streams of agony and his body began to convulse, seizing in a horrific display of his inner nightmares.

"Liar! What are you doing?" she howled, as she viewed his body thrash against its will while the tethers tried in vain to cease his outburst.

It was visually horrific, but he felt no pain, just rage and fear. Audrey shot to his side and gently wiped the tears from his reddened face. One of her delicate but strong hands placed on his chest was all it took to extinguish his writhing.

318

First Born by Janelle Gabay

She felt the electricity flow between their two bodies. She saw into his soul and he saw into hers. Flashes of visions of Joe crossed between them. Distant memories from centuries ago flooded into Tarian's mind, while Audrey saw such things as Tarian's birth and the horrible school bus accident that should have taken his life. Her true feelings for him as his for her crossed over in this unique gift of communication that Tarian possessed. Suddenly the flush of pleasure pivoted, turning into torment. Audrey jerked her hand away from his chest after she felt as if she had been stung.

She bent her head and whispered into his ear, "What is it, Tarian?"

"The clones." He looked into her soothing blue, silver eyes.

She turned to study them from his vantage point, and he saw the flash of his realization cross over her face.

"They are me and Delia," he stated in a surprisingly restrained voice.

Zachary refused to listen to Tarian's words. He was busy sterilizing equipment and marking notes down on a chart as if everything was normal.

"Aren't they!" The words flew from Tarian's mouth in a masculine deep scream.

"Yes," Zachary said again without emotion or reaction to Tarian's outburst. "Isn't it magnificent. They are not clones. That's the beauty of it. They are your offspring. Yours and Delia's."

"And my mother's." Tarian's body went limp.

First Born by Janelle Gabay

Zachary did not verify this fact, but Tarian knew it was true. The newborn had showed him in his touch. Zachary had created immortals concocted out of a powerful alchemical blood mixture.

Audrey spoke no words of comfort to Tarian, and no words of disgust to Zachary. It simply was too unbelievable. She slid her hand into Tarian's and they both out the window at the absurdity of his offspring, rows and rows of offspring.

As they surveyed the room once more, a figure came into view. It entered from the door at the other end of the long nursery, the same door Audrey and Tarian had entered over an hour ago. Her face quickly came into view. It was Eleanor but she was alone. Tarian now knew this meant she was either working with Zachary or trapped as they were. Zachary and his guards left the room when he saw her and locked the door.

First Born by Janelle Gabay

THIRTY-SEVEN
POINT OF THE NEEDLE

"Get me out of here," Tarian told Audrey.

She scavenged the chair and all of its gadgets for the control that released the implacable steel cuffs.

"He's taken it," Audrey said, and they both looked out the window to see Zachary holding a flat square pad. It was the control panel for his torture chair.

"You don't think Eleanor is going to negotiate with him?" he asked Audrey.

"No," she said, but offered no other explanation. "He's changed. His eyes..."

Tarian nodded. He did not need further explanation they had both seen the strange otherness that Zachary now possessed.

"He's stronger now too," she stated in words barely a whisper.

Tarian and Audrey watched as Zachary and Eleanor conversed for what felt like hours. The walls were sound proof so they could not hear a word, but visually it looked as if they were making an ordinary business deal. Zachary's wicked grin never shifted and Eleanor's green eyes never tensed. The conversation seemed civilized until Eleanor suddenly, with one unexpected move, stabbed Zachary in the heart.

"Oh my God! Did you see that?" Tarian's head jolted forward but the steel straps kept his body in place.

"She has Death Serum!" Audrey ran to the window.

321

First Born by Janelle Gabay

All Tarian could see was Eleanor and Zachary tangled on the floor. In unison, the men and women surrounding the perimeter began the emergency procedures they had been trained to execute. Half of them remained in place and raised their weapons, while the other half rescued the offspring. The guards quickly removed the crib-like, plastic containers and stacked them one on top of the other. They wheeled them at rapid speed toward an exit on the west wall. This escape route had clearly been meticulously practiced and well organized.

Audrey rushed to the exit, pulling and pushing, but it would not open. She kicked the door and banged the lock, but still it did not budge. Her immortal strength was useless against Zachary's modified steel and security controlled lock. Next she shot it with her gun and destroyed the lock, but the door remained sealed shut.

Outside, Guardians and military swarmed the nursery while Audrey and Tarian were forced to sit helplessly inside the white room and watch the bloody massacre unfold. They could not hear the sounds of the gunfire, the screams of the people, or the cries of the offspring, but through their sense of sight they could almost feel the events transpire. It was like watching a silent horror movie. Smoke, blood, bullets filled the space in front of their faces. Several times they shut their eyes avoiding the death and destruction.

"There's Lycott!" Tarian attempted to lift his arm and point, but it was immobile. He could not direct Audrey's eyes in Lycott's direction. "Over there, to the left, escaping."

Audrey scanned the room rapidly searching for a shadowy figure. "I see him."

First Born by Janelle Gabay

"We can't let him get away," Tarian said as he thrashed pointlessly in his entrapment.

Audrey took action and bombarded the door with bullets. It remained stubbornly closed. She rummaged through the many pockets in her SEAL suit and guard uniform overtop to find a small explosive device. She quickly detonated it. The door opened. She ran headstrong into the gunfire. Tarian could do nothing to help her. He watched as she rushed to Zachary's body. She wasn't trying to seize Lycott or save the offspring. She wasn't fighting at all. She wanted the control pad. She grabbed it and ran back towards the room. As she ran back towards him with a grin of accomplishment, Eleanor swiped the control pad out of her hands. The two women stumbled into the room.

"Eleanor, what are you doing?" Audrey asked, stunned at her maneuver.

"What has to be done," Eleanor said. "I'm sorry Audrey. Immortal DNA cannot be replicated. Zachary and I have been attempting to clone it for years."

"You knew about this operation?" Audrey asked.

"No. I gave up the cloning idea long ago when I found it was impossible to replicate our chromosome sequence and cell division. My attempts did not include taking over the world, but now I see the true evil that will come from our reproduction. I realize this cannot go any further. Zachary may be dead but he is not the only Guardian or mortal who may attempt this ill-fated mission."

Eleanor's words came together in Tarian's head. He was the missing link to the reproduction puzzle. He had to be

First Born by Janelle Gabay

terminated. He squirmed against the entrapment but it would not release. All he accomplished was bloody, bruised wrists and ankles. He stopped and prepared himself for death. His mind drifted away from this life and to his dad who would be waiting for him in the next. He would be able to experience what his dad had gone through. He would see him soon. He tried to hold onto these thoughts in order to stay positive, but his will to survive fought against this delusion and forced him to consider those left behind. They needed him: Chloe, Joe Jr., Teresa, Audrey, his mom. *Would Eleanor kill Mom too?* He fought again for his mother, but the solid steel of the cuffs was unbreakable.

He transferred his attention to Audrey; she was the only one who could change his fate. He saw her frustration and confusion as she listened to Eleanor. Eleanor was her leader, her chancellor, her sister. Audrey would never go against Eleanor's orders. His life was over. He prayed for his mother's safety.

Eleanor placed the chair's control pad on the counter and removed another Death Serum syringe from her pocket. Her emerald eyes locked onto Tarian's but she did not speak. In fact, she did not look apologetic at all. Tarian refused to speak as well. He glared at her and offered no excuses. His eyes stung and itched from dried tears, but he would not blink or look away. The two of them had an unspoken understanding. His immortality had been a natural phenomenon that provided a genetic gateway into the new scientific world. Unfortunately, mortals and Guardians could not be trusted with this power. Zachary had corrupted Tarian's existence. His dad had known this. He had known not to trust outsiders, never imagining an

First Born by Janelle Gabay

insider would betray him. He had died to save his life, to save many lives. *Wait!*

"No!" Tarian roared. His epiphany exploded before his eyes. He was not finished. He'd fight! His dad would not have died in vain.

His protest thrust life back into Audrey, wrenching her out of limbo. It was just enough of a distraction to allow Audrey to knock down Eleanor with a swift kick to the knees. She grabbed the control pad and pressed the release. Finally, Tarian was free. He sprung out of the horrible chair. It was two against one, but Eleanor held the lethal syringe.

She treaded towards them and he saw her calculating eyes dart around the room, examining her options. Eleanor could move objects at will, and Tarian feared her next move could come from any direction. Tarian instinctively pushed Audrey behind him to protect her. Audrey was his equal in strength and probably a superior fighter, but he wanted desperately to protect her from the point of the needle. Surprisingly, she accepted this submissive position yet her role was still vital. She had a gun in one hand, raised shoulder height around the side of his body, and aimed at Eleanor. With her other hand, she maneuvered her guard uniform to find her Death Serum tucked deep inside a protective pocket of her SEAL suit. Her shaking hands seemed unable to locate the serum, and her grip on the gun slipped. Her eyes teared and Tarian knew he could not rely on her to shoot an accurate shot, not this time.

Unable to grab a weapon, Tarian prepared to round kick Eleanor's hand that held the syringe. His goal was to destroy the serum, not Eleanor. She was out of line and too hasty, attempting

First Born by Janelle Gabay

to salvage a bad situation. If he could save everyone in this room, together they could arrive at a conclusion that did not involve death. He saw Eleanor look into his eyes and read his thoughts; then she acted. Tarian reacted too late to Eleanor's swift move. Eleanor stabbed herself with the needle. It took him a second to process that she had taken her own life instead of his, but Audrey was already by her side pulling the needle out of her body.

"No, Eleanor. No!" Audrey cried, as she knelt beside her friend. "Why?"

"It's okay, Audrey. I'm ready. I'm tired," Eleanor said, with tear-filled eyes. "I've lived far too long. I was willing to take the life of an innocent man to help the greater good. I've become what I hate."

"No you haven't. It's just all new and different."

"Yes, and I'm too old to do my job. I failed you. I failed Joe. I can't do it anymore." Eleanor closed her eyes and rested.

"It's not your fault," Audrey pleaded and hugged her friend.

"Virginia? Honey?" Eleanor's faded voice called out.

Eleanor opened her eyes. Her gaze transfixed on someone in the distance they could not see. Slowly she drifted away from their reality and spoke to people she saw in the next realm. She had a content smile on her face and as her eyes became still, they relaxed. The weight of her body substantiated and her breathing gradually silenced. Audrey sat on the floor stiff and tense cradling her friend's lifeless body and sobbed. Eleanor finally lay at peace.

First Born by Janelle Gabay

Tarian watched patiently as Audrey grieved and prayed for her friend, but he could not allow the grieving to continue after he heard the explosion.

"Get up Audrey!" he ordered brutally, trying to snap her out of her despair.

There's no time to mourn. She looked at him startled as if she did not remember the massive attack going on outside of the room.

"Take off the uniform." Tarian stripped down to his original SEAL suit. "We need to leave the building immediately. We have to find Gabe, Maria and Charlie."

She followed his orders like a veteran soldier, quick and precise. She then picked up Eleanor's body. He almost ordered her to leave it behind but then remembered Audrey's immortal strength and knew she was capable. As much as he admired Eleanor and wanted to take appropriate measures, all of his concern focused on Audrey's safety. His goal was to get them out of there alive and return safely to their home and their families. He was Audrey's family now, and he would make sure nothing happened to her.

He bolted for the door when he heard another explosion in the nursery. Metal, plastic, flesh, and blood flew from savage, ardent flames. Thick and unwelcoming smoke seeped into the apartment billowing above the floor. He turned and searched for another exit. There had to be another way in and out of this place. He frantically opened two closet doors and a bathroom entrance. Opening the last door, relief finally came he and Audrey exited into the hall.

327

First Born by Janelle Gabay

They ran. Every couple of seconds, he glanced backwards to ensure Audrey was still following him. Her silence felt disheartening, but she wore an encouraging look of resolution. She appeared determined to stay alive and that was all he wanted from her right now. Death seemed to be a gift for Eleanor and it scared him. Cognitively, he understood why after five hundred years and the loss of her daughter and loved ones, she would welcome death; but emotionally, he did not understand her desire to exit a wondrous world filled with so many admirers and friends.

Once again he looked back at Audrey. She was still running. He loved her. He had to destroy all the Death Serum. Selfish or not, he would not let Audrey leave him. If he was going to get through several hundred years, he needed her by his side.

"Faster, you are slowing down!" Audrey ran passed him.

Tarian now followed her. A sudden noise of destruction propelled them faster. The walls were caving in around them. With a jolt, they exploded through an exterior door.

Bright morning sunshine hit their faces. The drastic light blinded them, but they kept running until a whirling wind sucked them still. Several tiltrotors hovered overhead. Tarian aimed his weapon upwards until his eyes adjusted. The familiar badge of the Guardians of Dare emblem was stamped on the aircrafts. At once, Tarian felt the tackling embrace of Gabe, Maria and Charlie. Gabe retrieved Eleanor's body but Audrey could not let go. Tarian placed a hand on the lower part of her back, and she released her long time friend.

First Born by Janelle Gabay

When the heavy burden was physically and emotionally lifted from her, she looked as if she might float away. Tarian vowed he would not let her disconnect from him, not now, not ever. He had lost one love; he would not let another slip away. Aggressively and passionately, he grabbed her and pulled her into his arms as if his life depended on it. She returned his kiss with a hard, needy mouth. All of his doubts disappeared as their bodies melted into one, and he knew he would never be without her.

Maria yelled, "Let's go!" Her voice was harsh and authoritative, but she gave them both an enormous smile.

The eight tiltrotors, loaded with Guardians and Entente military, lifted in uniform grace towards the orange sky. A handful of men and women dressed in the black uniforms of Zachary's army ran from the burning building and began to fire at them, but they were already too high in the air for their bullets to reach the craft. The sight of the warriors disturbed Tarian. None of Zachary's army could be left alive, Tarian swore. He was not only thinking like a soldier, he was thinking like a man in love. The need to protect overpowered any of his guilt at the loss of life he was about to administer.

"We have to shoot them!" he yelled at the pilot. "Where is your gunman?"

"Look Tarian." Gabe pointed to the attack aircraft quickly flying into view.

Soon air-to-surface tactical missiles were launched, destroying everything in sight on the ground. As far as he could see, nothing, nor anyone would survive. He watched as the lifeless facility's blood red, bright orange and ink black colors slowly faded. As they created distance, the vast evergreen forests

First Born by Janelle Gabay

and snow-covered mountains of the region swallowed the colors. Quickly, it became invisible from his sight. However, his mind held the image. How had his birth turned into a massive evolution of an immortal army? Eleanor was right. If he has a DNA sequence that can reproduce unlike the other Guardians, this could happen again.

For once, he was eager to see Roman. He needed answers. Those newborns were not just a part of him; they were a part of Delia and his mother too. He would never tell them the whole truth. He would have to convince Roman to keep his secret. If Delia knew hundreds of her offspring had been destroyed in the name of science, she would snap out of control. She would hate immortals even more than she already did. And her father, how was she going to feel about his death? Relieved? Sad? Or would she rejoice?

Audrey's fingers intertwined in his, snatching him from the depths of his inner unrest. She looked exhausted and miserable, but she consoled him with her silvery aquamarine eyes and gentle touch. She kissed him again then laid her head on his shoulder. As long as he held her, he was happy to forget everything during the flight back to the village.

First Born by Janelle Gabay

THIRTY-EIGHT
THE FUNERAL

The dense drapery of clouds hung against the dark slate sky making for a gloomy February day reflecting everyone's mourning. Eleanor White Dare was dead and the world, itself, suffered. The weather conditions came as no surprise to Tarian, for she had lived in this world for over five hundred years.

Tarian sat in the luxurious, plush leather seat of a bulletproof, unmarked, dark green sedan in a line of thirty identical vehicles with Audrey by his side. Charlie sat in the front passenger seat with Guardian Warren Edwards at the wheel driving to Eleanor's prestigious farewell. Charlie now knew the entire absurd truth about Tarian's life and the life of their father. He took it quite well and offered his complete support to all the Guardians and Tarian.

Carolyn and Teresa also attended Eleanor's funeral. They rode in the car ahead of Tarian and the others with Eleanor's trusted lab partner, Patrick Wallace. When Teresa became a fixture at Eleanor's side in the lab, Patrick had welcomed her involvement and encouraged her participation. He promised he would continue Eleanor's work and insisted she continue to help him as she had Eleanor. Teresa promised him she would try her best, her grief too prominent in her heart to fully commit to the requested duty.

Tarian gazed out the car window as the many shops of the village rolled past. Usually major political figures' funerals were

331

First Born by Janelle Gabay

held in the Entente's National Cemetery in Boston, but with the unstable atmosphere, Audrey insisted on Quebec. The village was Eleanor's home, and the villagers would want to be a part of her funeral. Her actual resting place would be in Roanoke, next to her daughter and husband, however, that was not known to anyone other than the Guardians.

"It's not the same," Tarian said still regarding the village streets.

"I know," Audrey agreed.

The village had been magically expanded to accommodate the multitude of guests. The guests would never realize the true wonder of the village and the mortal villagers were accustomed to strangeness having lived through it for hundreds of years.

"It's not just the size. It's…it's…" He had no words.

Audrey looked at him with grief-stricken eyes and squeezed his hand.

The guests, villagers and Guardians wore black, stripping the streets of its colorful movement. Every aspect had dulled from the aromas escaping the bakery to the chiming of the bells on the doors. The magic and beauty of the cobblestone streets Tarian had enjoyed at Christmas time were now dismally idle. Tarian feared the exceptional enchantment had vanished with Eleanor's spirit.

The sedan stopped at the top of the hill. Tarian exited the vehicle and held the door open for Audrey. She teetered a little on her heel highs and adjusted her tailored skirt. Together they paraded through the mass of political heavyweights to their designated seats in the first row. As Tarian glanced around to

First Born by Janelle Gabay

view the extensive audience that included the president of the Entente, all Entente congressmen, heads of districts, and chancellors of justice from across the nation, apprehension overwhelmed him. He turned to look at his beautiful girlfriend and tried to appear confident.

"What are you so nervous about," Audrey asked, still fiddling with her skirt.

"I'm not nervous," he lied.

She smiled at him, placed a calm hand on his bouncing knee, but said nothing.

He forced his knee to stop bouncing. He wanted to shield her, not the other way around. He wondered how she could be so strong. In minutes, she would be giving the eulogy for the woman known around the world as the Entente's Secretary of Foreign Affairs, but who was actually the Chancellor of the Guardians of Dare, who had led and inspired the immortals since her journey to the new world in 1587. It was her daughter, Virginia, that had provided the first glimpse of hope to immortal procreation and her father, John White, had been the colony's governor. Simply by association, she had become the Guardian's leader and matriarch but then remained in power for hundreds of years due to her brilliant mind for politics and selfless characteristics. How could Audrey give Eleanor the eulogy she so rightly deserved?

"I can't do it." Audrey wiped the sweat from her palms and gritted her teeth together.

"What?" Tarian asked. Terror struck him as he was just thinking the same thing. He gathered himself together. He would not let her down in her time of need. He had to say

First Born by Janelle Gabay

something encouraging. "Yes, you can. Of all the people I know, you are by far the most qualified to speak for Eleanor. She would want you to speak for her."

"I know," she sighed. "But Eleanor was charismatic, never apologetic, always fair, admired by all. She was a natural born leader. How can I explain that? How?"

"Just like that." He touched her face gently. "You have rehearsed your speech to me a hundred times. It's perfect. You're perfect."

Silence fell upon the audience in anticipation of Audrey's speech. She took one long look at Tarian and stood up. She left his side and walked on stage alone. Standing tall behind the podium, she spoke with grace and truth.

"She's wonderful," said a familiar voice.

Tarian turned to see Piper next to him, sitting in the chair Audrey left moments earlier. Piper's smile widened as a tear rolled down her youthful face. She turned and cast her lavender eyes upon him. Her usual hyperactivity replaced with calm wisdom.

"Never doubt her love for you," Piper told him.

"I wouldn't," he said.

It seemed like a strange thing to say, and he wanted to question Piper, but he did not want to miss any of Audrey's eulogy. He turned his full attention back to the stage. Audrey ultimately received the satisfactory reward of a standing ovation. Tarian scanned the sea of people dressed in the color of shadows roaring with applause. Piper still next to him bubbling over with cheers, clapping wildly. He had never been more proud of

First Born by Janelle Gabay

Audrey and realized at that moment, she may accede as Chancellor.

As he watched her at the podium eloquently excepting the audience's praise, he imagined kissing her again. Amazed by her poise, style and beauty, he realized he had never been happier. Once the spectacular ceremony was over, he selfishly pried her away from the publicity piranhas.

"Finally," he said, as he tucked her warm, petite body into his.

They were back at Headquarters. It was midnight, and the two of them lay, embraced in her bed. He had been sleeping in her room ever since they returned, seven days ago. "Your speech was exceptional."

"It was?" she asked, surprised.

"Yes," he replied with a gentle kiss.

"I miss her. I miss all of them." The stressful events of the day had not yet released Audrey's spirit.

"I know." Tarian ran his hands down her body, caressing the softness of her abdomen and outlining the edges of her hips with his fingers. "You have me now." He kissed her again and forced his hands to stay in place. He wanted to run them all over her, to touch every inch of her, but he did not know if her desires were the same.

"Six hundred years is a long time to live," she said to him, and the words sounded frightening.

Confused, he pushed her to a distance where he could look into her eyes for answers. "Are you okay? Are you happy with me?"

First Born by Janelle Gabay

It sounded like an immature question, but fifteen people over six-hundred-years-old had just died, and he needed to know that she was not considering the option of death.

"Yes, I've never been happier." She turned her full attention to him and reassured him with a long, passionate kiss. "I meant, it's a long time. I wonder what's going to happen next. I thought I had seen and done everything, but now life is new again. It's both exciting and frightening."

"I'm looking forward to the next six hundred years." He slid his hands down her body once more, reigniting the desire.

Her skin stirred, and her voice moaned with delight, evidence that she hungered for him too. After their desires had been satisfied, she pulled him into her tightly, their bodies touching from chest to toes, her head nestled into his chest, his arms wrapped tightly around her; they fell asleep as one.

First Born by Janelle Gabay

THIRTY-NINE
AND YOU CRUMBLE

Several weeks passed since the funeral, and the halls of Headquarters gradually adjusted to Eleanor's absence. In a few days Audrey would be inaugurated Chancellor, and Tarian would not return to EMA with Maria and Gabe.

As Tarian strolled the familiar halls, he pondered visiting Delia. He had avoided her. He had gone so far as to not walk anywhere near the infirmary. His past visits with her never ended happily. His last visit ended with Roman escorting him out of the room with Delia yelling and her blood pressure rising.

"Tarian!" Roman's voiced echoed in the hall.

"Roman?" Tarian questioned the running body coming closer towards him.

"Delia needs to see you right away," Roman told him in a rough, ragged voice. He looked agitated, as if being away from Delia for any length of time was toxic.

Tarian understood this feeling. He felt the aching void whenever Audrey was not within sight. "Is she okay?" Tarian asked.

"No," Roman rushed Tarian down the hallway.

After Tarian studied his face more closely, he saw the dried crystals of tears staining Roman's cheeks. Tarian's heart sank. The gleeful butterflies that had fluttered inside Tarian's stomach every hour of his days with Audrey since surviving Zachary's inferno were now gone, and a hollow, hurtful pit dwelled in its place.

First Born by Janelle Gabay

Tarian had been so busy. The funeral arrangements, the paperwork, the lab work had all taken precedence. He had been consumed with planning an immortal future with Audrey. The last notion he wanted to address was a past pain. The girlfriend that left him, that hated what he was. He couldn't hide anymore and he was scared to look into her eyes and be held accountable for his absence. His life was exceeding his expectations and hers was slipping away.

"I'm sorry, Roman. I know I should have come to see her sooner." Tarian confessed while standing face to face on the elevator.

Roman's pale skin and swollen yellow eyes looked as if he had not seen the sun in weeks. "I don't expect her to make it through the night."

The words made it real. It shocked Tarian even though his mom and Teresa had kept him up to date on her decline. He had stubbornly refused to believe she would succumb to death. The Delia he knew had the will of a bull. Tarian had convinced himself she would live and when she got better, he would visit her. To face her now, on her deathbed, frightened him.

Roman looked back at him and said, "She's asking for *you*." He accentuated the word 'you' to insure Tarian would not retreat. "She has made peace with herself, her mother and brother, but she needs to see you before she can move on."

Tarian stopped and looked into Roman's bloodshot eyes. He wanted to refuse him, to refuse her. If he walked out now, she would keep fighting for life. She was that stubborn, he thought, and a smile flashed across his face as he remembered the old days of their courtship. Glimpses of the past rushed before

First Born by Janelle Gabay

him. He saw her when she was only sixteen, when they studied
in her father's library, and they walked through her vegetable
gardens. He remembered their awkward first kiss. It had
happened too quickly and he did not even remember how he had
approached her lips with his. He was sure he had done it all
wrong and that she would never kiss him again, when her lips
touched his once more. The second kiss was one he never forgot,
a passionate verification that she was his. She was the first girl
who loved him and not his better looking, overly charming, older
brother.

The buzzer on the elevator door shook Tarian out of the
past. Roman had held the door open for too long. The protesting
door and Roman's stern glare forced him to move forward.

"If you don't go in there now, you'll miss your chance to
say goodbye," Roman assured. "She can't fight it off any
longer."

Tarian exited the elevator but halted at the door leading
into her room. He tried but could not keep the watery tears from
building and slipping onto his cheeks. He hurriedly stroked them
away with the back of his hand, raised his head and straightened
his shoulders. He had no right to cry. He had no right to feel
bad. She was the victim. He had to be strong for her. He had to
give her the best of him. She deserved the best of him. With that
thought, Tarian flung open the door.

He saw a hint of Delia trapped inside a pathetic body of
bones: sunken eye sockets, piercing jawline and limp hair. The
best of him that he tried to give her fell apart. He turned around
and almost ran from the room but instead, he pulled himself
together and pivoted to face her.

First Born by Janelle Gabay

"Hi, Tarian." Delia's voice was strong. She sounded the same.

Her conspicuous eyes enjoyed watching him suffer but not in a vicious way. Instead, it was more the way an older sister feels when she has the upper hand or final word over her little brother.

"Hi Delia," he said, then silence.

The long, seizing pause smothered him with its thick, frigid air. The room felt like an ice chest. Shivers took over his skin at the thought of being trapped inside a human refrigerator that attempted to preserve the lives of the already deceased. Stifling panic struck him as he looked around trying to find something to focus on during this long silence. It felt like hours but was mere seconds. However, in the course of that brief moment, he took in all the surroundings: the cracks in the walls; the fingerprints of the many doctors, scientists and loved ones that visited; the medicinal products everywhere. This wasn't a room he would want to spend his last hours in. He needed to get her out of here, outside into the crisp, winter air. The sun shown brightly today and a few birds had returned home in the hopes of an early spring. Sweet melodies floated outside, and she was stuck in this stale white freezer. He began to suggest that she be taken outside when Delia spoke first.

"Is it true?" she whispered.

He could barely hear her. Her strong voice had faded. He moved close to listen.

"There were babies, innocent babies?"

"Yes," Tarian confessed, angered that she had found out the truth. But he could not lie to her. He owed her the truth.

First Born by Janelle Gabay

Lying would not make her passing into the next world any easier. It may relieve him, but he didn't have the right to deny her the truth for his own satisfaction, his own feelings.

"Tell me Tarian." Delia forced herself to sit up in her bed.

He told her most of the horrible truth. "Yes, they were cloned offspring. They looked like you and me." Tarian debated whether or not to reveal how the single newborn communicated with him. How he had the gift of transferring memories through touch, how he had seen his mother's contribution to these offspring. He resisted the urge to utilize his gift and release the terrorizing memories upon her. He protected her from the obscene knowledge that repeatedly haunted his dreams, and continued without anymore mention of the newborns. "I believe your father found a way to combine our genes to produce offspring. In the process he destroyed your cells. It's still unclear how he made it successful, but I assure you I will study it. I will find out so as to never let it happen again. Why he did it? We'll never know. He went delusional with self-righteous power." He refused to mention her father's infinitely black eyes, increased strength or otherworldliness.

"That's all Father cared about was power. He only cared about his precious immortals," she snarled, her anger giving strength to her voice again.

"That's not true, Delia," he said, defying her.

She looked deeply wounded by his betrayal. He briefly thought he should remain neutral and let her vent, but he could not.

341

First Born by Janelle Gabay

"Delia, don't you remember how he used to be when we were kids, how he took us so many places. We were little and my dad was alive and we went together to amusement parks and ice cream stores and the park. Remember?"

She nodded but did not speak.

"And Audrey has told me…"

She screeched a primal cry at him. "Don't mention her name! Don't mention any of their horrible, immortal names to me!"

He knew her words were meant to hurt him. She was in pain and didn't want her misery to be lonely.

She saw his wounded look. Her damage had been inflicted, so she recoiled back into her pitiful self. She continued her sentence in a less venomous tone, but her true intentions were clear. "Tarian, I know that you are an immortal. I know that you are the first hope. You will be different, but I don't trust the father I thought I had. He was always evil. You don't just discard people decade after decade if you are not evil. A mortal human could not do that. It's an immortal trait."

Tarian refused to continue this conversation. He turned to face Roman. "We're taking her outside. Unhook her from all of this."

"No, she's too weak. She's connected to these machines because they're keeping her alive," Roman protested.

"I don't want to be kept alive, Roman. If I can't live independently, then I'm not living."

"But Darling." Roman reached for her hand.

"Tarian's right. I may only have a few moments left. I don't want to spend them in here." Her voice quivered. Tears

342

First Born by Janelle Gabay

filled her eyes but she held her head up high and faced Roman
with dignity. "Do it! If I die after just one inhale of fresh air, it'll
be worth it."

They placed her gingerly in a wheelchair and wrapped a
cozy blanket around her. She smiled up at Tarian and reached for
his hand. They walked hands connected, as Roman pushed the
wheelchair forward. They passed a few Guardians, some
strangers and some friends. People looked at the threesome with
bewilderment and then sympathy, no doubt wondering what they
were doing with such a sick woman out of the infirmary.

Tarian gave each on looker a glare of stern confidence,
knowing pity was an emotion Delia despised. He noticed she
pulled her shoulders back and held up her chin as people passed.
She flashed her radiant smile. She would forever hold a place in
his heart.

The sun shown warmth onto their faces the instant the
doors opened to the exterior. It was the warmest Tarian had felt
it in months.

Delia exhaled a precious, joyful sigh. "Thank you,
Tarian. Thank you for the suggestion that we go outside." She
coughed a deep guttural cough.

Tarian panicked. "Is it okay? Do you feel okay? We can
go back inside."

The questions skidded off of Tarian's tongue like slippery
nails. He worried about his actions as Roman gave him a
distressed glare. He had stripped her from those horrid machines,
her life force.

The fear in Roman's eyes registered with Delia too.
"Roman, I'm fine." She looked into his eyes as calm and

343

First Born by Janelle Gabay

peaceful as if she were a healthy, immortal woman. "I know you're sad and confused, but I'm not anymore. Thank you for giving me a couple extra months of happiness. Thank you for being there when I had no one and no answers. You gave me hope. You loved me," she said, but her words gave out as her voice wavered. She paused to breath and swallow.

Tarian fidgeted as she confessed her love and appreciation to Roman. Yet, Roman had been there when Tarian could not, and for this, Tarian would be forever grateful.

She continued, "But I'm not going to survive any longer. I'm going to die. I'm going to die out here; outside in this beautiful sunshine with the two men I love most. The two men that have given me so much in such a short time. You've made my life full and definitely interesting." She grinned.

"Interesting," Tarian seconded.

They walked the path, strolling away from Headquarters towards the vibrant, hustle and bustle of the vendors and cafes in the village. Soon the cobbled street turned to reveal a quaint community park where Roman pulled the wheelchair up onto a small bluff. Here they watched the children play and listened to the birds chirp. They kept silent for at least ten minutes.

Tarian hoped she was enjoying the beauty of what surrounded her, dismissing thoughts of all she was leaving behind. He did not want her mind filled with worries about immortals, the Prevallers, the betrayal of her father. He hoped for those brief ten minutes, peace found her.

All of a sudden, a sharp pain grabbed Delia, and snapped her body forward. The poke of death, the pain of the inevitable, came to steal her away from them. She clasped her chest and

First Born by Janelle Gabay

looked at Tarian with panic-stricken eyes. She had something to tell him.

"What is it, my Love?" Roman knelt down by her side.

She didn't respond. Instead she wrapped her arms around him and kissed him for several seconds.

Tarian turned his eyes away.

"I love you," she finally said softly but adamantly, as if she never wanted there to be any doubt that he was her chosen one. Then she turned to look at Tarian and told him she loved him too.

"Please forgive me; I beg you. You must forgive me." The apologetic words flew from Tarian's mouth without hesitation or consideration. He had known and loved her all of his life. Her couldn't bear her suffering.

"I don't forgive you my sweet Tarian." She wore a mocking smile. "But everything happens for a reason. You've been thrown into a life you didn't choose. Both of our fates were chosen for us, and we had to make the best of it."

The pain gripped her again and she doubled over in agony. Roman and Tarian both embraced her, trying to ease her suffering. Tarian thought she was gone this time. He did not expect to hear another word from her lips, but she looked at him deliberately. She appeared desperate to tell him something. Her focus aimed at him and her posture straightened to that of a strong, lethal woman. Roman and Tarian pulled away from her fearing the look of determination in her eyes. Passionately, she clutched Tarian's arm and drew his face to hers so he could hear her last words while making sure Roman could not.

First Born by Janelle Gabay

"Don't trust her." She exhaled her last words with confidence but with a lack of strength, her voice forced and airy. Death's grip held her shoulders until her lifeless body doubled over and died in a pitiful lump of human frailty.

Roman quickly unfolded her to place her in a more dignified position.

Tarian felt his pain. His need to position her properly eased his distress. Tarian reflected on the absurdity of man continually 'fixing' reality. The reality was she died with words of hatred on her lips in a cold, metal chair in the awkward position that comes when deaths slaps you hard on the back and you crumble. Roman and Tarian, acting humanly, had tried to bring peace to her death but she knew better. Peace may have held her momentarily, but the cruel reality of her mortality had seized her. Only a fortunate few are genuinely ready to die; the rest fight death until the bitter end.

"I'm going to take her back now," Roman said in an admirably strong voice.

"Okay. Do you mind if I stay here?"

"No. I'd rather be alone."

Tarian felt the same. He remained at the spot where her life had evaporated. He sat against a tree, folded one knee up to his chest, and reclined back onto its trunk.

For an hour he sat alone in sober contemplation. Delia's last words haunted him. He focused on the children playing in the park and listened to their joyful laughter in the hopes that it would reassure him of the goodness in people. He found amusement as the kids stubbornly refused their mother's orders. He sympathized with the mother's plight, but secretly relished the

First Born by Janelle Gabay

kid's deviance. The children he witnessed were resilient. They fell down but got back up with even more energy and determination than before. Tarian smiled to himself.

A familiar, gentle caress startled him out of his reflection. Tarian glanced up to see Audrey. She sat next to him and entwined her warm arms around his. Then she laid her head on his shoulder. He welcomed her company.

"I'm sorry Tarian," she said, as they both looked straight away.

"Me too, Beautiful." He drew her closer into him.

He would never leave her, and he would never repeat Delia's last words. He loved Audrey, and he trusted her with all his being.

First Born by Janelle Gabay

EPILOGUE
Sleepers
Audrey

As Audrey stood alone and cold inside the dark, cavernous room, she examined the chocolate brown eyes of Joe Prescott, and thought, they would not look so different when they changed to black. She fooled herself. It wasn't the color of the eyes; it was the infinite depth of nothingness. The awakened eyes weren't just black they were empty.

Joe's milky colored, frigid body rested on one of the many beds inside the crypt. It was four o'clock in the morning, Audrey's usual working hour for this exclusive project, when she jerked wildly at the thud of the door shutting behind Patrick. His entrance always startled her even though his presence was expected.

"Audrey, come on! Maybe if you allowed yourself a little heat you wouldn't be so freaked out all the time," Patrick argued.

"I can't. They need the cold to survive." She snugly wrapped the lab coat around her narrow torso.

"*If* they survive," he corrected her.

She hung her head low suffering from her own inability to conquer the Awakening Serum. She and Patrick had been clandestinely working inside Eleanor's hidden, stone chamber laboratory for four months to no avail. They had no idea as to how long a Death Serum injected immortal could sleep. This was unchartered scientific territory for the Guardians.

348

First Born by Janelle Gabay

As she meandered around the beds, shuffling her wool-lined boots she gently touched each corpse-like body. She desperately wished they would rise up and scare the living hell out of her. She had spent endless hours inside the village church at the feet of an intricately sculpted Christ praying for answers, for help, for enlightenment, but only received the permanent stare of his sympathetic eyes chiseled out of wood. She understood why he offered her no help; she was not faithless, but she wasn't without doubt either. And she had not stepped foot inside a church for decades. At all her recent church visits, she vowed to be a better person, she promised to believe, and she did believe. She had seen the Devil, so she knew there had to be a God as well.

Eleanor had had the unquestionable faith and the brilliant scientific mind, but even she had not mastered this problem. Zachary had though. Zachary had somehow awakened himself from the grips of the Death Serum. Audrey had Eleanor's notes listing theories to explain many mysteries of Death Serum and its counterpart, but Eleanor's ingredients and equations were not producing the serum. Or maybe it was the amalgamation. Audrey was simply failing to apply all the parts correctly.

Audrey's horrible drop into the rabbit hole had begun when she journeyed alongside Eleanor's casket to the remote Roanoke burial site. Eleanor had left something for her to find. It had been buried under the dirt at the gravesite. The buried object was a formally sealed letter addressed to Audrey informing her of the secret underground laboratory where several sleeping immortals lie. The letter read like a fairy tale - sprinkle special awakening fairy dust over eternal, sleeping immortals and

349

First Born by Janelle Gabay

they will miraculously spring to life again. In this wicked fairytale, Eleanor told of the eyes of those having been awakened would be of the blackest black. However, Eleanor sadly admitted she had failed in her attempts to produce such an awakening. The fairytale was just that, a fictional tale. Only Eleanor confessed that it wasn't fiction, that Zachary had been successful at producing the power. As with all good fairy tales there was a horrible warning. Death cheating immortals strolled the halls of Headquarters wearing colored lenses to mask their transformation, a reality that made Audrey uneasy around all of her trusted Guardians.

At the gravesite after reading the last line of Eleanor's letter, she had crumpled the paper and thrust it as far away from her strained, tired eyes as possible. *Do not wake me! Let me rest in peace next to my family!*

Audrey shook off her memory and the guilt it brought, as she placed the thin white clothe back over Eleanor's still face.

Turning sharply to face Patrick, Audrey said, "Give me the bear."

"Please," Patrick teased.

"Please," Audrey added more docile. Her heart hardened inside the walls of this morgue, making it easy for her to snap at her trusted friend. She had loved each sleeping immortal inside this refrigerated, meat locker. Seeing them serenely resting with stunning magnificence of peace on their faces was too fascinatingly wicked for Audrey to handle.

Patrick handed Audrey Chloe's teddy bear. Audrey gently sliced it open at the seam as to leave no evidence once she restitched the bear. Placing her slender fingers inside the fluff of

350

First Born by Janelle Gabay

its belly, Audrey felt for the letter she expected to find.
Cautiously she pulled out the folded paper, caring not to harm
Chloe's bear. To Audrey's surprise she felt another object inside
the spun cotton candy filling. Pulling the object out carefully,
she saw it was a miniscule vial surrounded by a protective box.
She had never seen such an encasement before and had no way of
opening it. Audrey resisted the urged to slam it onto the ground
hoping to break it into tiny pieces, but she knew this action might
destroy its contents.

  Joe Prescott's note that was cleverly hidden inside the
teddy bear provided detailed chemical equations that Patrick
understood far better than Audrey. The arduously imprisoned
vial was a sample of the Awakening Serum, she was sure of it.
Another warning scrolled in ink on the paper. This horrible fairy
tale kept getting worse, and she hadn't had the heart to involve
Tarian. He already struggled with vividly, gruesome nightmares.
How could she possibly tell him his father was a sleeping corpse
in the basement?

  The final paragraph of Joe's note read:

  *This is new and unconquered biochemistry. As should be
expected, death comes to immortals in a form of sleep. The body
does not die, it hibernates and once awakened, it transforms.
This transformation produces a stronger, less human immortal.
Proceed with great caution!*

351

First Born by Janelle Gabay

Janelle Gabay

Janelle lives with her husband, three children and three dogs in Florida. She was born in Nebraska and grew up in the Philippines, Virginia, Alabama, Maine and Florida as an Air Force Brat. First Born is her debut novel. She spends her time writing, taking care of her dogs and watching her children play tennis and soccer. She is a graduate from the University of South Florida. You can visit her online at www.janellegabaybooks.com or on Twitter (@JanelleGabay)
janellegabaybooks@gmail.com

To purchase *First Born* and find out about upcoming books in the *First Born Trilogy* visit

www.janellegbaybooks.com